LOUISE ALLEN

---

*Surrender to the
Marquess*

HARLEQUINHISTORICAL

Recycling programs
for this product may
not exist in your area.

ISBN-13: 978-0-373-29920-1

Surrender to the Marquess

Printed in U.S.A.

Author Note

Some time ago I wrote *Forbidden Jewel of India*, a story I was passionate about, set entirely in India in the 1780s, the time when the East India Company ruled in uneasy alliance with the princes and rajas. Anusha is half Indian, her lover, Nicholas Herriard, an English officer and heir to a marquess, so when it was time for him to take up his title and return to England in 1816 I had all the fun of discovering how he and Anusha and their son and daughter adapt to English life.

I told Ashe Herriard's story in *Tarnished Amongst the Ton*, but I had no inkling of what happened to Sara, his sister—until now. So here she is, very much her mother's daughter, and determined to be her own woman, despite what the men in her life think—and certainly despite what Lucian Avery, Marquess of Cannock, believes is best for her.

I hope you enjoy following Sara's stormy path to true love as much as I enjoyed discovering it.

"Ladies need protection." Lucian stalked over to the balustrade.

Shaking the provoking creature would not be a good illustration of his case, kissing her even worse. "How did you get here this evening, for example? These streets and lanes are dark. Anyone could be lurking."

"By sedan chair with the same two reliable, burly chairmen I always use. They will come and collect me later. And should desperate footpads leap out and manage to fell both of them, then I can defend myself."

"How? With sharp words?" he demanded and took two strides to stand in front of her, his hands at either side, pinning her back against the balustrade. "Men are stronger, more vicious, than you could imagine."

"Also more vulnerable," she murmured. "Look down, my lord. It is not only my words that have an edge."

He did, just as he felt a pressure against the falls of his evening breeches. In the moonlight something glinted, sharp steel, held rock steady in her hand. Lucian stood quite still. "Where did that come from?"

Louise Allen loves immersing herself in history. She finds landscapes and places evoke the past powerfully. Venice, Burgundy and the Greek islands are favorite destinations. Louise lives on the Norfolk coast and spends her spare time gardening, researching family history or traveling in search of inspiration. Visit her at louiseallenregency.co.uk, @louiseregency and janeaustenslondon.com.

Books by Louise Allen

Harlequin Historical

The Herriard Family

Forbidden Jewel of India
Tarnished Amongst the Ton
Surrender to the Marquess

Lords of Disgrace

His Housekeeper's Christmas Wish
His Christmas Countess
The Many Sins of Cris de Feaux
The Unexpected Marriage of Gabriel Stone

Brides of Waterloo

A Rose for Major Flint

Stand-Alone Novels

From Ruin to Riches
Unlacing Lady Thea
Scandal's Virgin
Beguiled by Her Betrayer
Once Upon a Regency Christmas
"On a Winter's Eve"

Harlequin Historical *Undone!* ebooks

Disrobed and Dishonored
Auctioned Virgin to Seduced Bride

Visit the Author Profile page
at Harlequin.com for more titles.

To Lorna Chapman for encouraging me
to tell Sara's story. Thank you!

Chapter One

September 1818—Sandbay, Dorset

It was an elegant shop front with its sea-green paint-work, touches of gilding and sparkling clean windows. Aphrodite's Seashell. A *risqué* choice of name, Lucian thought, considering that Aphrodite was the Greek goddess of love, born from the sea foam when Cronus cut off Uranus's male parts and threw them into the ocean. Otherwise it looked feminine and mildly frivolous as befitted its function and location. Not a place he would normally set foot in unless absolutely desperate.

But Mr L. J. Dunton Esquire, otherwise known in polite society as Lucian John Dunton Avery, Marquess of Cannock, *was* desperate. Otherwise he would not be found dead within a hundred miles of an obscure seaside resort in the not very fashionable time of mid-September. That desperation had driven him to ask for advice and the landlord at the rigidly respectable Royal Promenade Hotel had recommended this place, so he pushed open the door to a tinkle of bells and stepped inside.

* * *

Sara gave one last twitch to the draperies and stepped back to admire the display of artists' equipment she had just set up beside the counter—easel, palette, a box of watercolour paints, the beginnings of a rough sketch of the bay on the canvas—all tastefully made into a still life with the addition of a parasol set amidst a drift of large seashells and colourful beach pebbles.

There, she thought, giving it an approving nod. *That should inspire customers to buy an armful of equipment and rush to the nearest scenic viewpoint to create a masterpiece.*

She replaced the jars of shells she had used on their shelf next to the other glass vessels full of coloured sands and assorted mysterious boxes and tins designed to stir the curiosity of the browser. A glance to her left across the shop reassured her that the bookshelves, the rack of picture frames and the table scattered with leaflets and journals looked invitingly informal rather than simply muddled.

Behind her the doorbells tinkled their warning. Sara turned, then modified her welcoming smile of greeting into something more restrained. This was not one of her usual clients. Not a lady at all, in fact. This visitor was not only unfamiliar, but male. Very male and a highly superior specimen of the sex at that. She kept the smile cool. She *was* female and most certainly young enough to be appreciative, but she had too much pride to show it.

'Good morning, sir. I think you may have gone astray—the circulating library and reading room is just two buildings further up the street on this side.'

He was studying the shop interior, but looked round when she spoke and removed his hat. That was a very superior specimen as well. 'I was looking for Aphrodite's Seashell, not the library.'

'Then you have found it. Welcome. May I assist you, sir?'

Aphrodite, I presume? The question was obviously on the tip of his tongue, but he caught it with the faintest twitch of his lips and said only, 'I hope you may.' He glanced down at her hand, saw her wedding ring. 'Mrs—?' His voice was cultured, cool and very assured.

She recognised the type, or perhaps breed was the better word. Her father was one of them, her brother another, although those two conformed only in their own unique way. Corinthians, bloods of the first stare, *non-pareils*, aristocrats with the total, unthinking, self-confidence that came from generations of privilege. But they were also hard men who worked to keep at the peak of fitness so they could excel at the pastimes of their class—riding, driving, sport, fighting, war.

Whether such gentlemen had money or not was almost impossible to tell at first glance because they would starve rather than appear less than immaculately turned out. Their manners were perfect and their attitude to women—*their* women—was indulgent and protective. Nothing mattered more than honour and the honour of these men was invested in their women, in whose name they would duel to the death in order to avenge the slightest slur.

It was not an attitude she enjoyed or approved of. She feared it. Nor did she approve of their attitude to the rest of the females they came into contact with. Respectable women, of whatever class, were to be treated with courtesy and respect. The one exception, in terms of respect, although the courtesy would always be there, was attractive widows. And Sara knew herself to be an attractive widow.

She conjured up the mental image of a very large, very possessive, husband. 'Mrs Harcourt.'

The warmth in his eyes, the faint, undeniably attractive, compression of the lines at their outer corners that hinted at a smile, was the only clue to what she suspected his thoughts were.

He was a *very* handsome specimen, she supposed, managing, with an effort that was deeply annoying, not to let her thoughts show on her face. He was tall, well proportioned, with thick medium-brown hair and hazel eyes. His nose was slightly aquiline, his chin decided, his mouth…wicked. Sara was not quite certain why that was, only that staring at it was definitely unwise.

'Sir?' she prompted.

'I have a sister. She is eighteen and in rather delicate health; her spirits are low and she is not at all happy to be here in Sandbay.'

'She is bored, perhaps?'

'Very,' he admitted. Then, when she made no response, he condescended to explain. 'She is not well enough for sea bathing and, in any case, she is unused to the ocean. That unfamiliarity makes her rather nervous of walking on the beach. She has no friends here and there are few very young ladies resident here, as far as I can see. At home, were she well enough, she would be attending parties and picnics, going to the theatre and dances, or shopping. At least her friends would be on hand. Here, she is not up to evening entertainments.'

'You hope to find an occupation for her, something that will help her to pass the time during the day. I can understand that it might help. Can she draw or paint?'

'Her governess taught her, but I do not think she ever applied herself to perfect her art. Marguerite was always too restless for that.'

If the girl was naturally active then convalescence and its restrictions must be even more galling. 'Can she walk at all?'

'A few hundred yards along the promenade seems achievable. Then she flags and asks to return. I cannot tell whether her reluctance is weakness or depressed spirits.'

'Would she come here and visit the shop to see what we can offer?'

'I do not know,' he admitted. 'Not if *I* suggest it.' He shut his mouth, tight lips betraying his anger with himself for allowing that flash of irritation to escape.

So, the young lady was at outs with her brother. Probably she wanted to be in London with her friends, however unhealthy that grimy city was for her. 'Then shall I come to her? I could bring some ideas for crafts she might like to try, some drawing equipment, perhaps.' As she spoke Sara made a slight gesture with her hand at the bounty of objects in the shop. 'Something might tempt her.'

'Temptation?' The word, spoken in that warm voice, was like a touch. He really could stand very still for a man of his size. It was faintly unnerving for some reason, even though her closest male relatives had the same quality of stillness. It came from power and fitness and the knowledge that they did not have to move to make their presence felt. But this was not her father or her brother. 'That would be most obliging of you, Mrs Harcourt. But who would mind your shop for you? Your husband, perhaps?'

That had been clumsy of him, the first maladroit thing he had done, and the rueful twist of those beautiful lips showed that he knew it.

'I am a widow, Mr—?' She did not expect for a moment anything other than a title, or at the very least a family name she would have heard of. She did not recognise him, but then she had been out only one Season before she married and moved to Cambridge with Michael, so it was perfectly possible to have missed him.

'Dunton.' He produced his card case and placed a rectangle of crisp pasteboard on the counter. 'We are at the Royal Promenade Hotel.'

'Where else?' Sara murmured. With that tailoring and manner even the best private lodgings in Sandbay would not do. She took the card, felt the depth of expensive engraving under her thumb, glanced at it and found herself surprised. *A plain Mister without so much as an Honourable to his name?* She was not altogether certain she believed that, but she could hardly challenge the man on no evidence. Besides, as long as he was not engaged in some criminal endeavour he could call himself what he liked.

Faint sounds of pans clattering emerged from behind the curtain screening the door to the back room. 'Excuse me, sir. Mrs Farwell, could you spare me a moment?'

To do him justice, Mr Dunton did not flinch when Dot emerged through the curtains, rolling pin in hand. She was a big woman, but then most of the dippers who commanded the bathing machines were. She glowered at him, which was her normal reaction when any man was close to Sara, and he returned the look with one of indifference. Dot gave a little grunt as though he had passed some test.

'I am accompanying this gentleman to visit his sister at the hotel. Do you mind managing by yourself for an hour? I am not expecting more than usual to this afternoon's tea and everything is ready to set out.' Sara handed her henchwoman the card. Dot was not much of a reader, but it did no harm to let him see that someone else knew where she was going with Mr Dunton. She might be independent to a fault, according to her brother Ashe, but she was not reckless enough to go away with a strange gentleman without taking basic precautions. Particularly with this one who, she was certain, was not who he said he was.

'Aye, all's prepared and ready. All I need to do is to pour the hot water on the tea. Sandwiches are made, fruit cake and plain scones with strawberry jam waiting to be set out and the boy brought up a good lump of ice, so the cream and the butter are cooling nicely. I'll take my apron off and come out the front.' Her accent might be pure local Dorset, but none of their customers ever had any problem understanding it. If fate had decreed that Dot had been born somewhere other than a fisherman's cottage, then she would have made even more of herself than she had already.

'This is also a tea shop?' Mr Dunton enquired as Sara took a basket and began to walk around the shop, selecting things to try and tempt his sister's interest. It was hard to decide what to take, for Miss Dunton might be a very fragile invalid or she might simply be a wilful and tiresome brat. Time would tell.

'We provide tea and refreshments twice a week. Customers come and work on their latest artistic projects, or their writing, perhaps. They exchange ideas and take tea. It provides a congenial place for ladies to congregate, somewhere they are not expected to confine themselves to idle chit-chat or to sit about looking decorative.'

'And it encourages them to replenish their supplies while they are here.'

'Exactly. This is a business, after all, Mr Dunton. The ladies encourage each other, take up new crafts having seen them being practised by their acquaintances and have an enjoyable few hours together. If you are ready?'

She put on a light pelisse, tied on her new, and pleasingly dashing, bonnet and added her reticule to the craft supplies. Mr Dunton reached for the basket, Sara held on to it. 'There is someone outside to carry it, thank you, sir. I will be back soon, Dot.'

He held the door for her and attempted again to do polite battle for the basket, but as they emerged Tim Liddle came trotting over from the mouth of the alleyway beside the milliner's shop opposite. He was eight and the main support of his widowed mother, so Sara gave him all the odd jobs she could find and some she had to create. He was clean but skinny, despite her best efforts to feed him up, and dressed in clothes that were worn and handed down, but his gap-toothed grin was cheerful.

'Here you are, Tim. Down to the hotel with it, if you please.' She handed over the laden basket, took Mr Dunton's proffered arm and sent him a slanting look from under her bonnet brim as they walked down the hill to the promenade. 'You did not really think I would go to a hotel with a strange gentleman, just like that, without any escort?'

'That lad would not provide much protection against some unscrupulous buck, I'd have thought.'

'No? If I do not reappear by the time I give him

Timmy will raise hell with the hotel staff, then run for Dot, then fetch the constable whose second cousin he is.'

'Ah, the formidable Dot. Now *she* would scare any ill-meaning male. She might well have assisted Cronus in his gruesome assault on Uranus, given the size of those brawny arms and the look she gave me. Does she not like my face in particular, or is she opposed to the entire male sex on principle?'

Sara did not rise to the bait of his reference to Aphrodite's birth. 'Dot was a dipper. They need to be strong women to deal with nervous customers who have never been in the sea before. Some of them fall over and have to be dragged out of the surf and others become agitated when it comes to being dipped and so have to be held tight and ducked under even more firmly. She hurt her back and could no longer do such heavy work, so she came to help me. She was grateful for the opportunity and, quite unnecessarily, has set herself to guard me against…importunity.'

That should suppress any inclination Mr Dunton might have to flirtation. Sara, who was not above enjoying the escort of a large, elegant gentleman—or the stimulating sensation of a well-muscled arm under her hand—allowed the silence to persist for the five minutes it took to reach the Royal Promenade Hotel at a gentle stroll.

The hotel was a straggling edifice consisting of a number of adjoining buildings tacked together with linking doors and added passageways. All had been unified by a coat of cream colour wash over the entire façade, set off by royal blue trim and the hotel's name in large gilt letters.

Mr Dunton removed the basket from Tim's grasp and

stopped in front of the reception desk where the proprietor was speaking to the clerk. 'Mr Winstanley, would you show Mrs Harcourt to our private sitting room while I fetch my sister to her?'

Nicely done, sir, Sara thought as she, and her basket, were ushered upstairs and through to a pleasant room with a bay window overlooking the promenade. *All very much above-board and using Mr Winstanley to establish his credentials as a respectable man who does, indeed, have a sister in residence. But there is still something not quite right about you, Mr Dunton.*

But whatever it was it did not affect the essential attractive masculinity of the man, even if something was making her antennae twitch with curiosity. He was very aware of her as a woman and she was equally as aware of him—the trick was going to be not showing that.

She settled herself at the table, took the sketchbook and a pencil from the basket and began to draw the scene from the window, concentrating on a rapid and amusing vignette of two ladies who had stopped to chat by the flagpole. One was large, the other thin, and both had ridiculously small lapdogs on ribbon leashes. When the door opened Sara stood up and dropped the book quite casually, face-up, on the table.

The young woman who came into the room with Mr Dunton at her back was obviously his sister, with the same brown hair and hazel eyes, but a straighter nose and less firmness to her chin. She was also very obviously young, had been unwell and was in a state of the sulks.

'Marg—Mrs Harcourt, might I present my sister, Marguerite.' Mr Dunton frowned at his own stumble and the girl sent him a sharp glance. 'Marguerite, this is

Mrs Harcourt whose shop I passed today. She has kindly brought down some things that might interest you.'

Miss Dunton bobbed the sketchiest of curtsies and sat on the other side of the small round table set in the window bay.

How very interesting. Dunton had begun to present her to his sister, which was correct if the girl was of higher rank. Then he had caught himself and presented the girl to her, the older, married woman. Which meant two things. Firstly he was treating her like a lady, not a shopkeeper, and secondly he and his sister actually ranked above a respectable married lady, even though he did not know to whom she had been married.

If you are not in possession of a title, my fine gentleman, I will eat my expensive new bonnet, feathers and all.

So what was he doing in Sandbay and what was wrong with his sister?

Sara summoned up her professional smile and a brisk but friendly tone of voice. 'Good morning, Miss Dunton. My shop provides everything in the way of rational entertainment for ladies.' That was met with a blank look so she tried for something more direct. 'I stock everything from hammers to hit fossils out of rocks to nets to explore rock pools with.'

Finally she had managed to produce a blink of reaction from the young woman. 'Hammers?'

'And art materials and plain wooden boxes and mirror frames and so forth to decorate with paint or shells or scrollwork. Fabrics and embroidery floss, knitting wool, water trays for making seaweed pictures, patterns…books, journals.' She nodded towards the basket. 'Perhaps you would like to take a look. Would you excuse me while I just finish my sketch of those two ladies outside, they make such an amusing picture.'

Behind her chair she gestured with her hand towards the doorway, hoping Mr Dunton would take the hint. After a moment, when she picked up the pad and pencil again, she heard the door open and close and bent her head over the sketch. To have the man out of the room was like releasing a pent-up breath and letting air into her lungs. He seemed to inhabit all the space, even when she could not see him.

Sara steadied her breathing and her pencil. She was not here for Mr Dunton's sake.

Chapter Two

From the corner of her eye Sara saw Marguerite hesitate, then begin to explore the basket. 'Why would you want to hit rocks?' She uncorked a bottle of little shells and let them run out into her palm. 'And what is a fossil?'

Sara sketched and explained about fossils, then mentioned, very casually, how liberating it was to scramble about at the foot of the cliffs, hitting things hard. 'I really do not think that young ladies have the opportunity to hit things enough, do you?'

'I often want to.' Marguerite picked up the hammer and weighed it in her hand as though visualising a target. Despite her apparent fragility she managed it with little effort. 'Aren't rock pools full of slimy things?'

'They are full of beautiful things, some of which are a trifle slimy. But the pleasure of taking off your shoes and stockings and paddling far outweighs the occasional slithery sensation.'

'No stockings? In public?' Finally, some animation.

'On the beach only, of course. There, what do you think?' She tipped the sketch up for Marguerite to see.

'Oh, that is so amusing! The large lady with the little

dog and the thin lady with the fat pug. How clever you are. I could never do anything like that.'

'It really isn't very good technically—I only sketch for my own amusement and rarely show anyone.'

'I don't know *what* I want to do.' The girl's shoulders slumped again, the moment of animation gone. It wasn't boredom or petulance, more as though she was gazing at blankness, Sara thought. This went deeper than a lowness of spirits after the influenza or a fit of the sullens at being dragged off to the seaside by her brother. 'I can't draw as well as you. I do not like embroidery...'

'Neither do I. Did your governess insist on you sewing tiresome samplers?' Marguerite nodded, so, encouraged, Sara pressed on. 'I hold afternoon teas at my shop where ladies bring their craft work or their writing and chat and plan new projects and eat wickedly rich cake. There is no need to socialise if you don't want to—some ladies just read or browse.'

'I suppose they gossip about their beaux.' The pretty mouth set into a thin line.

'Not at all.' *Interesting. Has she been disappointed in love, perhaps?* 'We do not meet to talk about men, but about what amuses us. And men, so often, are not at all amusing, are they?'

'No. Not at all.' Marguerite glanced towards the door, then stooped to rummage in the basket again and came up with a pamphlet. 'What is this?'

'How to make seaweed pictures. It is rather fun, only very messy and wet. I am holding a tea this afternoon at three, if you would like to come. It is six pence for refreshments and there is no obligation to buy anything.'

'What did Lucian tell you about me?' Marguerite asked suddenly.

There are going to be tears in a moment, poor child. Whatever is wrong? Don't lie to her—she will know. She isn't stupid.

'That you hadn't been well, that you were here for your health, but were very bored, and he hoped I might have something that would entertain you. Do you wish you were back in London? If that is where you live?'

'No… Yes, that is where our town house is, where my brother lives. I wish I were in France.' The hazel eyes with their lids that seemed swollen from crying gazed out southwards over the sea. 'I wish I was dead,' Marguerite whispered so softly that Sara realised she could pretend she hadn't heard that heart-rending murmur. What on earth could she reply that wasn't simply a string of ill-informed platitudes?

'I have never been to France. I was brought up in India.'

'Is that why your skin is so golden? Oh, I do beg your pardon, it was rude of me to make a personal observation like that. Only you are so very striking.'

'Not at all. I am one-quarter Indian on my mother's side. Her mother was a Rajput princess.'

That sent the threat of tears into full retreat. 'A *princess*? And you own a *shop*?'

'Because it amuses me. When my husband died I wanted to do something practical for a while, to get right away from everything that had been my life before. I found it helped.' *A little. It even keeps the nightmares at bay for most of the time.*

That would probably all get back to Mr Dunton, or whatever his name was, but her real identity was no secret in Sandbay. It would certainly serve to confuse the man, what with his assumptions about widows. Would he still flirt with a part-Indian descendant of royalty?

She glanced at the clock on the mantelshelf. 'I must go now. Shall I look for you this afternoon?' Sara kept the question indifferent, as though she did not much mind one way or another. This girl was being pushed to do things for her own good and her natural reaction was to push back, because that gave her some feeling of control. Sara reflected that she was all too familiar with that response herself. She began to gather up the scattered contents of the basket, pouring the seashells back into their jar.

'Yes, I will, thank you. Must my brother come, too?'

'Oh, no. We do not allow the gentlemen to join in. He may deliver you and collect you, of course.'

And, finally, she had earned a smile. Small and fleeting, but a smile. What on earth was wrong with the child? And with her relationship with her brother, for that matter.

They said their goodbyes, Sara deep in thought. The moment she closed the door behind her the basket was taken out of her hands.

'What response did you get?'

'Mr Dunton, I suggest you speak to your sister. I am not some sort of go-between for you and I am certainly not going to spy on her.' Then she saw the rigid set of his jaw and the anxiety in his eyes and relented. 'Miss Dunton would like to come to our tea this afternoon. Three o'clock, for ladies only.'

'These are all respectable ladies—' he began.

'Either you trust me, Mr *Dunton*, or you do not. Good day to you. I hope to see your sister later.' She did not stop to see if he reacted to the emphasis she put on his name. 'Tim! Take the basket, if you please.'

Respectable ladies, indeed. What does *he take me for?*

A fierce little beauty. Lucian was in half a mind to wrest the basket back from her tame urchin and walk Mrs Harcourt back up the hill. Then he recalled why he was here, which was not to flirt with shopkeepers, however well spoken. However beautiful. Mrs Harcourt was slender, except for a lush bosom, and she was blonde, grey-eyed and golden-skinned. She might have Italian blood, perhaps, although that imperious little nose did not look Italian. Very beautiful, very self-possessed and dressed in perfect, expensive, simplicity. This was not what he had expected to find when he had set out that morning to interview a shopkeeper.

He nodded to the porter who opened the front door for him and strolled across the road to lean back against the rail that protected the drop to the beach. From there he could watch Mrs Harcourt stroll up the hill without appearing to stare. Even in motion she had a poise that argued a much more rigorous upbringing than a shopkeeper normally had. And when she was near there was a rumour of perfume in the air, a scent shockingly exotic in the salt-laden air of this little Dorset town. Sandalwood and something else, something peppery. Temptation, indeed. His body stirred at the memory.

Her voice was not merely genteel and well modulated, it was unmistakably of the upper classes. What on earth was a lady, a respectable young widow, doing acting as shopkeeper in a seaside resort, guarded by her miniature police spy and her formidable assistant?

Lucian was conscious that the puzzle was doing nothing to dampen his very definite arousal.

How long had it been since he had been with a woman? Not since the beginning of this nightmare with Marguerite, he realised. Almost six months…a long time for him. Ever since he had been an adult he had been in a discreet relationship of some kind, sometimes simply brief *affaires*…more recently longer-term arrangements with a mistress. Lucian was naturally wary either of compromising his partners or of exposing himself to emotional entanglements. He was conscious of what was due to his name and his position and the reputation that his father had acquired as a womaniser did nothing to recommend a more flamboyant way of life to him. Finding himself responsible for a sister was an added incentive for discretion and the thought of next Season, when he had resolved to find himself a suitable young lady to court and marry, was another reason against setting up a new mistress. He had no intention of being an unfaithful husband.

But six months… No wonder the thought of taking a mistress was appealing. And pretty widows were often game for a brief liaison, ideal for a situation where his stay here was inevitably limited. But not, it seemed, *this* widow, who gave him the uneasy feeling that she was a mind reader and had no intention of reaching the end of the chapter as far as he was concerned.

Mrs Harcourt was almost out of sight now, still walking slowly, talking as she went to the lad beside her whose head was tipped to one side so he could look up at her. For some reason the slow pace seemed uncharacteristic—he could imagine her in rapid motion, swift, swirling, dangerous.

Dangerous? He really needed to get a grip on his fantasies.

That man had come out of the hotel and was watching her, she could feel it, even though she did not make the mistake of looking back. Sara kept her pace slow: let him look, she was not going to scuttle away like a nervous maiden and reveal how much he unnerved her.

'Just drop that at the shop, there's a good boy, and ask Dot for tuppence,' she said to Tim as he shifted the big basket from one hand to the other. She kept going past Aphrodite's Seashell and went into the third establishment she came to, Makepeace's Circulating Library and Emporium, the town's only library.

'Good morning, Mr Makepeace.'

James Makepeace was sitting behind the counter, making up an order for one of the page boys at the hotel to take down for a visitor. He stood up, bowed from the neck and sat down again. 'How may I assist you, Mrs Harcourt?' He knew perfectly well who she really was, all the town did, but he kept her two identities, the shop and her social life, scrupulously separate like everyone else.

'I wanted to consult the *Peerage,* if it is available, Mr Makepeace.'

If the library had been empty, which rarely happened during opening hours, he would stammer out *Sara* and she would call him James and he would blush rather shyly, his ears turning red, and offer her a cup of tea, which was as far as his notions of courtship dared go.

Sara did not encourage him beyond friendship, it

would not be fair. She liked him very well, although not in any romantic sense. Besides, she had one marriage to a sweet, unworldly man behind her and she knew that it took a special kind of gentleman not to be dominated by her direct approach to life. The librarian was a friend, and always an amiable one, and that was quite enough for her.

'It is on the usual shelf upstairs, Mrs Harcourt. Please let me know if I can be of further help.'

She murmured her thanks and climbed the short flight of stairs to the reading room with its panoramic view of the bay, one of its main attractions for those who were not bookish. Several people were out on the balcony in the sunshine using the telescope, two elderly gentlemen were engaged in a politely vicious dispute over the possession of *The Times* newspaper and a pair of young ladies came through from the lending section clutching a pile of what looked suspiciously like sensation novels.

Sara found the familiar thick red volume of the *Peerage* and settled down at a table. She had been out for less than a year before she married and she and Michael had moved immediately to Cambridge for him to take up his new post at one of the colleges. It was perfectly possible that she had missed seeing any number of members of the *ton,* including Mr Dunton, especially as her family had come to England from India only shortly before the Season began.

If I were going to take a false name I would keep it as close to my real one as possible so I would react to it without hesitation, she thought. Mr Dunton was about twenty-eight or nine, she guessed. His card gave his initials only, L. J., but Marguerite had called him Lucian quite naturally, so that was a start. She would begin with the Marquesses and work down the hierarchy because she was certain she knew all the dukes, at least by sight.

There was always the possibility that he was the heir to a title, which would slow the search down, but she was certain he was not a younger son. That gentleman had been born with a silver spoon, if not an entire table setting, firmly stuck in his mouth. Two pages…she turned the third and struck gold. There it was.

Lucian John Dunton Avery, third Marquess of Cannock, born 1790. Only sibling Marguerite Antonia, born 1800. Seat, Cullington Park, Hampshire.

She closed the book with a satisfied thump of the thick pages which made the elderly gentlemen look over and glower. She smiled sweetly at them and they went back to their newspapers.

So why was the Marquess staying at the hotel incognito? There was nothing unfashionable or shocking about taking a seaside holiday in the summer and a good half of the *ton* did just that, although this was a quiet resort and not a magnet for society's high-fliers like Brighton to the east or Weymouth, for the more sedate of the *ton*, to the west.

He was hardly outrunning his creditors and if there had been a great scandal involving him she must have noticed it in the papers, however little interest she took in society gossip. Or her mother would have written about it in the fat weekly letters that covered everything from the latest crim. con. scandals to the more obscure lectures at the Royal Society.

So the anonymity must be because of his sister and,

as there was no shame in being unwell and a large pro-
portion of the visitors were invalids or convalescent,
there must be a scandal to be hidden, poor girl. She
would need handling with even more sensitivity if that
were the case.

Sara slid the *Peerage* back in its place on the shelf
and went downstairs.

'You found what you wanted, Mrs Harcourt?'

She was so preoccupied that James's question made
her jump. 'Hmm? Oh, yes, thank you.'

'Will you be at the Rooms tonight? It is a ball night.'
Despite being shy James Makepeace loved to dance and
the Assembly Rooms' programme always included two
ball nights every week during the summer season. When
she nodded he asked, 'Will you save me a set, Mrs Harcourt?'

'Of course. The very first.' Even with the Assembly Rooms' rather limited orchestra it was a pleasure
to dance. She had missed that almost more than anything during her long year of mourning. At least the
very serious and straight-faced Marquess-in-disguise
was unlikely to indulge in anything quite so frivolous
as a seaside assembly dance.

Lucian was in half a mind to order a sedan chair for
Marguerite to take her up the hill to Aphrodite's Seashell, amused to see that the resort still provided them.
But when he suggested it she laughed, actually *laughed*,
and he was so delighted that he could not bear to put a
frown back on her face by insisting.

She had been so bitterly sad and angry—with him, of
course. This was all *his* fault, according to Marguerite.
Not that bas— All the spirit, all the restless enthusiasm

that was Marguerite, had been knocked out of her, replaced by a listless apathy in which he could not make the smallest crack. Even the anger had faded away, which was what had truly frightened him.

Marguerite was his only sibling and he was well aware that the difference in their age and sex had kept them apart. His childhood had been far stricter than hers—tutors, riding and fencing masters, carefully selected playmates from suitable local families had filled his days and provided his company. He could never forget that he was heir to an ancient title, great responsibilities, with a duty to the past and to the future. Marguerite had been spoiled and rather vaguely educated by a doting governess—it was no wonder that she had been hit so hard by what had happened.

'As though I want to be carted through the streets like an ageing dowager,' she said, pulling him back from his brooding, and slipped her hand into the crook of his arm, just like she used to do in the days before she ran away.

'Well, take it slowly,' he chided, not wanting to let his delight show. 'It is a hill.'

'I have to learn to climb hills again some time, otherwise everything would be abominably flat,' Marguerite observed as she unfurled her parasol.

Had that been a mild joke, a pun even? Perhaps this flight to the seaside had not been such a bad idea after all and he had been too impatient for results. She managed the climb well, without needing to pause for breath, and studied the shop windows as they passed with something like interest.

Lucian took her into Aphrodite's Seashell and let his gaze wander with seeming casualness over the women already gathered around the long table. Some were sit-

ting with craftwork spread out in front of them, others
stood chatting. Everyone looked up as he and Marguerite entered and then the ladies went back to what they
had been doing without any vulgar staring. They all
seemed perfectly respectable, well dressed and spoke in
educated accents. Their ages ranged from about twenty
to sixty, he estimated.

Mrs Harcourt was standing at the shelves, a number
of books in her hands, talking to a tall, earnest-looking
woman. 'You could either write the journal directly into
a book that is already bound and do your sketches on
blank pages, or do the entire thing loose-leaf and then
have it bound up, which might be safer—then if there
are any small corrections you want to make that page
can easily be replaced. But see what you think of these,
at any rate, Mrs Prentice.'

She excused herself and came over to greet them.
'Miss Dunton, Mr Dunton.' She looked at him and
Lucian found himself staring back into those intelligent
grey eyes that, surely, held a gleam of mischief. What
was there to amuse her? It did not seem to be malicious,
more, almost, as though they shared a secret. And once
more that inconvenient sense of attraction, of arousal,
stirred. It should not have surprised him, he thought.
This was a lovely woman with an intriguing mixture of
assured sophistication and youth.

He wanted to touch her, badly, and that made him
abrupt. 'I understand there is a small charge for refreshments?'

'Six pence, if you please, Mr Dunton.'

Lucian took off his glove to retrieve the loose change
from his pocket book and held out the small coin, rather
than put it on the counter. She extended her own hand,

palm up, and his bare fingertips brushed her skin as he laid the silver on it. He suspected she knew exactly what he was about, but she was perfectly composed as she broke the contact and placed the coin on the counter. Her hand had been warm and soft to his fleeting touch and Lucian had a startling mental picture of it, pale gold on his bare skin.

'Thank you, sir. At what time will you be returning to collect your sister? There is an excellent library just up the street on this side, if you choose to wait.'

So much for any thought of waiting in the shop to observe proceedings. 'Thank you, I will investigate it,' he said with a deliberately cheerful, open smile when he suspected she was anticipating something more laden with meaning, an invitation to flirt, perhaps. 'Half past four, Marguerite?'

'Mmm? Oh, yes, thank you.' His sister was already investigating the books and pamphlets. As he watched her a woman in late middle age smiled and indicated a book with a murmured comment. Marguerite took it down from the shelf and Lucian nodded to Mrs Harcourt, resumed his hat and left the shop.

Most definitely surplus to requirements, he thought, turning to continue up the hill in search of the library. It was a surprisingly good feeling to see Marguerite confident and engrossed. He couldn't even be annoyed that Mrs Harcourt was proving so resistant to his hints. She was a respectable lady with a position in the town to defend, no doubt, and, as a gentleman he had no intention of ruffling those feathers without a clear signal to proceed. Still, it was a pity, he enjoyed the unspoken conversation they seemed to be having. Or perhaps it was a duel.

Chapter Three

Two hours later Sara watched Mr Dunton—*the Mysterious Marquess*, as she was beginning to think of him—finally extract his sister from the shop, his arms full of parcels. She had suggested that Marguerite leave her purchases, and the shell-work project she had just begun work on, and she would have Tim bring them down to the hotel. But nothing would content her other than heaping them into her brother's arms, despite the fact that no gentleman—let alone a marquess—should be walking around town laden like a footman.

To judge by his expression, any number of parcels was worth the animation on the girl's face, the colour in her cheeks. Sara knew she ought to dislike him, or, at least, be completely indifferent to him, for he was exactly the kind of man she was living her life to avoid, but she admired his care for Marguerite.

She was still musing on the brother and sister—rather more on the brother, if she were to be truthful—as she locked the door, drew down the blind and began to deal with the contents of the cash drawer while Dot cleared away the tea things and washed up. The day's takings had been good, she saw with satisfaction, entering them in her ledger before locking the money bag away in the safe. She must make a trip to the bank tomorrow, which was very gratifying.

It was not that she needed the money, exactly, but profitability was her main measure of success in a business and Sara did not like to fail at anything she put her hand to.

'There you are, ducks.' Dot emerged from the scullery, flapping a drying cloth before hanging it on the rail. 'All done and dusted. Busy today, wasn't it? I liked that little scrap of a lass, the new one. Pretty manners and no side to her. Looks as though she's been having a difficult time of it though, bless her. It's a hard thing to lose a baby.'

'What?' Sara stood up from the safe so sharply that she hit her head on the shelf above. 'Ouch! What do you mean about a baby?'

'She's grieving and sad and she's thin—but not in her bubbies. And Mrs Pike knocked against her when she passed the scones and she flinched and made a little sound like it hurt. I reckon they're still sore, poor lamb, just like mine were when I lost our second.'

'But she's so young, only eighteen, I think. Oh, Dot, how awful.' No wonder her brother was so anxious and so protective and they were here under a false name. 'We must look after her, because I don't think she has her mother or a companion with her, no woman to talk to, only her brother—and her maid, I suppose. And I would wager this shop he's thinking most of the time about how to kill the man who fathered her child and not about how it has affected her.'

That was what men of breeding did, guarded the honour of their womenfolk whether the women wanted it or not. And people got killed as a result and the women in question were tied about with rules and restrictions because their menfolk cared so much and honour meant everything. *Their* honour, she told herself angrily. That helped stifle her own guilty conscience. A little.

The demands of honour had killed her husband, the man she had thought was above those antiquated notions about women and their lack of right to govern themselves and it had driven her here, a safe distance from the loving tyranny of father and brother. She could not turn away from Marguerite.

'We'll do our best for her, that's for sure.' The older woman threw her shawl around her shoulders and picked up her basket. 'I'm off home to make supper, then we're going down to the Dog and Mackerel, Farwell and me. What'll you be doing, ducks?'

'Dancing at the Assembly Rooms. I have promised Mr Makepeace a set.'

'He's sweet on you, you know, and he'll never say, a'cos of who you really are.'

'I know. I don't encourage him, Dot. I just want to be friends. It isn't because of who I am—it's because I don't think of him in any other way.'

'Aye, poor bugger. He knows it, so don't you be worrying about breaking his heart. He wouldn't do for you anyway, but he'll be hard put to compete with the likes of that other one now he is on the scene.'

'What other one?' *As if I don't know.* 'Honestly, Dot, shouldn't you be off home?'

Her henchwoman, superbly indifferent to hints, made herself more comfortable with one expansive hip propped against the doorframe. 'That Mr Dunton. If he's a plain mister, then I'm the Duchess of Devonshire. And he's taken a fancy to you. Not an honest one, that's true, but where's the harm in a bit of fun between the sheets, you being unattached and no maiden, as it were?'

'Dot, stop it this minute. *A bit of fun between the sheets* indeed! I wouldn't think of such a thing.'

Which is a barefaced lie. I haven't thought of much else since I set eyes on him. The Mystery Marquess. Only his presence here was not such a mystery now she knew about his sister.

'Aye, well, that's what you say. You have a good time and if the Rooms are too dull, you drop in at the Dog and join in the sing-song.' She took herself off on a gale of laughter at the thought, leaving Sara torn between amusement and exasperation.

Home for you, my girl. A nice bath, a few letters to write and then get dressed up and off to the Rooms for some wild dissipation, Sandbay-style.

Sandbay's Assembly Rooms were only a year old, the creation of a consortium of the town's leading businessmen who had raised the money for the construction. They had visited Weymouth and Brighton to seek inspiration and had returned to order a building containing a ballroom, card room, tea room and the associated retiring rooms, cloakrooms and entrance hall.

It was all very shiny, still smelled faintly of paint and had proved an instant success with the visitors and local gentry alike. Sara, who had a subscription for the season, paid off her sedan chair, left her outer clothing at the cloakroom and entered the tea room which served as the foyer during the evenings. A little flurry of new visitors was clustered around the Master of Ceremonies, Mr Flyte, who abandoned them with a smile and descended upon Sara.

'Dear Lady Sarisa, welcome, welcome.' She was his highest-ranking subscriber—unless *Mr Dunton* had subscribed and been recognised—and flattering her was far more important to the Master of Ceremonies than any number of newly arrived minor gentry.

'Mr Flyte, please do not let me interrupt. You were speaking to these ladies and gentlemen.' She bowed slightly in apology to the waiting visitors, annoyed that he had deserted them to toady to her, and went on through to the ballroom.

Although the music had not yet begun the room was already filling up, none of the subscribers feeling the need to demonstrate fashionable *ennui* and drift in halfway through proceedings.

James Makepeace appeared at her side, slightly pink and scrubbed around the ears, but smartly attired in his best evening suit. 'Lady Sarisa, good evening. You have not forgotten that you promised me the first set, I hope?'

'I have not.' She put her hand on his proffered arm and they strolled around the room, greeting old friends and stopping to chat with the local squire, Sir Humphrey Janes, whose grandfather had built the first lodging houses which had given the resort its initial impetus. His son had invested in the hotel and the bathing rooms and the present baronet saw it as his family duty to encourage the social life of Sandbay.

'You are in great beauty tonight, my lady.' He bowed over her hand, twitted the librarian mildly on his courage in leading out the belle of the ball and warned Sara to ready herself for a visit from his sister. 'She has plans for a charity bazaar and is scouring the town for committee members for the organisation. You would do well to flee to Brighton, if not Scarborough, to be at a safe distance.'

It was the laughter that caught Lucian's attention as he entered the ballroom, Mr Flyte at his side. Rich and musical, it sent a shiver of awareness down his spine.

'Now, Mr Dunton, you must not hesitate to call upon my services for any needs you have while you are a guest in our little town. We may be small, but we pride ourselves here in Sandbay on giving our visitors our most personal attention. Suggestions for tours, recommendations for the most reliable livery stable—'

'Who is that lady? The one in the amber and the emeralds? The one laughing.'

It couldn't be, surely? A shopkeeper in silk and gems? Perhaps they were paste, but he doubted it—the green glowed in the candlelight with the authentic fire in the eyes of a black panther.

'That, Mr Dunton, is our most distinguished resident, Lady Sarisa Harcourt—Lady Sarisa Herriard as was— the only daughter of the Marquess of Eldonstone.' The Master of Ceremonies beamed as though he was personally responsible for the appearance of so elevated a personage. 'A widow, you understand,' he murmured. 'We are fortunate that she recovers from her loss amongst us.'

'Mr Flyte, this morning I took my sister to a shop called Aphrodite's Seashell and met a Mrs Harcourt who bears a most uncanny resemblance to that lady.' Someone was playing games with him and he did not like it.

'Oh, hush, sir, I do beg you.' Flyte was positively flapping his hands in agitation at this indiscretion. 'A little eccentricity in a lady is something to be indulged, is it not?'

'It is?' Eccentric dowagers were one thing, beautiful young widows were quite another.

'Oh, most certainly. Lady Sarisa lends lustre to all the social and charitable occasions in the town and also amuses herself harmlessly by providing entertainment of a cultured and unexceptionable kind to ladies of all ages.' He cleared his throat and lowered his voice even more. 'We assist in keeping her ladyship's two, shall we say, *lives* quite separate.'

What the blazes her father the Marquess thought of this Lucian could not imagine. He had met the man, and his exquisite and alarming Marchioness, two years ago when they had come to England from India when Eldonstone inherited the title. The East India Company soldier and his exotic, half-Indian wife had caused a stir amongst the *ton* and there had been a son and daughter, he recalled now, but he had not met them because he had been called from London to his father's deathbed and the remainder of that Season had passed without him.

Lady Sarisa had inherited her mother's looks, but her father's blond hair and grey eyes, striking in contrast with the pale gold of her skin. For a moment he speculated that her marriage had caused a rift in the family, but if it had, she had not been cut off without a penny, because that gown and those gems had not been bought on a shopkeeper's earnings.

The small string orchestra struck up with a flourish and couples began to come on to the floor to form the first set. Lady Sarisa was led out by someone else he recognised, the gangling local librarian.

'I would beg the favour of an introduction to the lady when this set is completed, Mr Flyte.'

'Of course, sir. I would be only too happy to oblige.'

Lucian might be incognito, but he knew that Flyte had discreetly assessed his tailoring, his accent and his manner and clearly decided that he was suitable to make the acquaintance of Sandbay's grandest resident.

Lucian was wryly amused at his own reaction to that valuation. He had thought that somehow he kept his own self-esteem separate from his sense of what was due to his rank and position, but it seemed that his father's constant reminders of what was due to—and from—a marquess had made a deeper impression than he had thought. This was the first time that he had ever found himself in society as a plain gentleman and it was a mild shock to find how much he would have been put out to have been ignored.

He took himself off to the card room, reluctant to let Lady Sara see him standing waiting on her, watching her. If she wanted to play games, he was not going to join in, at least, not too obviously. But how to approach her now? Flirtation would be acceptable, he was certain, but anything else was another matter. This was not some dashing widow on the fringes of society.

When the set finally came to an end he was back in the ballroom, Mr Flyte at his side.

'Lady Sarisa.'

She turned at the sound of the Master of Ceremonies' voice, the movement wafting her scent to Lucian's nostrils. Definitely sandalwood, with an overtone of citrus, an undertone of pepper and a stimulating *frisson* of warm female skin, although that last might have been his fantasies at play.

'Mr Flyte.' The smile on her lips curved them into

a seductive bow and her grey eyes seemed to pick up green glints from the emeralds at her ears and throat.

'May I have the honour of presenting Mr Dunton of Hampshire to your ladyship as an eligible partner? Mr Dunton, Lady Sarisa Harcourt.'

Lucian bowed, she curtsied. Mr Flyte retired beaming.

'Lady Sarisa.'

'My lord.'

For a moment he thought he had misheard her, then he saw those grey eyes were alight with mischief. 'Just who do you think I am, madam? I confess that you have me confused.'

'I know exactly who you are. The Marquess of Cannock. Do you intend to ask me to dance, my lord? I am unengaged for the next set.'

'I would be delighted,' he said grimly, offering his hand as the musicians signalled the start. 'We need to talk, Lady Sarisa, but not here.'

'No, indeed. I will show you our seafront terrace after this set. It is delightful on such a warm evening as this.'

'I am sure it is.' Lucian made himself concentrate on the dance, a complex country measure that kept him busy negotiating the steps and gave little opportunity for speculation on the games *eccentric* young ladies might play on moonlit terraces.

'There is no reason we may not converse about general matters,' Lady Sarisa remarked as the convolutions of the dance brought them together for a moment. 'Unless you are a nervous dancer, of course, in which case I will observe strict silence. You only have to give me a hint. Do you intend a long stay in Sandbay, *Mr Dunton*?'

'My nerves will withstand a little conversation, I

believe. I had planned on a stay of a few weeks, *Mrs Harcourt.*'

She chuckled softly as the measure separated them and he remembered with a jolt that this was not some game between the two of them, but something much more serious. She knew he was keeping his sister from society, that there was something very wrong and he had no idea at all whether he could trust her discretion. Who did she know and, more importantly, who might she gossip to? If he had any hope of saving Marguerite's reputation then she must make her come-out next Season in good health and spirits without a whisper of suspicion that anything had gone amiss. Even then, it was going to be hard enough finding a suitor willing to overlook what had happened if it ever came to a proposal of marriage.

But he would cross that bridge when he came to it. For now, there was this woman to deal with. *This infuriating, teasing, beautiful woman.*

By the time the set had finished Lucian was quite ready to scoop up Lady Sarisa and dangle her over the waves if that was what it took to ensure her promise of silence. Somehow he managed to wait until they were off the dance floor and to make his words a suggestion, not a demand. 'Madam. Would you care to take the air?'

'That would be delightful. The terrace is this way.'

The Assembly Rooms building stood at one end of the promenade with its back to the sea at the point where the sweep of sand tapered into the beginning of low cliffs. At high water, which was the present state of the tide, the waves broke against the foot of the sea wall along which the terrace had been built. In a high wind they would have been drenched. As it was, with only the lightest breeze, and the moonlight enhancing the glimmer of lanterns set along the balustrade, it was a welcome escape from the heat and noise of the ballroom.

Lucian scanned the terrace along which at least half-a-dozen couples were strolling. 'We are adequately chaperoned, I see.'

'We will be alone soon enough, but I am not quite so careless of my reputation as to come out here when it is deserted to begin with, my... Mr Dunton.'

'If your reputation can survive spending half your time as a shopkeeper, Lady Sarisa, I would suggest it could stand most things.'

'Sara, please. Anywhere else it would not, of course, but Sandbay is not the resort of the *ton,* nor even the smarter set. One day soon it will begin to come into fashion and then I will have to become respectable all of the time or leave.' She lifted her hand from his arm and strolled to the balustrade.

Lucian felt as though he had stepped away from a warm hearth. 'You do not fear that irreparable damage has already been done by your masquerade as a shopkeeper?'

Lady Sara turned in a swirl of skirts and leaned back, both her elbows on the stonework. The amber silk settled into soft folds that hinted at the slender limbs and feminine curves beneath. He kept his eyes on her face with an effort that he feared was visible.

'It is not a masquerade. I *am* a shopkeeper, just not all of the time.' She sighed. 'I see I was right about you, Mr Dunton—you are one of those men who believe a woman begins and ends with her reputation and that what defines good and bad reputation is dictated entirely by the whims of society.'

'Hardly whims. The conventions uphold moral standards and protect the lady concerned from insult.' *Lord, but I sound like some crusty old dowager.*

'You believe that running a shop as I do somehow degrades my morals?' Sara seemed genuinely to expect him to answer such a shocking question. 'If I were running a milliner's and whoring out my assistants, which is all too common, then, yes, I would agree with you. It seems to me that society is too lazy to apply judgements on a case-by-case basis and so must make sweeping statements that mean nothing and only serve to imprison women.'

'The rules are there to protect women, not imprison them.'

'They do little to protect *women* who are without money or influence, those who have to work for their living. They trap *ladies*.' The passionate belief throbbed through her voice.

He could have shaken her because she was so mistaken. 'It is the duty of gentlemen to protect ladies. A matter of honour. You know your father and brother would say the same and your husband would have agreed.'

'Oh, yes, he agreed with them. In the end.' A tremor shook her voice and for a moment he thought she blinked back tears, then she was on the attack again. 'When you come right down to it this is all about *men's* honour because we are your possessions.'

'Ladies need protection.' Lucian stalked over to the balustrade and stood a safe six feet away. Shaking the provoking creature would not be a good illustration of his case, kissing her even worse. 'How did you get here this evening, for example? These streets and lanes are dark, anyone could be lurking.'

'By sedan chair with the same two reliable, burly chairmen I always use. They will come and collect me later. And should desperate footpads leap out and manage to fell both of them, then I can defend myself.'

'How? With sharp words?' he demanded and took two strides to stand in front of her, his hands either side, pinning her back against the balustrade. 'Men are stronger, more vicious, than you could imagine.'

'Also more vulnerable,' she murmured. 'Look down, my lord. It is not only my words that have an edge.'

He did, just as he felt a pressure against the falls of his evening breeches. In the moonlight something glinted, sharp steel, held rock-steady in her hand. Lucian stood quite still. 'Where did that come from?'

Chapter Four

Sara's smile was wicked as she watched his face. 'My sleeve. The current fashion for long sleeves on evening gowns makes life so much simpler. I am carrying two blades and three hairpins which are not really hairpins at all. And the cord threaded through my reticule is the perfect length for a garrotte. There are other things in my repertoire, but I shall keep them to myself in case I should need them.'

'Who the blazes taught you to use a knife?' *And a garrotte?* The dangerously intimate pressure eased and when he risked another downward glance the blade had vanished.

'My mother. At her uncle's court she and the other ladies were taught to fight. If an enemy had penetrated into the fort then they would have defended themselves and died rather than be captured and dishonoured. Their honour was in their own hands, you see.' She smiled, the moonlight throwing mysterious shadows across her face. 'My father and my brother added to my education, even though they are both European enough to want to fight the duels themselves on my behalf.'

'So I should hope.'

'Don't be so stuffy, my lord.'

Stuffy! His father's infidelities had hurt his mother deeply, not that she ever gave any obvious sign of even knowing about them. As a youth Lucian had watched and listened and, he supposed, he had judged his father. A gentleman behaved in a certain way—or, rather, he must be seen to behave that way. Appearances were all. But to Lucian that seemed like hypocrisy and he vowed he would not behave that way. Not only did one not hurt women, but one protected them, with one's life if necessary.

But to label him as stuffy because of that was the outside of enough. The music had begun again. Lucian was aware of movement along the terrace, then he sensed they were alone. A rapid glance confirmed it. 'You think me stuffy?' he demanded.

She nodded, so close that the movement brought her upswept hair close to his face. *Sandalwood, pepper, warm woman...*

Lucian bent his head and kissed her. He lifted his hands away from the balustrade so that she could slide sideways if she wished, then closed his eyes and sank into the sensual, dangerous taste of her. Her hands, innocent of any weapon, settled on his shoulders and he let his own close around her waist, feeling the delicious swell of her hips, resisting the urge to lift his hands to her breasts.

She had been a married woman, one who had enjoyed fully the sensual pleasures of the marriage bed—that was very apparent in the frank way she kissed him back, the sinuous glide of her tongue into his mouth, the way her body moulded itself to his. To kiss her, to hold her, was every bit as inflammatory as the fantasies he had been trying to push away since he had first set eyes on her. And now he wanted more. He wanted all of her, naked, in his arms, in his bed.

Lucian's kiss was every bit as delicious as she had been dreaming about, his hands on her body as strong. The subtle vibration running through his muscles told her how hard the effort to restrain himself was and that was reassuring. She had not misread this man after all. He wanted her, but he would ask for what he wanted and take *no* for an answer, she thought.

But the indulgence of a kiss was one thing, allowing him to assume her intentions went any further, as far as her desires, was quite another. It took an effort that surprised her to push Lucian away, her lips clinging for one last moment of contact.

His hands dropped from her waist and he stepped back, his face impossible to read in the poor light. 'I apologise.'

'Why?' She felt genuine surprise. 'If I had objected, you would have been in no doubt. I wanted you to kiss me.'

'Why?' he echoed her, standing very still. Sara realised that the lamplight fell full on her face and he was studying her expression intently.

'Because you are an attractive man, because I miss being kissed and because I was curious.'

'And is your curiosity satisfied now?' Lucian's voice was very dry.

'Perfectly, thank you.'

He moved slightly and the light caught the lower part of his face, betraying just the glimmer of a smile, a sen-

sual curve of those lips that had been so skilful, caressing hers. 'And?'

'And nothing more. I know why you are here under
an assumed name and I know what it is like to kiss you.'

'You know why? How can you?' Every ounce of sensuality had vanished from his voice. Sara found she was
glad of the support of the cold stone at her back.

'Because Dot knows what it is to lose a baby.'

The hiss of his indrawn breath was audible even over
the sound of the waves sucking at the shingle on the
beach below.

'Neither of us would dream of betraying her secret
and I do not think anyone else would realise unless they
knew how sad and fragile she is.' When Lucian said
nothing she risked putting her hand on his forearm.
'Marguerite is lucky to have your support.'

He shrugged. 'I feel helpless. I do not know how to
help her, to reach her. She rejects everything I try.'

'You have to give her time, she is mourning.' In the
ballroom there was applause as another set drew to a
close. 'We cannot talk out here for much longer or it will
be noticed. Tomorrow the shop is closed for the morning, come then. I would like to help Marguerite if I can.
A loving brother is a wonderful thing, but I suspect she
needs a woman to talk to.'

Lucian put his hand over hers as it rested against his
arm. 'What happened just now—'

'Was a moment that will not be repeated? Of course
it will not. I told you I was curious, not that I expected
an *affaire* and, besides, you do not want a woman with
whom you are having an irregular relationship anywhere
near your sister, do you?'

His cool silence said it all. Where had all that tingling

warmth gone to? Sara took back her hand, gathered up her skirts and moved towards a side door. 'I will go to the ladies' retiring room, it would be more discreet if we do not return together.'

And so much for your assumption that you were sophisticated enough to deal with any gentleman who crossed your path, she scolded herself. No wonder he had become cool. She had sent messages that she was available and then backed away. He must think she was an outrageous flirt or a horrid tease and either possibility made her feel hot with an embarrassment she hadn't felt for years.

The room set aside for ladies to repair their complexions and hair, and to have drooping hems and split seams attended to, was mercifully empty, except for the maid on duty. She stood up when Sara entered, bobbed a curtsy and then waited in the background while she sat at a dressing table and made a pretence of fussing with her hair.

What did you expect? she scolded herself. Sinking with embarrassment was not going to help matters, she needed to understand herself. She had wanted a moment of madness, the touch of a man's mouth on hers, the affirmation that she was not rushing towards a sexless middle age, she supposed, and Lucian had assumed she expected more, probably a full-blown affair, she guessed.

Perhaps that is *what I really want*. She hadn't expected to miss sex. It had been lovely with Michael, of course. She had loved him and he had been tender and careful. Perhaps, thinking about it in retrospect, a little too respectful. All the whispers, the gossip from other women, portrayed sex as exciting, thrilling, sublime. Her experience had been that it was pleasant, and occasionally exciting, and the intimacy and trust had certainly brought her and Michael closer together. But sublime and thrilling? That kiss just now had been thrilling, it had made her toes curl, but perhaps that was simply because it was not a married kiss but a shocking one.

The Marquess of Cannock was a physically attractive man who apparently found her attractive, too, which was, in itself, arousing. But he was precisely the kind of man she had avoided marrying, the sort who wanted to smother all his womenfolk under the all-enveloping cloak of his honour, to control them, however benevolently. Daydreams and frankly erotic night-time dreams were no reason to risk entangling herself with a man she would have no intention of marrying.

Sara frowned at her own face in the mirror. It had taken long enough to recover from Michael's death, she would be insane to risk her still-tender emotions on a man so very different, so very…dangerous.

She gave herself a little mental shake. The fact that she was attracted to a man was an encouraging sign that she was returning to normal after her mourning—that was all. The really important person in all this was Marguerite and she could do nothing about the girl until tomorrow. Now she was going to go out into the ballroom to dance and enjoy herself and if Mr Dunton was making himself agreeable to all the ladies, then that would be excellent.

Lucian climbed the hill to Aphrodite's Seashell next morning, prey to more uncertainty regarding a woman than he had experienced since he was eighteen. Lady Sara… Mrs Harcourt rather, as this was daylight and she seemed to change at nightfall like some magical creature, *Sara* was not indiscreet or mischievous or uncaring. However she felt about him after that kiss she would do nothing to harm his sister. But what had that been about? She was sexually experienced and yet she had treated it as no more than a moment's diversion, not the invitation to a full-blown *affaire* that he had taken it for.

Was she actually that sensual, that beautiful, that free and yet that innocent? He reached the door, which had the blind drawn down and a sign reading *Closed,* and knocked.

When the door opened it was the redoubtable Mrs Farwell who stood there. She came right out into the street before ushering him in and Lucian realised she was demonstrating to anyone who happened to have seen him that Mrs Harcourt was very adequately chaperoned.

Lucian knew himself to be experienced, sophisticated even, in the relationships between men and women. It was strange and more than a little disconcerting to feel a faint apprehension about this meeting. Sara had kept him wrong-footed from the beginning, although if he was honest with himself, she had done nothing and he had fallen into one misapprehension after another about her identity, her likely morals, her availability. And he did not feel very comfortable about any of that, he realised as he waited inside the shop for Mrs Farwell to relock the door.

'Lady Sara's out on the balcony,' Mrs Farwell announced with a wave of her hand towards a door in the back wall. 'I'll brew some tea. Expect you'd like some cake, most men do.' Having reduced a marquess to the level of a small boy greedy for sweets, she stomped off through the curtained opening.

Lucian knocked on the door she had indicated and opened it to find himself apparently in mid-air over the sea. He covered the instinctive grab at the wall by closing the door and remembered that the hill that the street climbed was in fact a cliff, so the houses on this side of the road were built virtually to the edge. On either side the owners had cultivated tiny strips of clifftop garden but Sara's shop, and a few other buildings, had balconies stretching along the width of their properties.

'Good morning. You have no fear of heights, I see.'

Lady Sara was leaning on the elegant but terrifyingly spindly balcony railings facing out to sea. Lucian hitched one hip on the rail, leaned against an upright, and ignored the same unpleasant sensation low in his belly that he had experienced crossing Alpine passes on his Grand Tour. He itched to reach out and pull her back against the wall, away from danger.

'Nor have you.' She smiled as she turned her head and the heavy plait of hair slid over her shoulder to swing over the waves crashing below.

His stomach swooped in sympathy even as he admired the unconventional simplicity of her hairstyle. 'Loathe them,' Lucian confessed. 'But it doesn't do to give in to things.'

'Does that work, or do you simply become good at dealing with the fear? I am afraid of snakes, which is a ridiculous thing in this country. In India there are a whole variety of lethal ones and it was quite rational to be wary of them. But here, my brother assures me, I would have to find an adder and then prod it with my finger to encourage it to bite me.' He laughed at the image of Sara experimentally prodding an adder, but her smile faded. 'I have never before come across a man who is actually prepared to admit that he is frightened of something.'

'You see that as a sign of weakness?'

'No, certainly not.' She straightened up, very earnest now. 'I think it admirably honest, though surprising.'

'It depends what it is and to whom one is confessing. I wouldn't admit a weakness, any weakness, to another man or to anyone who I suspect might want to do me harm: that would be a foolish thing to do, like showing a housebreaker where you keep your front door key. Besides, if it was something I was afraid of, but didn't have the guts to confront, then I doubt very much that I'd own up to that, to you or anyone else.' The fleeting look that she gave him expressed considerable doubt that he was keeping that kind of secret. Which was flattering.

'A man challenging another to a duel, or accepting a challenge—he would be afraid, wouldn't he?' Sara asked, abruptly.

'He'd be a fool not to be, just as a soldier going into battle must feel fear. The knack is not to show it, to harness it so that it sharpens you, not blunts you. Why do you ask about duels?'

'Oh, no reason.'

She is lying, he thought, and waited.

'Did you challenge the father of Marguerite's child?'

Ah, so that was what this is about. 'No, not yet,' he admitted.

'Not yet? You mean he refused your challenge?'

'No, it means that I have not been able to lay hands on the bas—on the swine yet.'

'Will she not tell you where he is? Or who he is?'

'Oh, I know who he is all right. I trusted him, employed him, in fact.' He hadn't even managed to keep danger out of the house, but had invited it in to share the place with his innocent sister. 'He abandoned her. She denies it, says something must have happened to him, but he walked out on her because of the baby and because the money had run out, I would wager anything on that.'

'Oh, poor girl, she must be heartbroken, to lose both him and the baby.'

'She is well rid of him. This is not some damned romance,' Lucian snapped as the door opened and Mrs Farwell brought out the tea tray.

'Language,' she said, giving him what he categorised as A Look.

'Thank you, Dot, that is delightful.' Sara gave him the twin of the look and reached for the teapot. 'Tea, my lord? Do take a scone.'

Lucian gritted his teeth into a smile at Mrs Farwell who looked less than impressed as she marched out, leaving them alone again.

'Tell me about it if you can. I am exceedingly discreet.' Sara handed him a cup and settled down on a rattan chair. He took its twin, glared at the scones, decided it would hurt no one but himself to ignore them and heaped on strawberry jam and cream.

'I employed Gregory Farnsworth as my secretary eighteen months ago. He was just down from university, the third son of our rector. He proved intelligent, hard-working, personable. I began to include him in dinner parties and so on when I needed an extra man and before long he was part of the household. I trusted him implicitly.' He took a bite of scone, savoured the delicious combination of cream and jam and made himself go on with the story.

Whatever your doubts, whatever errors you make, you keep to yourself, his father had told him. *Remember who you are, what you are.* And here he was, spilling out every detail of his failure to a woman he hardly knew.

'Marguerite was just turned seventeen. Not yet out, but free of her governess and in the hands of my cousin Mary to acquire some polish before she made her come-out next Season. Mary apparently noticed nothing between them and I certainly didn't, fool that I was. Not until that is, the young puppy comes in one morning and announces that he is in love with Marguerite, that his affections are returned and that he wants my permission for them to be formally betrothed with the intention of marrying when she was eighteen.'

'How old was he?'

'Twenty-one.'

'Not such an age gap and not at all unusual, if he waited until she was eighteen.'

'But he didn't, did he? He lured the girl into believing herself in love with him instead of doing the honourable thing and waiting, keeping his distance, until she was out. I should add that he is probably the most beautiful young man I have ever seen—blond hair, blue eyes, Classical profile and so on and so forth. Even Mary admitted it gave her palpitations just to look at him. When I get my hands on him he is not going to look so pretty, believe me.'

'You refused him permission, I assume.'

'Of course I did. She was far too young, he had no prospects and no money beyond the salary I paid him. How did he think he was going to support the daughter of a marquess in the manner she was accustomed to? By sponging off me, I suppose.'

'Perhaps she would have been happy to live more modestly?' Sara ventured. 'And if he is a good private secretary he might have hoped for a career in a government office or the Bank of England.'

'That is academic. I refused him and warned him that if I ever discovered him alone with my sister, or writing to her, I would break his neck. I should have booted him out there and then, but his father the Rector was an old friend of my father's, a decent man, and I hoped to keep this from him. Then I had to deal with Marguerite. I was an unfeeling brute, I had ruined her life, cast dishonourable aspersions on the motives of the man she loved, et cetera, et cetera... She threw an inkwell at my head and refused to talk to me.'

'Go on.' Sara poured more tea and Lucian realised he had drained his cup.

'I had no idea that he had gone behind my back, but Farnsworth must have set out to seduce her almost immediately, if he hadn't already. I worked it out when I eventually found her and talked to the doctor who told me how far along the pregnancy was. Two months after I forbade the match Mary came to me in strong hysterics, waving a note from Marguerite. I had forced her to take desperate measures, she said, so they had eloped and would be halfway to Scotland before I read the note.'

Chapter Five

Sara's gaze was fixed on his face. 'Did they make it to Scotland?'

'It was a bluff.' Lucian blanked out that nightmare journey to the Border and back from his mind with the same concentration that he had applied to stay sane, to keep thinking and find their trail. 'He took her to Belgium, to Brussels, thinking that they would find an English cleric there to marry them. They did find one. When I finally got on their track and found him he told me he had refused point blank, guessing that she was so much underage. It seems they then decided to try in Paris. Since Waterloo the Continent is full of English visitors and it was a reasonable assumption that they'd find someone, if not at one of the Anglican churches in the cities, then a private chaplain or tutor accompanying tourists.

'They finally located a cleric, in Lyons. Their money was running out and Marguerite was six months pregnant. Farnsworth left her in a lodging house, telling her that he was going to interview the clergyman. He never came back. You may imagine the state she was in when I found her three days later.'

'I can guess at it.' He was so lost in the black misery of that time that he almost jumped when Sara put her hand over his. 'And you must have been beside yourself with worry and exhaustion if you'd been chasing them the length of England and back and then across Belgium and France.'

'Me? What I felt did not matter. I found my sister, *my little sister*, having a miscarriage in a run-down French lodging house with a landlady threatening to throw her out if she didn't get paid. There was no hope of saving the child and for days I thought we would lose Marguerite as well. Even when the doctor said she was out of danger she simply turned her face to the wall. All she would say was, *"He must be dead. They are both dead. I want to die, too."*'

Marguerite was all the family he had and he loved her and he had failed her.

'And you have been looking after her ever since. How long?'

'Three months.'

'Is your mother alive? Are there no female relatives to help? Your cousin Mary?' Sara's warm hand was still over his, her fingers firm and comforting.

I do not need comforting. I am a man, I should be able to cope with this. It was surely a sign of weakness that he couldn't bring himself to draw his hand away.

'My mother is dead and I do not trust our aunts to know how to help her—they would be shocked and disapproving. Mary was in hysterics, it was all I could do to get her to be silent about it. Of course, I should have married as soon as I inherited. If I had found the right wife then she would have seen what I did not, but I had put that off, believing I had ample time.' Another failure on his part, the selfish reluctance to plunge into the Marriage Mart, try and sift through the seemingly identical mass of pastel-clad, simpering misses to find the perfect Marchioness.

'I thought it best to take Marguerite where no one would know her and gossip about her looks and her low spirits. Then, when she's stronger, she can come out next Season, find a husband. If there is someone she takes to, then I will make certain her dowry will be large enough to ensure he doesn't think about her past.'

'But she will still be mourning Gregory,' Sara protested. 'She will not be ready to think about another man by then.'

'He seduced, deceived and deserted her. Once she recovers from the miscarriage she will realise what a fortunate escape she has had.'

'Idiot!' Sara pushed away his hand abruptly and got to her feet. 'I hardly know your sister, but I can tell she is no fool. And she is loyal. She has had to keep her feelings entirely to herself with no one to talk things through with, so how do you expect her to realise if she was mistaken? Or how could she convince *you*, for that matter, if she was *not* wrong about him? If she truly does love him, then you will have to find out what happened to him so she can begin to heal.'

'If I thought he was still alive I'd be on his heels with a pistol, believe me.' Lucian found he was on his feet, too, toe to toe with the maddening woman on the narrow balcony.

'Oh, that would be very helpful!' Sara prodded him painfully in the sternum with one long finger. 'How do you expect her to cope if her brother kills the man she loves?' She jabbed him again. 'And it is not for her, is

it? All this sound and fury is because of *your* honour.
You believe you did not protect her. You failed as a self-
appointed watchdog, so now you have to restore your
own self-esteem, whatever the cost.'

'I *did* fail to protect her and it *was* my duty to do so.
And stop prodding me.' He caught her hand in his just
before the nail made contact for the third time.

'Why? You deserve to be hit over the head with the
tea tray, you and every other muddle-headed, bloodthirsty, honour-obsessed man.'

And then he realised that she was not simply angry,
she was on the verge of tears. They gathered shimmer-
ing in her eyes, making them look like two great moon-
stones. With an impatient gesture she dragged the back
of her free hand across them and Lucian pulled her towards him, against his chest, and wrapped both arms
around her. 'Don't cry, I'm sorry, don't cry, Sara.' He
was not sure what he was apologising for, but he felt
sick, as though he had struck her.

She stamped on his foot, pushed against him. 'Let me
go! I am not crying, I never cry. I am *angry*.'

He released her warily and reached into a pocket for
a handkerchief, aware it would probably be thrust back
into his face. And, finally, his brain started working,
started piecing clues together. 'How did your husband
die?'

'In a duel. A pointless, stupid duel with his best
friend who is somewhere out there—' she waved a hand
vaguely in the direction of France '—with his life ruined
and Michael's death on his conscience.'

'Why?'

'Because they got drunk and Francis, who, it seems,
had a perfectly harmless *tendre* for me, was teasing my

husband, the man who I thought was above all this stupid, patriarchal nonsense about women's honour and duelling. And Francis, in his cups, went too far and… I don't know what was said. Michael wrote in the letter he left that he never believed for a moment that I had been unfaithful to him and yet I cannot understand how he couldn't see that Francis was drunk and a bit jealous, perhaps, and didn't mean it. They told me that Francis had intended to fire wide, but he always was a hopeless shot…'

'My God.' He thrust the handkerchief into her hand, she stared at it as though she had no idea what it was for, then swiped at her eyes with it, blew her nose with inelegant force and threw the crumpled linen to the floor.

'I suppose you think he did the right thing? Even my father and brother, who were appalled at his death, obviously understood why he had made the challenge.'

'What else was he to do if his wife was insulted?'

'Oh, let me see.' Her voice dripped sarcasm. 'Wait until they were both sober? Ask Francis to explain himself? Blacken his eye? Act like the reasonable, reasoning, intelligent human being that he was?' Sara turned from him and stood looking out over the sea. 'Can you imagine what it is like for someone you love to get themselves killed and to leave a letter telling you that they did it *for you*? The guilt is hideous. Can you imagine how Marguerite will feel if her brother kills the man she loves *for her*?'

'Gregory Farnsworth should be punished.'

'If he is alive, if he really is a heartless seducer, then, yes, he deserves punishment. But you are not judge, jury and executioner, Lucian.' When he didn't reply she looked round at him and all the anger drained from her face, leaving only a small, bitter smile. 'I haven't convinced you at all, have I?'

'I am appalled at what happened to you, but the circumstances are not the same.' He stooped and refilled the cups. 'Come and sit down and have some tea.'

'Of course. We are English, are we not? Anything can be made more bearable by tea.' Sara sat, seemingly quite calm now, and took the cup he passed her with a murmur of thanks. 'But the question of Gregory is neither here nor there while you have no idea of where he is, or even if he lives. When I was grieving it was talking to my close friends that helped more than anything. Let me see if Marguerite will talk to me.'

Lucian looked at her as she sat, poised, beautiful, controlled again. And yet so much anger and grief and guilt boiled under that exquisite exterior. He wanted her, he realised, wanted to taste her again, to hold her, to strip every scrap of clothing from her body and possess her, wanted all that with an urgency that shook him. What did that make him, when he should be thinking about nothing but his sister's welfare, when the woman he desired was still shattered by her husband's tragic death? It simply made him male, he supposed, capable of thinking about carnal matters even in the midst of situations of great seriousness.

In the end all he could find to say was, 'Thank you. I know I can trust you with her.'

Lucian was right to trust her to do her best to help Marguerite, but she would do nothing to help him bring down the errant lover, not if the girl still had deep feelings for the man. Sara sipped her tea and looked out to sea, watching Lucian from the corner of her eye. He was

a brave man not to have fled when she had unleashed all
that misery and anger about Michael's death.

He was very attractive, she thought, and perhaps the
fact that she noticed, that she wanted to kiss him again,
wanted far more than that, was a sign that she truly had
come through her mourning. She would never forget
Michael, never stop loving the memory of him, or feeling anger at his death—and anger at him for challenging Francis and guilt herself for... No, she had promised
herself not to dwell on her own guilt because it would
drive her mad. She was a different woman now, a new
Sara who had to decide what she really wanted in this
moment, today. And tomorrow.

'You are very thoughtful.'

*And you, with all your demons, are an uncomfortable
companion for my thoughts!*

'I was brooding on the future, what I will do when I
leave here. The shop was always something for a year
or so, something completely different from everything
that had gone before. And it was creative, I could build
the business, which was interesting. I have one grandfather who was an East India merchant and perhaps I
have inherited his trading instincts.'

Restless now, she put down the cup half-emptied and
went to look out over the sea again. The tide was turning and the little fishing fleet was making its way out
to sea, red and buff sails vivid on the blue water as they
butted through the waves. 'Sandbay is changing, developing. There is perhaps one more year when I can live
my dual life and then I will be too much of an oddity.'

Lucian came to join her at the rail, resting his hands
on it as she was, their little fingers—his right, her left—
just touching. A tingle like the spark from a cat's fur in

a thunderstorm shot up her arm. Did he feel it, too? His hand moved, covered hers, his thumb stroking slowly over the pulse in her wrist. *Oh, yes, he feels it.*

'Sara. Last night you said you were curious. Are you still?'

'Yes,' she admitted and closed her eyes as the world narrowed down to the sensation of his caress on the tender skin, the awareness of his body next to hers, the brush of the breeze on her face. 'But...'

'Ah. The *but.*'

'You should not allow your lover to associate with your young sister—and that is what we are talking about, isn't it? Not just a kiss or two, but an *affaire.*'

'That is what I desire, yes.'

Looking out to sea, with only Lucian's voice to judge by, undistracted by his expression, she could read the layers of meaning. Yes, he wanted her. Yes, an *affaire* was what he meant: this was most definitely not a proposal of any other kind. And, no, he would no more bring his lover into contact with his sister at the moment than he would his mother, had she lived.

The silence hung there for the time it took a seagull's scream to die away and then he said, 'And you are quite correct, of course, about Marguerite. Her needs must be paramount.'

He was going to kiss her, she felt him shift against her as his breath touched warmth to her wind-chilled lips, then she was in his arms, moulding herself into his blatantly aroused body. There was no pretext now that this was curiosity or flirtation taken a little too far. This was an exchange of desire and demands that they both knew would go no further.

One of them had to stop and she supposed it had better be her. Sara rested her cheek on Lucian's chest and listened to his heart beat and imagined it over hers as they lay in bed, then put the fantasy firmly away.

His hands dropped from her shoulders and she opened her eyes to see him outlined against the sun dazzle on the sea, already moving towards the door. 'We will be in all day if you call. Marguerite would be pleased to see you. Thank you…for the tea.'

Marguerite was occupied with her new sketchbook at the window of the private sitting room at the hotel when Sara called. It had taken an hour to regain some composure and to think about how to best approach the younger woman. Now she perched on the table next to her and admired the drawing of the cliffs which was lively, if amateurish. 'How is the shell mirror frame coming along?'

'It is drying over there. I need some more small shells for the rim around the glass. Have you seen Lucian today?'

Was that a question with a hidden meaning, or simply a genuine enquiry? Sara bent over the mirror and spoke casually. 'He dropped into the shop this morning to tell me you would be at home all day. Would you like to go out on the beach? I need to collect seaweed to make some pictures and it is lovely weather.'

'I…yes, I would, I think, if it is safe. I can't swim, you see, which makes the waves rather frightening. What should I wear?' Marguerite looked dubiously at her very pretty morning dress with its frilled hem.

'We won't be doing anything more perilous than paddling, I promise. Wear something cotton, the kind of thing you would put on at home in the country to go into the garden to gather flowers. Something that doesn't matter if you get salt splashes or sand on it. And no stockings, just some old, sensible leather shoes.'

'No stockings?' Marguerite looked mildly shocked.

'It is far less immodest to walk across the road with no stockings on than it is to take them off on the beach. We will be getting our feet wet.'

'Oh!' She sounded dubious, then seemed to make up her mind. 'I expect I have something. I won't be long.'

The tide was ebbing as Sara led the way across the beach to the foot of the cliffs where the retreating sea exposed firm, flat sand. 'If we go around the little headland then we are into Bell Bay, which is quite small and secluded. There is some talk in the town about creating a path over the headland and making that the ladies' bathing beach with no men allowed until after noon on the sands or the part of the headland that overlooks it. It would mean room for some more bathing machines and the shyer ladies might feel more comfortable.'

She kept talking, chatting casually about trivial town affairs until they were around the headland, then she perched on a low rock and pulled off her shoes. 'You do the same and then we can leave them on top of the rock. There, isn't that pleasant? And walking on the sand smooths the feet beautifully.'

Marguerite grimaced at the feel of the cool, wet sand, then smiled, the first really wide, uninhibited, smile Sara had seen on her face. 'It is lovely. Ooh—if I wriggle my toes I start to sink.'

'There are no quicksands in this bay, we are quite safe. Now, if we walk across to those rocks over there we can explore the rock pools.'

* * *

It took no more than half an hour of splashing along the surf line and picking up shells and driftwood for Marguerite to relax. She finally came to rest on top of a smooth rock to catch her breath while Sara dipped glass jars into the rock pools under the cliff.

'What does Sarisa mean?' she asked after a while. 'Is it Indian?'

'It means charming.' Sara straightened up and held out a jar to Marguerite. 'See? A little crab. I'll put him back in a moment. Papa said I was a perfect charmer, right from the beginning, so that is what they called me.' She tipped the crab back into the pool and watched it scuttle under a fringe of weed. 'Marguerite means daisy, doesn't it?'

There was silence, then a wrenching sob. Appalled, Sara dropped the jar into the water and took Marguerite in her arms. 'I am so sorry, what did I say?'

'That's what he called me. Gregory called me his… Dai… Daisy.'

Sara gave her a handkerchief, sat down on the rock beside her and held her until the storm subsided into sniffles. 'Do you want to tell me about it? I guessed about the baby. And Gregory is the father?'

'Oh!' Wide, tear-drenched hazel eyes gazed into hers. 'Did Lucian say anything? I think he believes it is better that I lost her, but he doesn't say that, of course.'

'I told him that I had guessed and asked if I could help you. I'm sure he would never wish that you had lost the baby, although probably he would prefer that she never existed in the first place.'

'I am certain he does.' Marguerite blew her nose de-

fiantly and sat up. 'I am sorry to be such a watering pot.
I try to be brave, but I worry so.'

'About Gregory, your lover?'

'He was only my lover because Lucian wouldn't let
him marry me. I know he is still alive, I feel it in my
bones. And I know he would never leave me, so something horrible must have happened to him and he is lying
in a pauper hospital in France, or he has been press-
ganged or something dreadful.'

'Would it help to talk about him?'

Chapter Six

It seemed it would help Marguerite to talk. The story poured out, essentially the same as the account Lucian had given, but with one vital difference. 'I seduced him,' Marguerite said defiantly. 'He wouldn't do more than kiss me, he said we must wait until we were married. But when Lucian was so horrible and refused even a long engagement I went to Gregory's room when he was asleep and got into bed with him with no nightgown on.'

'Ah. I suppose matters were already out of hand before he was properly awake.'

Poor man! So much for Lucian's illusions about his innocent little sister. Doubtless she had been untouched, but she knew exactly what she was about when she got between those sheets.

'Yes. It was clever of me, I thought, because Lucian couldn't blame Gregory. But Gregory was upset and he felt guilty anyway and he wouldn't let me go and tell Lucian that I had seduced him.'

Despite the seriousness of the story Sara had to bite the inside of her cheek to keep from smiling. She could just imagine poor Gregory, his masculine pride crushed as it was explained to the infuriated Marquess that he was the one who had been taken advantage of. No wonder he refused point-blank to allow Marguerite to tell her brother. Marguerite might know how to seduce a man, but she had no idea how their minds worked.

'And then I discovered that I was pregnant.'

That reminder chased away all inclination to smile. 'Didn't you think your brother would let you marry then, even if he disapproved?'

'No.' Marguerite shook her head vehemently. 'He would have whisked me away to one of my horrible aunts in the country and I'd have had my baby and they would have taken her away from me and Lucian would have called Gregory out and killed him.'

It was difficult to argue against that, Sara thought. It sounded exactly the kind of solution Lucian would have come up with, especially the calling-out. 'So you decided to run away together?'

'Yes, Gregory said we must marry as soon as possible. We thought if we went to the Continent then he might be able to find work as a secretary over there and there would be English clergy—but all the ones we found were so difficult because of my age. They could tell I wasn't a servant or a tradesman's daughter so they thought there would be a scandal and they would be in trouble if they helped us.'

'Lucian thinks Gregory left you because of the baby and not having any money?' Sara risked the question and was rewarded with an indignant denial.

'No! Gregory was going to find work, any work at all, in Lyons. He would have dug ditches for me, but he had heard of a merchant who needed someone who could speak English because he wanted to export fans and small luxury items to England. Gregory was going to see him after he had spoken to the clergyman we had been told about. We hoped if we were married then the merchant might let us have a room in his house.'

It all seemed perfectly reasonable to Sara. 'Did you tell Lucian this?'

'When he found me I was too ill and it was almost a week before I realised that Gregory had vanished. I thought Lucian had killed him at first, but he swore not and he wouldn't listen when I told him about the clergyman and the merchant. He said Gregory had been hoping to extort money from him and I was just an innocent, gullible child who had fallen in love with a handsome face.' She blew her nose again with a defiant, inelegant snort.

'And so I did—I fell for a man who was as lovely inside as he was outside. Gregory wouldn't have asked Lucian for money, he was far too honourable and proud. He explained to me before we ran away that we would have to live very modestly on what he could earn and that if I didn't think I could bear that, then it was best to go and confess all to Lucian.' She gave Sara a sideways look from under her lashes. 'I suppose you think I am wicked and silly and gullible, too.'

'No. I think you really did love Gregory and that he was worthy of your love.' Marguerite was a mixture of innocence and feminine wisdom, but she was also intelligent and honest. If there had been a false note in her lover's protestations she would have heard it. If the vicar's son had managed to fool Lucian into giving him a position of trust and responsibility and then seduced Marguerite with such skill that she had believed him utterly, then he was a great loss to the English stage, or the best confidence trickster in the country.

'Thank you.' She scrubbed at her eyes as the tears welled again. 'I wish I knew what to do. I can't ask Lucian to find Gregory because I know what will happen if he does and I don't know anyone else who could afford to send an enquiry agent to France and who would cross Lucian into the bargain.'

No, but I do. If it came to it then she would write to Ashe and ask him to track down the handsome blond Englishman in Lyons. Her brother would know who to send and he would not ask endless infuriating questions if she told him it was important. 'I will think about it,' Sara promised. 'There must be some way around this.'

'Thank you.' Marguerite's chin was up now and her eyes, although red-rimmed, were dry. 'Show me what is in the rock pools, please.'

They splashed about, soaking the hems of their old cotton dresses, laughing as they chased shrimps that darted into crevices, grimacing as seaweed wrapped itself around their ankles.

Sara collected several jars of brown and pink and black weed and some discarded crab shells and Marguerite's handkerchief was stuffed with shells and sea glass in jewel colours, worn smooth by the waves. As they explored they chatted. Sara told stories about her family, their life in India, the dismay at realising that they must leave because her father had inherited the title and how strange England had seemed.

Marguerite asked questions and, her guard completely down, dropped little nuggets of information about her romance, about her lover, that Sara stored away to brood about later.

She kept an eye on the state of the tide and finally dragged Marguerite away. 'See how it has come in? If we don't go back now, we'll have to walk back over the headland and there is no proper path. It is quite hard going and your brother will not thank me for exhausting you. Besides, it is time for luncheon.'

'Lucian wants the best for me, I know. He just doesn't understand.'

'Men think about love differently from us.'

'You mean because they can just have sex when they want to so it doesn't mean much to them and then they get sex and love muddled up?'

'Er...'

'Gregory wasn't like that.'

'No, neither was my husband. And my parents and my brother made love matches. But Lucian is protective of you and he's ambitious for you. He wants you to marry someone of your own class who can give you the life you should expect as the daughter of a marquess.'

'Your father is a marquess and he let you marry a commoner.' Marguerite was beginning to drag her feet through the sand like a tired child.

Sara linked her arm through the girl's and slowed her pace. 'My parents are very unconventional and Ashe knew Michael really well by then. But it seems to me that most men are happy if they have a companionable wife who makes them a comfortable home, children—and, as you, say, there is the sex. The fact that they would be even happier if they *loved* their wives doesn't appear to occur to most of them, although actually I think a lot of them do and just don't recognise that is what they feel.'

'It would be better to be the daughter of some shepherd on the Downs, I think sometimes.'

'No, it wouldn't. You would not want to live in a little hut and besides, even then your father would be on the lookout for a son-in-law with a prize ram or who was handy training sheepdogs or something.'

That made Marguerite laugh and they were still making up the requirements for every kind of tradesman's son-in-law by the time they reached an overturned boat by the low jetty and sat down to put on their shoes.

'A butcher would want skill in getting all the meat off a carcass and his daughter would want a big chopper!' They both doubled up in thoroughly unseemly laughter at the *double entendre* until a shadow fell across them.

'I am not going to even ask what that was about.' Lucian was on the jetty, hunkered down just above their heads.

'Housekeeping,' Marguerite said pertly.

Sara was sitting on the upturned rowing boat, her legs stretched out in front of her, her skirts almost to her knees as she let the sunshine dry her skin so she could dust off the sand. She leaned back on her supporting hands and saw that Lucian was studying her bare legs. She straightened up slowly, refusing to be put out of countenance, as she let her skirts slide down and brushed the sand away. When he lifted his head and met her gaze he had a heavy-lidded look of concentration that she had no trouble deciphering at all.

She pulled on her shoes and stood up to find he was still crouched down, buckskin breeches stretched tight over strong horseman's thighs, the tails of his coat brushing the cobbles, his hat in his hands. 'You have been riding, sir?'

'I was just going to, but I wanted to be certain Marguerite had luncheon and a rest before I left.' He straightened up and began to stroll back along the jetty parallel with them as they made for the steps. 'You look well, sweetheart. There is colour in your cheeks.' Tactfully he made no mention of the signs of tears.

'I liked it, Sara showed me so many things. But I am tired now. Thank you, Sara.' She turned and kissed Sara's cheek, gave her hand a little squeeze, then climbed the steps to her brother's side.

'Do you ride, Mrs Harcourt?' he asked. 'Would you join me?'

'I do, Mr Dunton. But it will take me half an hour to get home, change and have my horse brought round from the livery stables.'

'If you give me directions I will fetch it to you, which will save some time.' The severe mouth curved into a sensual smile. 'I find myself very eager for a good gallop.'

Wretched man! A good gallop, indeed. I know exactly what he means and he knows perfectly well that neither of us is going to give way to whatever it is that makes him look like that and turns my knees to jelly. It is basic lust, I suppose, and we are both grown up enough to deal with it.

Her house, one of a row of neat, newly built, terraced villas with a desirable view of the bay, was a brisk five minutes' walk uphill. Maude, her maid, scurried for the clothes press when Sara swept in, breathlessly calling for her riding habit.

'The English one, my lady?'

Sara hesitated. It was very tempting to see Lucian's expression if she appeared in the Rajput clothing that she and her mother used for riding in the privacy of the family's country estate, but she had to remember that in daylight she was still Mrs Harcourt and it was not good policy to upset the precarious balancing act that was her social standing in the town.

She was changed, hat on head, boots on her feet when Maude twitched the curtain to look down on the street and reported, 'There's a gentleman outside with your mare, my lady.'

Sara jammed an unnecessary pin into her hat, pulled down the veil and ran downstairs, amused to see that her staff were all peeking from various places to see her gentleman caller. Besides Maude she employed a footman and a cook and a maid of all work who came in daily—a size of household that partly soothed her father's worries about her living alone and which filled the small house to its limits.

'My lady.' Walter the footman opened the door with a flourish and handed her a riding crop. He, at least, had good reason to be in the hall.

'Come and assist me so that Mr Dunton does not need to dismount, Walter.' The footman beamed and she guessed he would now go back and give the other staff a detailed description of the gentleman, right down to the toes of those glossy boots.

'That's a pretty animal,' Lucian remarked as she settled into the saddle and twitched her skirt into place.

'She is indeed.' Sara gave the arched dark grey neck an affectionate pat as she turned the mare's head uphill. 'My brother bred her—Twilight by Moondancer out of New Dawn. I thought to go along the clifftops to the west. That way is perfect for the good gallop you wanted.' And she would give him exactly what he asked for, she thought with an inward smile.

The livery stables had done Lucian proud with a raking chestnut hunter that was a good match for Twilight, its long legs eating up the ground with ease while the gallant mare had to work hard to keep abreast. But like Sara she was not willing to be bested by a male and she was still in contention when they reached the spur in the track leading to Merlin's Bay.

'Down here,' Sara called as she reined in and the chestnut thundered past. It gave her an opportunity to admire Lucian on horseback without seeming to stare as he rode back to her. Being in the saddle was his natural habitat, she guessed, and it suited him, brought animation to a face that sometimes seemed severe in repose and showed off a fine physique.

'Where does it go to?' he asked when he reached her.

'Merlin's Bay, which is a recent renaming. I think it was originally something prosaic like Murdle Bay or Mumbles Cove, but it is a local beauty spot and it was given a more glamorous title to attract the visitors when Sandbay began to be more popular.'

There was just room to ride side by side as the track descended into the little valley, woodland crowding in on either side. 'It seems very isolated and intimate,' Lucian observed.

'I'm afraid that is an illusion.' As she spoke a second, wider, carriage road joined them from the right and the track levelled out into a wide space where two carriages were already drawn up in the shade and grooms were walking three horses up and down. 'It is a popular tea rooms and gardens now. I thought that we could take refreshments here.'

'I would very much like to make the better acquaintance of your mama,' Lucian remarked as he swung down from the saddle and came to help her to dismount.

'You would?' Sara kicked her foot out of the stirrup and allowed herself to slide down into his perfectly proper and impersonal grasp.

Lucian lowered her to the ground and gestured to one of the grooms who came forward to take their mounts. 'She has sent you out into the world perfectly equipped to deal with importunate males, hasn't she?'

'I cannot imagine what you mean, Mr Dunton,' Sara said demurely. 'You tease a little—that is all.' *At least, I hope it is teasing. I* think *he will behave as a gentleman should.* 'There are some pleasant places to sit amongst the trees along the shoreline and we can order food and talk with no danger of being overheard.'

There were about a dozen people visible in the little pleasure grounds and they had no difficulty finding a table with benches under an arbour. A waiter came to take their order and Lucian sent him away to fetch cold meats, salads, bread and butter, ale, lemonade and a selection of cakes. 'You missed your luncheon,' he pointed out when Sara protested that Twilight would buckle at the knees if she ate all that.

'Marguerite looked happier than I have seen her since before this whole miserable business began,' he said abruptly when the food had been delivered. 'And I had almost forgotten what she looks like with roses in her cheeks. You have worked a miracle.'

'I fear not. The fresh air and some gentle exercise put those roses there and the opportunity to talk to someone who is completely unconnected with the emotions behind all this helped, I think.' Sara ate some cold chicken while she pondered how to talk to him and then decided to simply say what she thought. 'She loves Gregory, she believes in him and it is tearing her apart not knowing what has happened to him. But she fears you looking for him because she believes you will kill him when you find him.'

'I will call him out,' Lucian said grimly. 'Then it is in the lap of the gods.'

'No, it is not,' Sara snapped back. 'It is in *your* hands. Do not try and tell me that a young man from a vicarage can match you with either rapier or pistols. If he is dead already in some accident, or the victim of footpads, then she will mourn him, but eventually she will recover. If you kill him, she will never forgive you.'

'He is a predatory seducer.'

'I very much doubt that. Marguerite might be young and inexperienced in the ways of the world, but she is not foolish, nor is she a bad judge of character, I think. You need to ask her what happened the first time they… were together.'

'What do you mean?'

'It is not my story to tell.'

He stared at her, frowning for a long moment, then gave a bark of laughter. 'The little minx seduced *him*?'

'I imagine that there are some circumstances when a man, especially an inexperienced young one, might find things are well out of his control before he knows what is happening,' Sara suggested carefully.

'They should have come to me.'

'Really?' She stopped, her glass halfway to her lips. 'I should imagine they were terrified of you!'

'Nonsense. He is a man—it is up to him to do the right thing even if he *is* terrified, not go dragging my sister all over the Continent. The only mercy is that she appears to have had the sense not to go about in Brussels and Paris and be recognised.'

'Marguerite thought that if she stayed then you would send her away into hiding and then take her child from her.' When he stared at her, speechless with what she hoped was outrage at the suggestion and not guilt that she had guessed rightly, she pressed on. 'If you can only find it in you to promise Marguerite that you will not call Gregory out if you find him alive it would make all the difference to her. She would tell you everything she knows about what he was doing in Lyons and you might well be able to find him.'

'And you know what he was doing, where he told her he was going?'

'Yes,' Sara admitted, reluctantly.

'Then tell me.'

Oh, yes, those two young people would have had every reason to be scared of Lucian, she thought as the hazel eyes focused sharply on her face and she read the barely leashed anger and intent there.

'No. Marguerite told me in confidence. If I have to, then I will employ my own investigator to locate him for her, whether it is his person or his grave. At least then she will be able to find some peace.'

Lucian put down his glass of ale with a deliberation than was more frightening than if he had slammed it on to the board. 'It is not your affair to interfere in.'

Chapter Seven

The mouthful of bread and butter Sara had so unwisely taken turned to sawdust in her mouth. She swallowed and took a sip of lemonade. 'You made it my affair.' She let that sink in, then added, 'And I like your sister, I would like to be her friend.'

Lucian's mouth hardened into a thin line. 'I am beginning to wonder if that is a good thing. All I wanted was for her to be encouraged to develop a few interests, to get out and about and not be moping inside.'

'*Moping inside?* She is mourning a lost baby, frantic with worry about the man she loves and racked with guilt because she has disappointed her brother and you call it *moping*?'

'I want her to forget him,' Lucian said stubbornly.

There was more than anger in his expression now. There was pain and frustration and something very like despair. He had always been able to make the world right for his little sister, Sara realised, and now he had come up against something that was outside his experience, something that money and power and intelligence could not knock into submission. She had seen it in the faces of her brother and father when Michael died and they could do nothing to put it right for her except kill his killer, as if that would help—and Francis had fled out of their reach.

She trampled on the surge of sympathy. 'She will never forget and there is nothing you can do about it except promise her you will not call Gregory out, will not hurt him—and then go to Lyons and find what happened to him.'

'I cannot promise that.'

'Then you risk losing your sister,' Sara stated bluntly and saw the involuntary grimace at her harsh words. 'She *wants* to understand why you acted as you did, why you are still so obdurate, and she wants to forgive you for it, but I have no idea how long that will last.'

'Are you threatening me?'

'No, you stubborn man! I am warning you.' Her temper snapped like a dry stick. One moment she was sitting there with a glass of lemonade in her hand trying to reason it out, the next she found herself striding across the lawn between the scattered tea tables under the curious gaze of the other visitors. Behind her she heard raised voices, presumably the waiter demanding payment from Lucian.

'Your help to mount, if you please,' she said as she approached the grooms watching over the horses. 'The gentleman will pay you in a moment.'

One of them tossed her up into the saddle and Twilight began to sidle, catching her mood. 'Thank you. Come on, my lovely.' She gave the mare her head towards the track up to the clifftop, riding on a loose rein. They both knew the way and the ground was sound.

If she thought that unfamiliarity with the track and a

natural caution would hold Lucian back, she was mistaken, she realised, as she heard the hooves pounding behind her. Of course, no *gentleman* would allow a lady to ride unaccompanied, she fumed. Goodness knows what dangers might await her. *Rabid rabbits,* Sara muttered as they emerged from the woods and on to flat ground. *Sex-crazed smugglers, unhinged hedge-layers...*

The hoofbeats behind her were getting closer, much closer. She risked a backwards glance and realised that the only danger to her just at that moment was the Marquess himself. He looked as though he wanted to throttle her.

Sara twisted back round, wishing she was riding astride and not wearing this so-fashionable habit with its trailing skirts and broadcloth that slid on the saddle. As she thought about sliding a buzzard flapped up out of the long grass, a rabbit in its talons. The mare jinked, stiff-legged, swerved back and Sara lost her stirrup, lost her balance and went over Twilight's shoulder down to meet the turf with a thud.

Instinctively she rolled, tucking herself up into a ball as her great-uncle the Rajah's *syce* had taught her. The clifftop was almost as hard as the sun-baked Indian plain, she thought as she tumbled, arms around her head, braced for the hooves of Lucian's horse.

There was the sound of furious, inventive, swearing, then she came to a stop, untrampled, and lifted her head warily in time to see Lucian dismount from a rearing horse in a muscular, controlled slide.

'Sara!'

He was by her side and she closed her eyes strategically to postpone his anger and in sheer self-preservation. He had looked like a god just then and she could put no reliance on her own self-control. 'Mmm?' she managed.

'Are you hurt?'

Yes, was the honest answer. Her left shoulder hurt, her right wrist stung and her pride as a horsewoman was severely dented. 'No,' she said and opened her eyes.

'Excellent,' Lucian growled. 'Because I fully intend wringing your neck.'

'Why?' Indignant, Sara moved too quickly, found several other things that hurt and was hauled into an upright sitting position. 'Ow! What are you doing?'

'Checking.' His hands worked along her collarbone, wriggled her fingers and prodded her ribs. 'Move your feet. Let me see your eyes, your ears. What day of the week is it?'

'Thursday.'

'Correct.' Then he kissed her.

It was probably less life-threatening than having her neck wrung, but as she found herself flat on her back on the turf again Sara was hazily aware that it was probably more dangerous. Lucian was angry with her and she was not very pleased with him, but that only seemed to touch a flame to the tinder of feelings that had been simmering inside her ever since that kiss on her balcony.

They were both wearing far too many clothes, she thought as her hands slid into his hair to hold his head so she could kiss him back with as much fervour as he was kissing her. His mouth moved from her lips to her cheek to her ear and she arched her neck to give him better access, shifting so he was lying fully on her, his pelvis cradled against hers, the heat of his erection like a brand.

She opened her eyes on a sigh as his hand slid between the buttons of her jacket, seeking her breast, blinked against the sun dazzle and gave a yelp of alarm. 'Lucian!'

'What?' He came up on his elbows, which felt alarmingly wonderful as his hips pressed down tight into hers. 'What's wrong?' He looked distracted, but then she felt more than distracted herself.

'*Wrong?* We are in the open, on the clifftop. There is no cover. This is a public bridleway. You are undoing my clothes. We agreed we were not going to do this! Is that enough *wrong* for the moment?'

'Hell.' He rolled off her, sat up and looked around. 'I am sorry. We do appear to be alone, if that is any consolation.'

'There is no need to apologise, I kissed you back. It seemed preferable to having my neck wrung.' Which was untrue. She had just wanted to kiss Lucian, have his hands on her, put hers on him, and she hadn't been thinking at all.

'I'll get the horses.' He rose to his feet and walked towards them. Twilight was well trained enough to stay when her rider fell off and the hired chestnut was standing nose to nose with her. They allowed themselves to be caught with no trouble and Lucian led them back as Sara fumbled her jacket closed and tried to make some order out of her tangled hair.

'Your hat.' He held it out as he jammed his own back on his head, then held out his hand to pull her to her feet.

Sara hissed with pain and Lucian moved close to take her arm. 'You said you were not hurt.'

'I am bruised. I fell off a horse. Naturally it hurts.'

'Can you ride?'

'Of course. If you will just give me a boost.' She settled into the saddle and managed not to wince, or to look at Lucian as he swung up on to his own mount.

'Why did you run off like that?' he demanded as they set off again at a walk.

'I lost my temper with you and rather than ring a peal over you in a public place I decided to leave.'

'I was perfectly in the right—'

'You were perfectly *within* your rights as an autocratic male head of household. But you are certainly not right about how to deal with your sister.'

'She has to accept that Farnsworth abandoned her. I refuse to believe that an able-bodied, educated young man could meet with some fate so severe that he could not get a message back to a woman he cared for, one that he had left totally vulnerable.'

'You might feel quite secure wandering around a French city, *my lord*. You have wealth and power and experience. Gregory was near-penniless and, however good his French, I would wager it was his first time in that country. How could he have coped if he had ended up under arrest for some innocent misunderstanding? Or in the charity ward of a hospital after being set upon by footpads?'

Lucian could hardly throw up his hands in exasperation, not with both of them holding the reins, but he could feel his shoulders twitch with the desire to do just that. Somehow he managed to get the desire that was burning through him like a wild fire under control, but his body held the memory of hers under him, of her softness and heat where his erection had burned and throbbed. *Focus*. 'You will not encourage my sister to hold on to these hopeless dreams.'

The frustration and guilt were beginning to undermine his control, he thought grimly as they rode in frigid silence. He had failed Marguerite by not protecting her against the wiles of an unsuitable man, which meant he had failed in his basic duty to his family, to protect them. Now, somehow, he had to restore her lost honour—and his—and Sara's inability to understand that, let alone sympathise with it as she should as a well-brought-up lady, was wreaking havoc with his temper. He must be mad to think of taking her as his mistress, of allowing her any deeper into his head, destroying his single-minded concentration on his sister.

It must have been her unconventional upbringing in India, he supposed. Her father and brother had seemed normal enough in their attitudes, from what little he had seen of them and from what Sara had said, but her mother was a different matter. She was a stunningly beautiful woman with an imperious manner who struck him as more than likely to take the defence of her own, and her daughter's, honour into her own hands. And those pretty hands, he rather suspected, would be holding something as sharp as the knife Sara had drawn on him the other evening.

But that definition of honour must be very different from his if Lady Eldonstone had calmly allowed the newly widowed Sara to take herself off and set up as shopkeeper like this.

'What am I to say to her, then, if Marguerite speaks of Gregory?' It sounded as though Sara's teeth were gritted.

Lucian forced away the memory of how that mouth, now so tight-lipped, had softened under his, how her tongue had felt, impudent and demanding in his mouth. 'You will tell her that I have forbidden discussion of him and that if she wishes to keep you as an acquaintance that subject is out of bounds.' His mother had never defied his father, Marguerite had never disobeyed either parent. His father had acted as though opposition to his will was unimaginable and, without uncles or elder brothers to model himself on as a youth, Lucian had tried to follow his example in everything except his womanising. So, was he lacking in essential authority to have lost control of the situation like this?

The unladylike snort that greeted that pronouncement was answer enough. *And I do sound damnably pompous,* he thought. Good God, if looking after a sister was difficult, what would it be like when he had children of his own?

'Why are you looking at me like that?' Sara demanded.

'Like what, exactly?' Now the conversation was descending to schoolroom levels. Somewhere there were beautifully behaved, elegantly minded young ladies who behaved with perfect decorum at all times and would be charmingly deferential to the men in their lives. Why was he surrounded by the complete opposite?

'Speculatively,' she said, after a moment's frowning thought.

'I have no idea why I should have been looking at you *speculatively,* which leads me to assume that you are reading more into my expression than was there.' *Pompous again.* He had been trying for authoritative.

'Very well. If Marguerite mentions Gregory, I will tell her what you say. She has heard my views on the matter already, so my silence now will make little difference.'

As olive branches went that one was decidedly shrivelled, but he decided to accept it. 'Thank you. A lack of encouragement will have to suffice.' That appeared to have effectively flattened all conversation. After five minutes, as they entered the lane down from the cliffs into the town, he added, 'I will take your mare back to the stables.'

'Thank you, my lord.' When they reached her house she permitted him to help her down, then hesitated with one foot on the lower step up to the front door. 'There is an early evening concert at the Rooms tonight. Just a short one of light, popular pieces with refreshments afterwards. Marguerite might enjoy it.'

He felt his irritation with her vanish like sea fret in the sunshine. He did not want to be at outs with this woman. He wanted...to be what...to be *friends*? Surely not. He was never friends with his mistresses. They had a civilised, cordial, passionate business relationship and that was all. 'Thank you, I am sure she would like that very much. Will you be attending?'

'I expect so. Until later then, Lucian.' And her smile was as warm as that sunshine he had been imagining. Sara, it seemed, did not hold grudges.

He found he was looking forward to an evening of undemanding music and tepid tea. His brains were obviously addling in the sea air.

Chapter Eight

'How well you look.' Sara tucked Marguerite's hand into the crook of her elbow and took her off towards the refreshment room. 'We've just time for a cup of tea before the performance starts.' The younger woman had colour in her cheeks, her languid air had vanished and her eyes were positively sparkling.

'I had such a lovely walk along the promenade this afternoon. I took my maid, of course,' she added.

'I am glad to hear it,' Sara said, wishing Lucian was within earshot to hear her sounding so respectable. 'Did you just walk? There are some tempting shops in that direction.'

'I discovered that little hat shop, just beyond the church, and then I went up to the library to look at *La Belle Assemblée* so I am completely *au fait* with the very latest fashions.' Her smile suggested that she gained more satisfaction from perusing the latest hemlines than Sara did.

'I wish I was,' Sara said ruefully. 'Mata keeps sending me prints from all the journals and pointing out that I must be in the direst need of a smart new crop and the most thorough review of the London shops.'

'Is that the Indian word for mama?' When Sara nodded she added, 'Does she not come and visit you here?'

'She doesn't dare let Papa loose on me down here because he'll try and dragoon me back to town. Besides, the two of them are a trifle noticeable in such a small place, which does not help my attempts to blend in.'

'And are you perfectly conventional when you are in London?' Marguerite not only secured a cup of tea, but added two cream scones to her plate.

'Yes, I suppose I am. I still feel like a fish out of water there. I had such a short Season and then I lived in Cambridge, but I suppose I will soon learn to spend large amounts of money, attend every fashionable event until I am absolutely exhausted, gossip with the best of them and flirt outrageously.'

'And then escape down here before the bills, the gossip and the flirtations catch up with you?' Marguerite suggested saucily.

'Of course.' Sara smiled, but she was puzzled. Was Lucian's sister putting on a most convincing front of happiness and recovered spirits or was she more resilient, or perhaps less in love, than Sara had thought? The recovery from the weeping girl on the beach was incredible. 'Here comes your brother to take you through to find your seats.'

'Yours as well—you will join us, won't you?'

'Thank you.' Sara smiled when Lucian reached their side and curtsyed and made small talk and did her level best not to think outrageous and improper thoughts lest they show on her face. What with trying not to show any distinguishing attention to *Mr Dunton* that would stimulate wagging tongues, puzzling over Marguerite's welcome, but unexpected, cheerfulness and attempting

not to fantasise about ripping Lucian's exceedingly elegant tailcoat off his broad shoulders, she could feel her
expression freezing into one of well-bred *ennui*. And her
bruises from her fall were beginning to ache, which did
not make sitting elegantly any easier.

If the infuriating man was taking any notice of her
at all he should feel thoroughly cold-shouldered, given
that she was presenting him with her profile and not a
single smile. The trouble was, she thought, listening with
half an ear to the slow movement of one of John Field's
piano concertos, he was more than capable of ignoring
anything that did not fit in with his determined view of
how matters ought to be.

'Marguerite seems in good spirits,' she remarked low-
voiced during the interval, unable to resist talking to
him any more.

Lucian's gaze followed his sister as she went to locate even more scones. 'Yes. I have to agree with you,
talking about things with another young woman has
helped her. I feel more confident that she will continue
to improve now.'

'You are?' Sara had difficulty believing in this sudden improvement. Surely Marguerite was not pinning
all her hopes on Sara's promise to investigate and feeling
full of false confidence that Gregory was alive and well?

'We lost my mother to a virulent fever when she was
just ten years old and she is my only sister. I was twenty.
I knew nothing about girls and my father coped by handing her over to her governess.' He smiled fleetingly.
'Then it was a shock when I found myself the Marquess
so suddenly—that was during your first London Season, I think. There was a lot to learn, but I resolved that

I was going to raise my sister to be as perfect a young gentlewoman as if her mother was still alive.'

The smile no longer reached his eyes and Sara thought she glimpsed the grieving man pitchforked into awesome responsibility and determined, somehow, to be perfect.

'My father had years to become used to the fact that he would inherit the marquessate,' she said, recalling the frank family discussions about what the inheritance would involve. 'Which was a good thing because Mata was horrified at the thought of it and almost refused to marry him when she found out. We stayed in India until the last possible moment, but he was fully prepared when it happened and my brother Ashe was older than you were when you inherited, so he was a great support. Mata said that after an Indian royal court Almack's and St James's Palace were simplicity themselves to negotiate. I cannot imagine poor Ashe finding himself responsible for me, though.'

'I couldn't let her down, I thought,' Lucian said grimly. 'She was without her parents just as she was becoming a woman—I had to make things perfect for her. And I failed.'

'Perfection is impossible. And besides, what about you? You were bereaved, too, you must have been swamped with responsibilities and decisions.'

'It was my duty to cope, that I did know. I am a man and head of the family. My sister's future, our honour, were in my hands.'

'Honour and duty,' Sara murmured. 'And what about happiness?'

'One thing my father taught me was that persons in our station in life should not expect personal happiness, although we might hope for it.'

'I am *so* sorry,' she blurted out. 'Oh, don't poker up at me!'

'I do not need your pity,' Lucian said, his voice frigid.

'It was *sympathy*, you prickly man,' she snapped back. Mrs Prewitt, the mayor's wife, was watching them with raised eyebrows and Sara fixed a smile on her lips. 'And it is rapidly evaporating,' she added in honeyed tones. 'Here comes Marguerite.' Which was a good thing because she wanted to take him by those perfectly-cut lapels and shake him.

Fourteen shillings plus two pounds plus three pence four farthings plus...

Sara jammed her pen back into the inkwell and glared at the page in front of her. The previous week's takings should be perfectly easy to total and reviewing sales and what needed re-ordering was simply a matter of routine. But last night's concert kept intruding between her and the page and Sara found she was still brooding on Marguerite's mysteriously good spirits and Lucian's attitude. That, of course, was now no mystery at all.

Raised by a father with a rigid attitude to duty and then pitchforked into high position as a young man, where all he had to cling to was the imperative to live up to that upbringing, it was no wonder he had made a mull of understanding his sister. But it did not explain why such an intelligent man appeared incapable of learning from his mistakes.

The sound of the shop door bell and raised voices brought her to her feet, but a peep around the curtain showed that it was only Miss Denver, a nervous and voluble spinster who was being dealt with by Dot.

'There, there, you sit down and I'll fetch you a nice

cup of tea, Miss Denver. Yes, it must have been a shock, but these poor fellows can't help the way they look. Wounded in the war, I've no doubt…'

Miss Denver was still wittering on when Sara closed the account book and came out to the shop. 'And in the circulating library of all places! I only went in to look at the new patterns for tatting in *Ackermann's Repository*—and I found such a pretty one—and I said to that nice Mr Makepeace, you shouldn't let such a…a *Janus* in to frighten decent ladies.'

Sara had a momentary fantasy of two-faced Greek gods inhabiting the circulating library. Lucian was the only god-like being around and he definitely only had one face, which was quite enough. She pulled herself together and went to distract Miss Denver before any of the other customers became totally exasperated with her. Last week she had been rabbiting on about the dangerous presence of gypsies on the heath—'We'll all be murdered in our beds…'—and had succumbed to strong hysterics when Dot had remarked that she welcomed the opportunity to buy a new supply of clothes' pegs.

'I have some charming new shades of cotton in. They might be just the thing for that pattern you found. You have such good taste, Miss Denver, you must tell me what you think of the colours…'

By the time the twittering had finally subsided, the accounts were straight and the orders written, Sara felt in need of some company that did not make demands, require direction, brood with dark sensuality or worry her. She made her excuses to Dot, went up the road to the circulating library and sank wearily on to the chair at the counter.

The lower part of the library was empty, save for the shop boy on hands and knees pursuing spiders out of corners with a feather duster. 'James, say something soothing. I have just been dealing with the accounts for Indian ink, which would not tally, the inability of my paper suppliers to read what is written on an order and, worst of all, Miss Denver, who you sent to me in strong hysterics.'

James blushed as always when she used his first name, but leaned confidingly across the counter. 'I am sorry and it *is* rather a problem. I am going to have to warn ladies before they go upstairs, after that nice Miss Dunton was in tears yesterday and now Miss Denver is so upset. But I cannot forbid the library to a gentleman whose manner and dress is perfectly acceptable, simply because he is scarred, poor fellow. So tragic, under the circumstances. What if it is an honourable war wound? I would never be able to live with myself if he was snubbed and insulted on my premises.'

'No, of course not, poor man.' Strange that Marguerite had not mentioned being reduced to tears when she said she had been to the library, but perhaps she had felt ashamed of her reaction, or it had simply been a result of her heightened sensibility.

'May I be of assistance now you are here, Sa—? Er... Lady Sara?' His ears had gone red, which meant, she guessed, that he had almost dared to use her first name in public.

'Have you any new novels in? I want to lose myself in something thoroughly entertaining.'

'Indeed yes. There is *An Angel's Form and a Devil's Heart* and *Secrets in Every Mansion* just come in, both from the Minerva Press. Or, if you are in a mind for something more unusual, there is this.' He produced three volumes from under the desk. 'To be honest, I would welcome your opinion as it seems rather dark in tone and possibly may alarm many of my readers. It is from a small press.'

'*Frankenstein; or, The Modern Prometheus,*' Sara read and flipped through a few pages. '*"I started from my sleep in horror; a cold dew covered my forehead..."* I can see I am going to be reading this in broad daylight, James. But I will borrow it and both the novels you suggest. Could you have them sent round? I will go and see if I can wrest a copy of the *Morning Post* from the Colonel and immerse myself in what the society pages have to say.'

She really did want to see if there was a review of the latest theatrical productions, but she also wanted to show the unfortunate gentleman with the scars that not every woman would recoil from him in horror.

The stranger was sitting next to the window reading a newspaper, the strong light from behind throwing his face and figure into silhouette. Sara suspected the position was chosen deliberately, for it made it almost impossible to see his face in any detail. He was wearing an eyepatch, that she could tell, and he seemed quite young.

She settled down with the *Morning Post*, made a note of one production to avoid and one to see, if she did as she was inclined to and travelled up to London in a week or so.

She left after twenty minutes, called in at the shop and found it quiet, so went down to the promenade for a breath of fresh air. An open carriage bowled past with

Lucian sitting next to his sister. He raised his hat, Marguerite waved and Sara waved back.

Would he do the right thing and find out what had happened to the mysterious Gregory? she wondered as she watched the carriage disappear in the direction of the coast road to Weymouth. And if he did and the man was alive, would he be able to restrain himself from calling him out?

Men! They were impossible to live with and yet she definitely did not want to live without them. If she went back to London Papa would be anxiously looking for a suitable new husband for her, however much he tried to hide it. Ashe would be circling anyone who showed the slightest interest and warning off any man who was not—in his opinion—perfect. And if anyone made the slightest reference to her unconventional decision to marry a scholarly commoner, let alone her current eccentric lifestyle, they would both be bristling in her defence and more than ready to issue a challenge.

If they were not careful, she thought, she would wed a librarian—that would rattle them. Not that she wanted to marry poor James, even if he ever plucked up enough courage to court her. The only man she wanted, the one by now half a mile out of town, would drive her to distraction within days, she was certain. Not, shamefully, that marriage was what she wanted him for.

Sara made herself smile at a party of ladies strolling along the promenade, stopped to admire Miss Wheatley's new parasol and advise Mrs Carlow on the best place to collect seaweed, bought herself an entirely unnecessary length of lace, two cream tarts and a fashion journal she could have perfectly well read at the library, and finally went back to the shop where Dot had hung up the *Closed* sign in order to eat her noon meal.

'Hmmph,' Dot remarked at the sight of the packages. 'I'll put the kettle on the hob and get a plate for those tarts. Eating cream cakes won't get that man in your bed, although cakes are a lot less trouble in the long run.'

'Dot!' But the reproof was half-hearted. 'He *is* very attractive. And loyal to his sister and intelligent when he is not being an idiot about honour above everything else.'

'And he must be rich and he's your class and that's where you ought to be, and you know it, not hiding down here.'

'I am not hiding.' That was half-hearted, too. Sara rather thought she *was* hiding, not so much *from* anything but because she had absolutely no idea what would make her happy and she was avoiding making a decision. 'And taking that man as my lover is not going to do anything for my social standing.'

'Not as a lover,' Dot mumbled through a mouthful of cream cake. 'A husband.'

'Lucian? He's the Marquess of Cannock, you know, only he's incognito because of Marguerite's situation. And I know what you are just about to say, that it makes him even more suitable. But he would be impossible to live with, he doesn't want me—' Dot snorted '—not to marry, and besides I do not want to marry anyone.'

Dot made a face and took the other cream tart.

'That's mine!'

'They make you fat. Doesn't matter for me, my man likes me big, but that Marquess, he'll want a wife who looks elegant.'

'I told you, I do not want to marry the man. I think he is rather attractive, that's all. Anyone would. A girl can look, can't she?' She took herself off in a huff to drink her tea on the balcony with the door closed on Dot's wickedly inventive suggestions on just what a girl could do besides looking.

I am young still, she thought, staring out to sea. *And sometimes now I cannot see Michael's face clearly. I want a family of my own and a man who loves me and who wants to grow old with me and who is exciting in bed and interesting to talk to and who stops to wonder whether I would prefer him risking his life to defend my honour or alive and simply punching someone on the nose for being offensive. And that includes some of the Lady Patronesses of Almack's.*

The thought of Lucian felling—and silencing—Lady Jersey with a well-aimed left hook when she made snide remarks about Sara's ancestry was so ridiculously funny that she stopped sulking and went to open the shop door with a smile on her lips.

'Oh, yes, Lucian…there…oh, please, more…' Sara was vaguely aware of her own voice, her incoherent pleas and moans, but she was beyond pride or shame. She only wanted his hands on her body, his lips on her mouth, on her breasts, between her thighs. 'Oh, *yes*, Lucian. There, like that.'

His hair was rough silk to her clutching fingers, his skin was hot, his body hard and any moment now—

The dream shifted in the maddening way dreams did and now she was alone in the bed and Lucian was swinging a sledgehammer against a great slab of teak. He was naked, of course—that was logical. He had only just got out of her bed, after all. His body was magnificent, his legs long, the muscles elegant, his hips slim, his erection—

'My lady! Do wake up, my lady, please.'

Sara blinked her eyes open to see Maude, her hair in curl papers, clutching the edges of her wrapper together with both hands. 'What? What time is it?'

'Just on five, my lady. And there's this man at the door hammering and he won't go away and he says if I don't open up and let him talk to you he is going to break it down.' The continual hammering of the door knocker confirmed that. 'Walter's got his shoulder to it, but that's no help.'

Sara scrambled out of bed, dragged on her wrapper and went out on to the tiny balcony. It was, of course, Lucian. For a confused moment, as the mists of the dream faded, she was surprised to see that he was fully dressed, although bare-headed.

'Be quiet,' she called down softly. It was a miracle that half the street weren't hanging out of their windows to see what was going on.

He looked up, his expression grim. 'Where is she?'

'Marguerite? She is missing? No, don't answer me, we cannot talk like this. I will open the door.' She stepped back into the room. 'Maude, go down and tell Walter to let Mr Dunton in and put him in the drawing room while I get dressed.'

She had thrown off the wrapper and was in her nightgown rummaging for a day dress when the bedchamber door banged open. 'Lucian!'

He ignored her protest and her state of undress, and went directly to the dressing-room door, opened it, looked inside and turned on his heel to confront her. 'Where are you hiding her?'

Chapter Nine

'Marguerite is not in this house and I have no idea where she is if she is not at the hotel. I have not seen her since the concert, you have my word on it. Now will you kindly get out of my bedchamber, Lord Cannock?'

For the first time Lucian focused on the furious woman in front of him and realised that Sara was wearing nothing but a flimsy muslin nightgown which, as she was standing with her back to the window, might as well not have been there. His body reacted with an inconvenient inevitability, despite the anxiety that consumed him.

'Your word?' He put the slightest doubt into the question and it was enough to keep her gaze, fixed and furious, on his face and not any lower.

'Do you not believe that a woman can have honour to pledge? You would like to search the house, perhaps? Look under my bed? Check the roof? The bread bin? Please, go ahead.'

'I believe you. I apologise.' He should have known better, should have trusted her. The stinging contempt in Sara's voice was enough to extinguish a forest fire, let alone a brief flare of lust. He was duly grateful. Lucian dug the note out of his pocket and held it out. 'I will go downstairs and wait. I would value your assistance with this.' He was reduced to begging, but Marguerite was more important than his pride, especially with Sara. With her he did not seem to have any protection for his feelings or his emotions and certainly not for his weaknesses.

'No, wait.' To his amazement Sara pulled on her robe, jerked the sash tight and curled up in the armchair, with a wave of her hand towards the *chaise* at the foot of the bed. 'Sit down while I read this.'

He deserved to have the *chaise* thrown at his head, he was very well aware. Lucian sat, marvelling at the infinite unpredictability of women, and tried not to tear his hair as he watched Sara's face as she read, then re-read the note, her lower lip caught between her teeth. She was beautiful even with her hair tousled and her face shiny with sleep.

'Where was the note?' Sara asked.

'In the sitting room. I woke up thirsty, realised I had left the water carafe on the table last night and found the note was propped up against it. Normally I would have slept another hour and a half, perhaps two. It was simply luck that I had forgotten to take the carafe into my room.'

'So, her Gregory is alive and has come for her and they have run away to marry,' Sara summarised as she looked up from the note. 'But why did you come here? I would have expected you to be giving chase.'

'Because if I were her I would go to ground here, in Sandbay, until her wretched brother had gone galloping off in pursuit to the Border and then I would follow at a safe distance.'

'That would take strong nerves and a degree of cunning.'

'Which is why I thought they might be here,' he confessed. She was the most intelligent woman he knew, one of the most intelligent people, come to that, and she had the nerve to take risks and to think around corners.

Sara regarded him through narrowed eyes and then gave a gasp of laughter. 'Thank you for the compliment, if that was what it was. They are not here, but Gregory cannot have been in Sandbay long and finding his lodgings might give us a clue.'

'How do you know how long he has been here?' he demanded, his suspicions resurfacing.

'Marguerite's mood at the concert. Looking back, I can see she was happy, truly happy, not putting a brave face on things as I thought at the time. She must have seen him that day, I think. Oh, what an idiot I am—*of course*, the man in the library.' She jumped to her feet and began to pace, her skirts swishing around her, untied ribbons fluttering.

'One of my customers was upset yesterday because a man with a severely scarred face was in the circulating library. When I went in later and spoke to Mr Makepeace he said that Marguerite had been tearful the day before when she saw this person—and yet she did not mention it to either of us, did she?' When Lucian shook his head, she nodded. 'I thought so and it would have been very natural for her to speak of it. She was weeping because it was Gregory and he had been injured, not in revulsion at the sight of a maimed stranger as Mr Makepeace thought, or simply because of heightened sensibilities.

'I went into the reading room myself, through curiosity, I have to admit, but could only see him against the light, which was no doubt intentional. From where he was sitting he could have heard anyone come in and, if *you* had entered and he recognised your voice, he would have been able to hide behind his newspaper. I think only one side of his face was injured—my customer referred to him as a Janus—and that also explains something odd that James Makepeace said. *"So tragic, under the circumstances."* You told me Gregory was very handsome and James would have thought the disfigurement even worse if it marred such a face. He was wearing an eyepatch.' She came to a halt in front of him, her face alight with triumph at having worked it all out.

'He will have trouble disguising that eyepatch, it will make him easier to track down.' At last something positive.

'I can discover where he was lodging—but only if you promise me that you are not going to harm him,' Sara offered.

A moment's thought brought him to the same conclusion that her reasoning had. 'I have no need to negotiate on that.' Lucian ignored the way her brows drew together in a frown. He rather suspected that Sara Harcourt would rarely approve of anything he said that related to his sister. 'He would have registered with the circulating library if he wanted to use it and I imagine Makepeace knows the town well enough to spot a false address. I will ask him. Where does he live? Over the library?'

For a moment he thought she would defy him, then Sara got to her feet. 'Let me change and I will come with you, otherwise you will simply go and find a directory and look it up, you stubborn man.' She tugged the bell pull and when the maid appeared, her face a picture of barely suppressed amazement and speculation, told her to go and wake the cook. 'Coffee for both of us as soon as possible, then ask her to fry bacon and make sandwiches.' As the maid scurried out she shrugged and made shooing gestures towards the door. 'If you have to give chase, you may as well do it with a packet of sandwiches in your pocket. Now, let me change.'

Cook, it transpired, had been awakened by the noise and was already making up the range and he had hardly finished a scalding cup of coffee when he heard Sara coming down the stairs. Or, rather, he assumed it was her, but the person who walked into the drawing room and took the second cup from the tray was almost unrecognisable.

The slim figure was dressed in a full-skirted, fitted coat of some dull dark blue brocade, high at the neck and split to the waist front and back. Trousers of the same colour tucked into soft leather boots could be glimpsed beneath the skirts and a tight black turban completely covered the hair.

'I thought it best to dress for travelling,' Sara said calmly as he tried not to choke on the coffee, his throat closing with a mixture of outrage and desire. 'This what my mother and I wore to ride in India and we still use it at home in the country. We have to check here first, of course, but if Gregory and Marguerite have fled and you are determined to follow and stop them, she is going to need a female chaperon if we are to contain the scandal. It will obviously be a hard, fast journey.'

Over my dead body, clashed with, *That makes some sense.* 'I hardly think that if you are seen dressed like that—' Lucian began, working out why he actually felt pleasure at the thought of Sara's company. Which was inexplicable. This was a crisis, a nightmare and most definitely not a pleasure outing.

'I have a small portmanteau. I assure you, if I am seen with your sister by anyone likely to recognise us I will be dressed with the utmost propriety, but I refuse to go haring about the countryside in stays and trailing skirts.'

A plump woman looked into the room. 'Shall I begin breakfast now, my lady?'

'No, thank you, Cook, we have no time. Make bacon sandwiches, pack a flask of cold tea, anything else that you think will be useful and we'll be back soon.'

'Anything else that will fit in a curricle,' Lucian interjected. It seemed he was doomed to have Sara's company if they did not find the eloping couple in some Sandbay lodging house, but he was damned if he was going in pursuit encumbered with a load of luggage.

The clock struck six and he reined in his impatience. If Farnsworth and Marguerite were on the road, then they had the Lord knew how long a start and fretting over half an hour was not going to help.

'James lives next door to the library, luckily.' Sara swung a cloak around her shoulders and pulled up the hood.

It took ten minutes to reach the librarian's door which opened, after determined knocking, to reveal a flustered manservant and the admission that Mr Makepeace was in, but most certainly not At Home.

Lucian set his foot against the door and leaned until they were both in the hallway. 'Kindly give him my card and say that if he cannot join us in five minutes then I will join him.'

In the event Makepeace came down in his robe, his

nightcap askew on his head, his face a picture of confusion when he saw Lucian's companion. He blinked in bemused recognition. 'Lady Sara? What—'

'No time to explain, James.' She was already pushing the man towards the door. Lucian found he could admire an organised and forceful woman, just as long as it was some other poor devil she was forcefully organising. 'Get your keys to the library, please. We need to consult the register for the address of the man with the scarred face.'

'But I can tell you that. He's at Mrs Thompson's lodging house in Dolphin Lane…'

'What name is he using?' Lucian demanded.

'Er… Mr George…no, Gregory Tate…'

'Thank you, James.' Sara was already running back down the steps. 'This way, we can cut through the alleyway. I'll watch the back while you go to the door.'

The landlady was already up and beginning her day when Lucian knocked. She was indignant at the hour, then flustered by his card—he had dug out the ones with his real name—and finally agog at his questions.

'He's gone,' he confirmed when he re-joined Sara. 'She recommended Lambert's Livery to him when he said he wanted to hire a post-chaise. I'll go and rouse them out and get a curricle.'

'You promise you'll pick me up?' Sara demanded, her hand tight on his arm.

He should say no and not involve her. He knew that. But Marguerite liked and trusted her and she seemed to understand his sister. She needed Sara, he told himself, and tried to ignore the little voice that murmured that so did he. *Desired her,* he corrected. *Lusted after her, wanted her. I do not* need *this woman.*

* * *

It took an hour to get back to her, sixty minutes while he forced himself to plan and stay coldly rational. The last time he had done this it was to find Marguerite at death's door—now, Lucian told himself, he would find her safe. At the hotel he found an apologetic note from his sister tucked into his wallet. His very empty wallet. *Cunning little hussy*, he thought as he raided his emergency funds hidden in the false bottom of his writing desk. He stuffed all the ready money he had into his wallet and found a road book while his valet, Pitkin, stowed the bare necessities into a valise. He loaded his pistols, tucked the case with his rapiers under his arm then set out, Pitkin on his heels, to find the livery stables.

By ill chance it was not the one he had used before, so there was all the delay of establishing who he was, where he was staying, convincing the owner that, yes, he might want the curricle for as long as a week and he did want his best pair.

Lucian couldn't fault the speed with which Sara whisked down the steps from her front door, tossed her valise in with his and swung up on to the seat beside him. He had left Pitkin to deal with the hotel and to hold their suite for a week and, with no groom up behind, the light vehicle rattled over the cobbles.

'Which route do you think?' she asked, settling the folds of her cloak around her. 'If I was them I would take the Dorchester road, then Yeovil and Bristol.' Lucian grunted his agreement as he reached the top of the hill and let the pair canter. 'I was trying to work out how much of a start they have. What time did you retire last night?'

'Midnight and I suppose I was asleep by one. I haven't been keeping town hours here.'

'And she would know that, so, if she crept out at two…I wonder how she got past the night porter. Did she take much baggage?'

'Two valises. And the man dozes at the front desk. If she went down the back stairs quietly he wouldn't see her.'

'So, it was eight o'clock when you picked me up, say eight miles an hour…forty-eight miles. They could be halfway to Bristol by now.'

'Farnsworth's got the contents of my wallet to add to whatever he has been able to raise and Marguerite's only had her pin money for a couple of days, so they are not going to be short of funds to change horses when they want.' Beside him Sara was wriggling out of her cloak. 'What are you doing?' Lucian demanded as she stuffed it under the seat and sat up straight beside him again, arms folded.

'It was too hot, I don't need to hide now and I am your groom. You are eccentric and have an Indian one.'

'Give me strength! I am not so eccentric as to have a *female* Indian groom.'

'People see what they expect to see.' She glanced downwards. 'It is a tight coat.'

Lucian told himself that he was not going to study the effect on her curves and kept his gaze fixedly between his horses' heads. 'How are you going to explain your absence from Sandbay?'

'I do not have to explain. Maude will tell Dot to open the shop, or close it if it is inconvenient for her. I am, after all, the daughter of a marquess. People expect me to do exactly what I want. The fact that I do not normally choose to flaunt my rank, or to put people out because of it, does not mean I can't if I have to.'

It was easy to forget that this stubborn, independent, infuriating woman was of the same rank as his sister and that, however unconventional her upbringing had been, she was Lady Sara, part of his world. What would he have thought of her if he had met her in a crowded ballroom or at a fashionable concert? Beautiful, desirable, intelligent...

The pair jibbed and Lucian yanked his attention back to what he was doing. They were still not on the turnpike road and he dared not risk a cracked axle or a broken wheel.

'The road book is in my valise, if you can reach it. I need to plan ahead for changes and to make certain we do not miss our road.'

'I know it well as far as Dorchester.' Sara turned on the seat, knelt up and leaned precariously over the back.

'Take care!' Lucian jammed the reins into his whip hand, brought his left down to grab what he intended to be the waistband of her trousers and found himself cupping a deliciously rounded buttock. He let go and Sara squirmed back on to the seat, pink-cheeked and clutching Cary's *Great Roads*.

'I apologise, I was trying to—'

'You have a case of pistols in your bag,' she stated, ignoring his inadvertent fondling. 'Tell me you are not going to call Gregory out.'

'I am not setting out on a journey that could last for days without weapons.'

'That is not what I asked. Lucian, this has gone too far, you are going to have to let them marry. It is obvious from what I saw of his injuries that Gregory could not possibly have returned to her, whether it was an accident or he was set-upon. And she loves him, she has carried his child.'

He knew it and he knew, too, why admitting the inevitable was so difficult. If Marguerite married Gregory Farnsworth now, then all his opposition, their elopement, her miscarriage and misery—and presumably whatever had ruined Gregory's face—had been for nothing. If he had handled things differently from the beginning, then he would have spared his sister all that grief.

Which meant that he had failed in his most basic duty, to protect his family. At home there was a Long Gallery, filled with portraits, the earliest dating back to the reign of Henry VII. His father and grandfather had walked the line of them regularly with him, telling the stories, the history. Men of honour, all of them, building the fortunes of the family until they were placed in his hands to safeguard. It was not Marguerite who had lost her honour, it was he who had lost his. And he was damned if he was going to admit any of that to this woman who held male honour so cheaply.

'Killing Farnsworth is not going to help matters now, I agree.' But he could still beat the living daylights out of the man, he thought grimly. And Lady Sara was not going to stop that.

Travel with the Marquess of Cannock was rapid, uncomfortable, occasionally alarming but exceedingly efficient, Sara discovered. Ostlers ran to fetch horses when he stopped for a change and their choices were quality animals. Landlords bustled out with ale and offers of the house specials and stopped to listen sympathetically to the tale of his ward who had run off with an unsuitable chit of a girl and who needed to be rescued for his own good.

'He isn't quite clear in his thinking since his accident,' Lucian would explain, neatly building Gregory's injuries into the narrative. 'He was easily imposed upon by the little hussy.'

They picked up the trail in Charminster, just north of Dorchester, where the eloping couple had made their first change of horses at four o'clock, then again at Yeovil.

Sara had decided she was his lordship's valet, which meant she could keep her distance from the ostlers and grooms and, as she had predicted, it was her clothing that attracted the attention, not the feminine face beneath the turban.

It was almost four in the afternoon when they reached Bristol and saw the spire of St Mary Redcliffe church. Lucian reined in his tired pair in the yard of the Greyhound and climbed down.

'How are we going to search?' Sara joined him and looked around. 'I have no idea how many posting inns there are in the city.'

'We are not. We are going to eat something, because that packet of bacon sandwiches was a long time ago. And while we eat, the urchins of the city will search for us.' He snapped his fingers at a hopeful-looking lad hanging around waiting for the chance to carry bags for a tip. 'You see this?' He held up two crowns and the boy's eyes widened.

'Cor, two troopers? Yes, guv'nor, I sees 'em.'

'They're yours if you and your mates can find out about a post-chaise that came through Bristol earlier today. It had a yellow body, four horses, two postilions.

There were two passengers, a young lady and a man with a badly scarred face and an eyepatch. I want to know when they set out again, what road they took and if the carriage or number of horses has changed. Got that? I need the information within two hours. If you can do it in one, there's another bull's eye for you.'

'Cove with a shutter on his ogle and a bloss in a yellow bounder with four tits. I got it, guv'nor.' He took to his heels, whistling a shrill note, and a handful of urchins appeared as he ran out of the gate.

'Two hours?'

'They'll have it in less than that,' Lucian said confidently. 'And now you and I are going to have a civilised meal.'

She looked down dubiously at her brocade coat. It was one thing pretending to be a valet in exotic dress, quite another eating with Lucian in one of Bristol's smarter hostelries.

'Don't worry. This is a port city and you will not be the most exotic thing they have seen, not by a long chalk.'

Sara resisted the urge to put out her tongue at the broad back in its caped greatcoat as Lucian strode towards the entrance and discovered that she was amused and feeling quite in harmony with him. She doubted it would last.

Chapter Ten

His lordship's title produced a private dining room, the landlord's personal attention and the assurance of a meal equal to any they might enjoy in London.

'What will you do when we find them?' she asked when the soup tureen had been put on the table.

'If Marguerite still wants him, then she must marry him, I suppose. If she has changed her mind, then I am most certainly not going to insist.'

It did not escape Sara that Lucian's answer did not cover the first encounter with the errant pair. She wondered if she could hide the ammunition for the pistols, but there was a sword case as well and Lucian was doubtless as willing to run Gregory through as shoot him. Besides, if she did unload the guns then they would probably encounter a highwayman, Lucian would be wounded and it would all be her fault...

'What are you brooding about?' he asked as she ladled oxtail soup into bowls, lost in thought.

'Highwaymen. I had wondered whether I should hide all your ammunition. But you have rapiers, don't you? And it would be tempting fate too far to be careering about the country unarmed.'

Lucia took his bowl and regarded her much as if she had grown an extra head. 'Have you any idea what I would do to you if I found you had hidden my ammunition?'

'No.' The soup was exceedingly good. Sara concentrated on it and not the fact that she was alone in a private room with this man, was travelling for goodness knew how long with him and that what she really wanted him to do was leave the eloping couple to their own devices and bespeak a private bedchamber here.

'Neither do I. I suggest that we do not put it to the test.'

The soup was followed by a fricassee of chicken and baked fish in cheese sauce. They ate in edgy silence broken only by stiltedly polite requests for the bread or the salt.

Lucian cracked first. 'Just what do you think I should have done when Farnsworth asked for Marguerite's hand in marriage?'

'Agreed to a private engagement if they would wait for eighteen months. If he is a decent young man, he would have agreed. You made them feel as though they had been backed into a corner, with no choice. They are young and everything is so immediate when you are Marguerite's age. It was black and white to her and a dramatic flight with the man she loved was not only emotionally right but it also had all the glamour of a fairy-tale romance.'

'Which just goes to prove my point that she was far too young.'

'And you are so old and sensible? How old are you, my lord?'

'Twenty-eight. Men grow up faster, are more worldly-wise.'

'My mother says that all men are little boys and all little girls are women. Think about it—you did the equivalent of putting up your fists and saying, *I'll black your eye if you touch my toy soldiers*. Marguerite calmly set about seducing Gregory.'

'So you implied the other day. How, for goodness sake?'

'I was not going to tell you, but I think I must. She took off her nightgown and crept into his bed when he was asleep. What do you think happened then when he woke up? In fact, he probably was beyond the point of no return by the time he was properly conscious. Can you really blame him for that?'

It was a struggle, she could see it in his face, but Lucian eventually shook his head. 'No, I cannot. I suppose by the time he realised it was not some particularly vivid erotic dream things had gone too far. *Hell*.' He threw her an apologetic glance for the language. 'I really do not want to imagine it. This is my little sister we are talking about. Wherever did she get such ideas from?'

'I do not know where men get the notion that young women are total innocents. It is no wonder that you prowl around looking ferocious, protecting us against shocks and surprises that are no surprise at all.' Sara stabbed a knife into a blameless apple pie. 'Unless a girl is dim-witted, completely unobservant and has neither friends nor access to books, then of course she knows about these things. The actual mechanics may well escape some of us until our wedding night if we have the sort of mother who mumbles worrying messages about *duty* and the compensations of children, of course.'

'I suspect that was not your mother's approach. And however comprehensive a young lady's theoretical knowledge might be, that still does not protect her from some predatory rake with seduction or worse on his mind. Nor from the consequences of being compromised in the eyes of society. Do pass me that pie before you stab the unfortunate thing to death. I very much doubt it is male.'

'I have nothing against men when you are behaving reasonably.' Lucian narrowed his eyes at her, but made no comment. 'As for Mata, well, she was raised in an Indian court and received the full *theoretical* erotic education expected for a well-educated woman.' The slice of pie that Lucian had just cut fell off the knife with a soft splat. 'Which, naturally, she passed on to me.' She could have sworn he stifled a moan. 'Are you in pain?'

'Not at all. I bit into a clove. That is all.'

His eyes had lost focus for a moment, which was very gratifying. If she could only keep Lucian thinking about his own masculine frailties then perhaps he would be less inclined to murder Gregory for his.

Sara was contemplating how best to add fuel to the flames when there was a tap at the door heralding the innkeeper.

'There's a scrubby lad asking for you, my lord. I saw you talking to him earlier or I would have sent him on his way with a flea in his ear.'

'Bring him in, would you?'

The urchin was escorted in, one ear firmly held between the man's finger and thumb. 'A proper limb of Satan, this one, my lord. Do you want me to stay and keep an eye on him?'

'No, thank you. We have a business agreement.' The

landlord went out, his expression a silent comment on the strange ways of the Quality. 'Well? It is an hour and a half.'

'Sorry, guv'nor. Only it was the Black Swan they changed at and that's right off on the outskirts of town to the east. But they hitched up three bays and a black to the same yellow bounder and they're headed for Gloucester. They left nigh on two.'

'Not going to London, then. You did well.' Lucian tossed three crowns to the boy who snatched them out of the air and ran before the nob could think better of his generosity. 'This makes it easier—if they vanished into London they'd be the devil to find and there's always the chance Marguerite would be recognised. Are you ready to go? This is where we drive hard and fast and begin to reel them in.' He drew on his driving gloves and jammed his hat on his head, his expression grim.

He's hunting, she thought with a shiver, then saw that Lucian had ordered a team to be harnessed in place of the pair they had used on the country roads. Now they would be driving over turnpiked highways for miles and, despite the anxiety about Marguerite and the anticipation of an uncomfortable journey, there was the secret thrill of speed with a real whipster holding the ribbons.

'Worcester.'

Lucian's voice jerked Sara out of a troubled sleep into darkness lit only by the glow of the carriage lamps on the hedgerows and a twinkling mass of light ahead. Her head bounced painfully on something hard and she realised she was slumped against his side, her temple on the point of his shoulder.

'Oh, I am sorry—have I been asleep long?'

'Only since the last change.'

They pulled into an inn yard as a nearby church clock struck midnight. Sara hurried off in search of the privy and came back to find the horses already hitched and Lucian draining a tankard.

He passed her another. 'We are gaining. They came through four hours ago and the ostler told me that they had to settle for a second-rate team. The ones we have got, which *do* look like quality, were not rested enough to send out then, in his opinion. That and night driving means we'll pull them back long before they reach the Border.'

'Let me drive.'

To her amazement Lucian did not immediately refuse. 'You can drive a team?'

'Yes. I have driven both my father's and Ashe's teams and they both keep only blood horses. And I have driven at night.' Only in India, though, and at a walk, but she was not going to tell him that. Lucian seemed tireless, but he wasn't made of iron. Even if he did no more than catnap it would do him good to rest his arms and shoulders.

'Very well.'

His ready acceptance shocked Sara into immobility. She hadn't expected him to agree, not really. Her father and brother would never have let her take the ribbons with a strange team and at night. She couldn't decide whether he had a flattering belief in her ability or was simply applying common sense and snatching some rest.

'Well, come along.' Lucian was waiting to give her a helping hand into the driver's seat.

Sara climbed up, collected up the reins and took her time sorting them carefully in her left hand. She would not be pushed into haste by a desire to impress him. When Lucian was settled beside her she took a firm grip on the whip, made herself relax her wrist and ordered, 'Let them go!'

She kept the team at a collected trot, learning them as they passed through the streets which were, however irregularly, at least lit. 'Go to sleep,' she said without turning her head to look at the man beside her.

'In a minute or two,' he said as a dog rushed out of an alleyway, barking hysterically at the leaders. They jibbed and she collected them up and drove them on. Lucian kept his hands where they were and, she realised, he hadn't so much as made a twitch to take the reins from her.

'Thank you for trusting me.'

'You have the confidence and the steadiness that is required and now I see you can keep your head and are strong enough to hold them together. Wake me if I snore.'

'I will be sure to.' Not that he would fall asleep immediately, she was certain, however relaxed the big body against hers was. It would take more than witnessing her deal with a minor incident before he would trust her entirely, she knew, but the show of confidence was as welcome as it was unexpected.

Have I misjudged him? Sara wondered as they left the town and her eyes adjusted to the moonlight. The road stretched on, pale against the darker verges. They were fortunate that the moon was full and that it had been dry so that the dusty road was not dark with rain. The team were well balanced and responsive and she let them extend their trot. Was Lucian not the domineering male she had categorised him as, or was he a pragmatic man aware that he could not keep going all the way to the Border without rest?

There was a heavy pressure against her side as he relaxed into sleep and she felt her mood soften even further into something perilously like tenderness. Surely she was not falling for this man? Desire was one thing, but developing a *tendre* for a powerful, opinionated man with traditional views on honour and the independence of women was quite another. An *affaire* could be ended in a civilised manner when it had run its course, she assumed—not that she had any experience of that kind of thing—but unrequited feelings could be nothing but painful. And she was not going to let herself explore exactly what those *feelings* might mean.

Sara thought Lucian woke before they reached the next posting inn in Kidderminster, but he kept silent beside her, allowing her to drive, and she was glad of his forbearance—and glad to stop when she reined in outside the Blue Boar.

'They're a good team and you handled them well,' he said, swinging down from the seat. He waved away the ostlers who came running out. 'They'll do until Wolverhampton, it's only about another fifteen miles. Move over.'

With Lucian up beside her Sara flexed her aching hands surreptitiously and rolled her shoulders. She would not have admitted it for the world, but she was glad to hand over to him and his praise, delivered in perfectly matter-of-fact terms, was both a surprise and a pleasure.

'Cold?' he asked as he gave the team the office to start.

'No, just a bit stiff.'

'There's a rug under the seat.' Lucian reined in and wrapped the reins around the whip handle so she could reach down. 'Put it around your shoulders, it will keep the muscles warm.' When she fumbled with fingers still cramped from the reins he tugged it straight and tucked it around her, then drew her against him and kissed her, long and slow. 'Mmm. I prefer this to driving with a groom.'

Sara found she had nothing to say when he collected the horses' attention again and drove on. That kiss had been tender and yet somehow possessive. Surely Lucian was not beginning to feel… No, of course not, he was simply tired and affected by the moonlight and the unconventionality of their closeness on this long, long drive.

She had made herself close her eyes and doze so she would be able to take her turn with the reins later and this time slept solidly until the curricle turning sharply into an inn yard rocked her against Lucian. 'Where are we?'

'Stafford.' He smiled at her, despite the dark shadows under his eyes and the tightness of the skin over his cheekbones that betrayed his weariness. 'You slept right through the last change. We'll get down here, stretch our legs.'

She watched him as he talked to the men unhitching the team, saw them react to his natural authority and the easy way he spoke to them as he helped out by taking a trace, lifting the shaft. As she leaned against the wheel, sleepily content in the shadows, she wondered where the stern, authoritarian man had vanished to.

Then, as Lucian turned, he froze, his attention on a

vehicle on the far side of the yard. He asked a question, his voice sharp in the almost deserted space. Then he strode towards her, all trace of that tired smile wiped from his face. 'They are here.'

'Thank goodness.' The relief was heartfelt until she realised what might happen now. As Lucian turned to reach into the back of the curricle for the valises—or his pistols, she did not stop to see which—Sara ran across the yard and through the door of the inn. A sleepy waiter in the hallway jerked awake as she shook him by the shoulder. 'The young couple who arrived earlier. Which room are they in?'

He gaped at her clothing, seeming not to comprehend the educated English combined with such exotic garb, but when she repeated the question he pointed at the stairs. 'Number six, on the left…'

Sara took the stairs two at a time, blessing her trousers, and skidded to a halt in front of a door with a faded number six painted on it. She knocked, then, as the front door banged open again, turned the handle and went in. There was a gasp and a scuffle from the shadow that must be the bed, then she knocked against a chair, spun it round and jammed it under the door handle. 'Marguerite?'

'*Sara?* Gregory, it is Sara.'

'For heaven's sake, light a candle,' she snapped as footsteps came closer along the uncarpeted landing. There was a scrabbling, a scraping and then a flicker of light that grew as the man in the bed touched it to the candle wick.

'Open this door.' Lucian kept his voice low, but the tone was enough to have Marguerite turn white.

'In a moment,' Sara said, then glanced at the bed. 'I

suggest you both get into something less likely to in-
flame the Marquess than your bare skins.' She turned
her back as the door latch rattled, but kept talking. 'Do
you want to marry him, Marguerite? Be very certain.'

'Oh, it *is* you in those clothes! I didn't... Yes, oh,
yes, of course I want to marry Gregory. But Lucian will
kill—'

'No, he will not.' Sara realised she was standing on a
pair of breeches and tossed them behind her on to the bed
as a fist thudded into the door. 'Hurry up! It will only
enrage him further if he finds you in bed together—'

The lock broke and the chair went flying. Lucian
stalked into the room, kicking pieces of wood aside.
His hands, Sara saw with a gulp of relief, were empty.

'Lucian, she wants to marry him, you can't kill him
now.'

He brushed past her as though she wasn't there. Sara
spun round to find that the young man with the scarred
face was on his feet wearing nothing but breeches and
his eyepatch. With a courage that Sara could only mar-
vel at he moved round the bed until he was face to face
with Lucian who was four inches taller and far broader
in the shoulders. 'I am at your disposal, my lord.'

The right hook sent him sprawling on the floor.
Lucian grimaced and blew on his knuckles. 'Get up. I
can't talk to you down there.' Gregory got unsteadily to
his feet, lifted his chin until he could look Lucian in the
eye and stood there swaying.

'It did not occur to you to come to me and tell me
what had happened in Lyons?'

'I begged him not to.' Marguerite, her nightrobe half
off her shoulders, scrambled across the bed and clutched
Gregory's arm.

'And you *still* want to marry this fluff-headed chit?' Lucian asked, his tone verging on friendly curiosity.

'I… Yes, my lord. I love her.' Gregory's face reflected complete surprise at the question.

'You will give me your word that you will both stay here tonight. In the morning we will discuss what is to be done. Yes? What is it? Don't you knock on your guests' doors?' He turned on the unfortunate landlord who stood on the threshold, nightcap askew, a truncheon in one hand.

'There is no door! You broke it open!'

'I broke the lock and a chair. And I will pay for the damage,' Lucian said coolly. 'I want two decent bed-chambers for myself and my valet.'

Sara stepped back into deeper shadow as Lucian advanced on the landlord, making him step back on to the landing. 'Give me your word you will not run away again,' she said to the young couple, low-voiced and urgent. 'I promise you he will allow you to marry.'

'My word on it,' Gregory said, his voice shaking. Marguerite burst into tears and Sara, her head spinning with tiredness, looked round the door, saw the landlord in full retreat and joined Lucian. 'They will stay there,' she told him, closing the damaged door behind her as best she could.

'That is the good news,' Lucian said. 'The bad news is that a severe storm two days ago took most of the tiles off the back of the roof. There are only two habitable bedchambers and that—' he jerked a thumb to the room she had just left '—is one of them. I'll sleep in the bar.'

As he spoke the landlord came up the stairs, dumped their luggage at the top with a glare and stomped back down again.

'No, you will not.' Sara scooped up her valise. 'We will both sleep in the remaining bedchamber.'

'Sara, we agreed about this.'

'We agreed that you would not want your lover befriending your little sister. Well, your little sister is in there in bed with a man she is not married to and you need a good night's sleep because you have a lot of thinking to do in the morning.' She blinked at him, almost too weary to focus. 'Please, Lucian. I will only lose sleep worrying about you otherwise.'

Lucian picked up the pistol and sword cases. 'Anything to keep you from worrying.' His smile was wry as he added, 'I really do not think I am a threat to any woman's virtue tonight.' He led the way down the passage and pushed open a door. 'This is the one, I think. Yes, it does appear to have a ceiling.'

Sara stumbled into the room. She was beyond tiredness, she realised hazily, and hardly aware of what he was saying. She tugged her turban loose with one hand and began to unbutton her coat with the other. On the far side of the bed Lucian was dragging off his clothes in just as random a manner. When she fell into bed dressed only in her shirt she was barely conscious of the covers being pulled over her shoulders or of Lucian's breath warm on her ear as he murmured *goodnight*.

Chapter Eleven

Fingers drifted across his chest, encountered a nipple, sifted through hair, then drifted on, downwards. Lucian woke slowly, coming up through layers of sleep to the awareness of that erotic touch, to the realisation that this was not a dream, that this was not his bed, that his shoulders ached dully and that something was lurking that he did not want to deal with. But just now, at this moment, there was nothing but pleasure. *Sara.*

He opened his eyes, savouring the sensations, unwilling, yet, to hurry anything. The weak light filtering through thin cotton curtains at the window showed it was early, not much past five. He turned his head on the pillow, his cheek touching the rough silk tumble of Sara's unbound hair and realised that she was still no more than half-awake.

The fan of her lashes fascinated him, thick and long and much darker than her hair. Her lips were slightly parted, her breathing light and fast, her cheeks faintly flushed. She was aroused, he realised, even though she was still virtually asleep.

Her wandering hand slipped down, making the skin

tighten beneath its warmth, then the tip of one finger found his navel, dipped inside, and Lucian doubled up with a snort of laughter.

'Mmm—?' Sara blinked awake.

'I am ticklish there.' Lucian came up on one elbow so he could kiss her. 'But do not let me stop you exploring,' he murmured against her lips.

Sara kissed him back, slowly, languorously, as her hand bumped against the blatant evidence of his arousal and she enclosed him in a perfect grip, firm, unhurried, wickedly skilled.

'Sara, we had agreed not to do this,' he said, coming fully awake with a jolt, reaching for self-control with an effort that hurt.

'Why on earth did we do that?' she asked, sounding as distracted as he felt.

'Shocking Marguerite, as I recall. That seems a little redundant now.'

Sara nodded. 'Absolutely.' She gasped as he let his fingers roam.

He had forgotten, somehow, that she had been married, that she would know exactly what she was about—and that she knew what she needed also, he realised, as she arched up to meet his own seeking fingers.

Mouths joined in an endless kiss, they moved together, became one undulating, shifting, yearning body, stoking fires even as they soothed them, teasing and tormenting, then gentling, caressing. Sara was like liquid silk in his hands, against his body, demanding, yielding, giving, challenging him to demand more, give more.

When he finally rose up over her, caging her between his elbows, fitting himself into the cradle of her curves, she became still, gazing up into his eyes from the fathomless moonstone-grey of her own. 'Lucian. Yes. *Yes.*'

It must have been some time for her, he made himself remember that, made himself go slowly and she let him lead, quivering in his arms with little moans of encouragement as she opened like a flower to take him, then held him within her, tight, hot, still. And she stayed motionless in his arms, as her inner muscles rippled and stroked with a subtle, devastating pulse that had him shaking with the effort to hold back his climax.

'Wicked, clever woman,' he whispered and finally let himself move, take over the rhythm, drive them both tighter and higher into a spiral of pleasure that became a sharply focused endless moment of sensation made up of the sound of their bodies working together, their mingled, sobbing breath, the scent of their arousal, until he knew he could not hold on much longer. 'Come, come for me now…'

And as Sara arched up, eyes wide, lips parted on a keening cry of pleasure, he wrenched himself from her and shuddered to completion on the silken skin of her belly.

'I suppose we should move,' Sara suggested as she lay with her cheek pressed to the admirably hard planes of Lucian's chest some unfathomable time later.

'Yes,' he agreed, his voice rumbling under her ear. 'Excellent idea.' He did not stir.

'It must be seven o'clock.' He grunted, sounding suspiciously like a man drifting off to sleep again. Sara blew on his nipple, which produced some reaction, although one that was not very conducive to getting out of bed.

'Someone has to be strong-minded,' she announced,

mentally cursing eloping couples and her own sense of responsibility that told her she must somehow create a happy ending for Marguerite and Gregory.

'Are you a nag, madam?' Lucian sat up, catching her by the shoulders to pull her up with him. 'Am I to rise and go forth and deliver lectures and chastisement?'

'No. You are to rise and think of some way of extracting those two from this pickle with reputations intact.'

'London is quiet. I could get them back to the town house and married from there by special licence. Or St George's, Hanover Square, with a show of openness, but safe in the knowledge that virtually everyone is out of town.' Lucian got off the bed, stooped to give her a rapid kiss, then threw on his robe and pulled the bell rope.

Sara burrowed down under the covers when a tap on the door heralded a maid servant who was promptly sent for hot water. 'And plenty of it. And breakfast in half an hour.'

'That all seems rather hole-and-corner,' she remarked ten minutes later as she sat up in bed, arms wrapped around her knees, and admired the view of Lucian, naked, shaving. *He really does have the most excellent backside*, she thought, indulging in a long, sensual stretch. 'Especially with her not being out yet.'

'I know it. What I need is a house party, if only I knew who to trust. Then the pair of them, finding themselves away from the normal environment of my town house, can make the startling discovery that they are in love.'

'And you can be persuaded, in full view of the interested onlookers, to yield to the pleas of young love and all will be well?'

'Exactly.' Lucian tipped the water into the slop bucket

and began to dress. Sara took his place at the washstand, marvelling at how easy it was to be like this with him, so at ease and yet tingling with the awareness of his closeness, of his body.

'The only problem being, I do not know anyone I can trust well enough to turn up, out of the blue, with a battered secretary who has been absent from the scene for months and a wan-looking little sister.' He raised his chin and squinted into the glass as he tied his neckcloth.

Sara dipped the brush in her toothpowder and scrubbed at her teeth, rinsed, spat and straightened up with an idea. 'But I do. My parents have a house party and the first guests arrived yesterday. We can join that. I think you will need to tell them something of the background, but you can trust them absolutely to keep the secret and to play along with the deception.'

'Whereabouts?' Lucian stuck a pin in his neckcloth and turned. 'It would be perfect—if they agree.'

'Eldonstone is in Hertfordshire, near St Albans. About one hundred and fifty miles from here, I suppose.' She took the walking dress out of the valise, gave it a shake, frowned at the creases and put it on anyway. This was where respectability began.

'It would be perfect,' Lucian repeated, slowly, 'if you and I had not just become lovers.'

'That is simple. We are not lovers for however long we are at Eldonstone,' Sara said, rather more firmly than she felt. 'Quite simple. We met at Sandbay, I became friends with Marguerite and invited you both to the house party. You have a great press of business, so Gregory comes, too. He has been away for some time recovering from whatever caused his injury and he and Marguerite see each other differently in these new surroundings.'

'While you and I behave with great circumspection,' Lucian said with resignation. 'The things I do for my sister.'

She laughed and he turned from packing his valise to look at her, his expression serious but unreadable. 'Are you all right? This morning—'

'This morning was bliss and I cannot wait to do it again and I am very much all right, Lucian.' She hesitated, wondering how to say this right, word it so that he understood she had no expectations beyond this relationship. 'I feel free. Free to have made the choice to be your lover.' Now she knew what she was doing, she had choice and there was nothing to feel guilty about in her relationship with this man. She had experienced more than enough guilt to last her a lifetime.

'Good.' He nodded, still serious. 'That is good.'

So, Lucian had no desire for this to be anything but a coming together for mutual pleasure either. That was excellent, just what she wanted. Of course it was.

'How good is your acting?' Sara asked Marguerite as the chaise bumped off the cobbles and on to the road towards Lichfield. The relief of discovering that she could marry Gregory safely, or perhaps the effects of a night in her lover's arms, had put roses in Marguerite's cheeks and a glow in her eyes. *I wonder if it has done that for me.* She certainly felt physically transformed. Looser, warmer, more alive.

'My acting?' The young woman bit her lip in puzzlement. 'I have no idea. Why?'

'Because you are going to have to seem to either fall gradually for Gregory or to have a *coup de foudre*, a sudden revelation that you love him. What we must avoid at all costs is any impression that the two of you felt anything for each other before this house party.'

'I can do that—in fact, I can see it all perfectly.' Marguerite smiled. 'I think perhaps I will be solicitous of him because of the injury. Lucian will be working him too hard and I will try to help. That will bring us close and then we will realise that we have loved each other all along and did not recognise it.' She glanced out of the window at the front of the chaise, past the bobbing backs of the postilions, to where Gregory sat beside Lucian in the curricle.

The imperious blast of a horn behind them had both vehicles pulling over to let the mail coach sweep by. 'That should be carrying my letter to my parents,' Sara said. 'I am hoping it will arrive at least an hour before we do.' It would certainly help if Mata spoke about inviting Sara's new friend and her brother in advance of their arrival. She had racked her brains to try to recall who was expected, but one could never tell with Mata, who might take the fancy to entertain anyone from a bishop to an actress, or sometimes both at the same time. Hopefully there would be at least a few pillars of the establishment, which was what was needed to ensure no shadow of gossip attached to Marguerite.

'I cannot thank you enough for persuading Lucian to accept the match and to only hit Gregory once,' Marguerite said earnestly. 'I cannot believe how forgiving he is being.'

'I suspect it is a mixture of realising he cannot shut the stable door given that the horse has bolted not once, but twice, and a reluctance to pulverise an injured man. What *did* happen to Gregory in France?'

'A roof tile fell off a building that was being repaired.

It did not hit him right on the head, thank goodness, or I think he would have been killed, but it tore right down the side of his face as you can see. He was taken unconscious to a nearby nunnery where the sisters cared for him and sent for a doctor, but they could not save his eye. He was unconscious, then in a high fever and in no state to explain himself, let alone get out of bed. It was two weeks before he could persuade someone to go round to the lodgings to find me and by then I was on my way back to England with Lucian.' One fat tear ran down Marguerite's cheek and she dashed it away. 'He says I must not think about it, but I cannot bear to think of him in so much pain and so worried.'

'That is all behind you now. This evening we will make certain that we are all telling the same story and everything will be well.'

'You parents must be very kind for you to be so certain that they will welcome three extra guests at such short notice,' Marguerite ventured. 'But I expect they will be pleased about you and Lucian.'

'About—what on earth do you mean?' Mata might not turn a hair about Sara taking a lover if that made her happy, but her father and Ashe would react in a way that was completely predictable.

'You are going to get married, aren't you? I am so pleased about it. We will be sisters and—'

'No, we are *not* going to get married,' Sara snapped, too startled to control her reaction. 'What on earth makes you think that?'

'But…' Marguerite's cheeks were pink with embarrassment. 'But you…he… Last night, there were only two bedchambers,' she finished in a rush.

Sara gritted her teeth and kept her voice reasonable.

'Marguerite, I am a widow. A discreet liaison in those circumstances is, shall we say, overlooked, by society.'

'But don't you love him?' Marguerite looked mystified. 'I was sure you loved him.'

'I find your brother very attractive. I admire his desire to protect you. I also find him infuriating, stubborn, single-minded, authoritarian and domineering. He is the last man I would wish to marry.'

'Truly? And he does not want to marry you?'

'No.' *He made that perfectly clear.* 'He wants an *affaire*, has wanted it ever since he realised I was possibly…available. I have no doubt that next Season Lucian will be choosing a bride from the young ladies making their come-out.'

'I think I know who he will choose.' Marguerite wrinkled her nose. 'She was out last Season and she lives near us in the country. Lady Clara Fairhaven. She is *perfect*.' The emphasis was not one of approval. 'She is pretty and dull and has all the right connections and never puts a foot wrong and her father would be delighted if Lucian marries her. I thought he was going to make a declaration last Season, which was infuriating because I wasn't out so I couldn't do anything to stop him.'

'Such as?' Sara asked, fascinated despite herself at the thought of anyone thinking they could stop the Marquess of Cannock once he had made up his mind to something. 'What could you do to prevent it?'

'I could get her drunk at Almack's or bribe some rake to flirt with her outrageously or put a mouse up her skirts at a dinner party,' Marguerite said darkly. 'She would make him dull, too. You wouldn't.'

'I am one-quarter Indian, I am a widow, my husband died in a duel and I have led a somewhat unconventional life since his death. None of that makes me a suitable wife for your brother, certainly not set against a well-bred young lady of perfect deportment. Even if I wanted to marry him, that is. Which I do not.'

Even as she spoke she could think of nothing but waking that morning in Lucian's arms, the tender fierceness of his lovemaking, the pleasure they had exchanged and shared, the harmony she felt with him. And yet…and yet, this was the man who had only permitted his sister to marry for love when every other option had been removed, the man who would have killed Gregory and thought it was his duty, an honourable thing to do, the man who seemed to have no understanding of her own need for freedom or her anger at what Michael had done in his misguided desire to protect her honour.

There were fleeting moments when she imagined being with Lucian, sharing ideas, impressions, laughter. And there were long hours when she could see what would be the reality, a conventional husband expecting a conventional wife and exerting all the power that men had to enforce that.

'I definitely do not,' she repeated and looked away from the broad shoulders of the man driving ahead of them.

'I suppose it will make it awkward for you, going to your family house like this,' Marguerite ventured. 'With Lucian, I mean.'

'I have no intention of carrying on an *affaire* under that roof, you may be certain. And neither will you. Everything depends on the other guests witnessing the beginnings of a love-match and you behaving like an innocent young lady not quite out.'

'Yes, Sara,' Marguerite said meekly, making her feel forty-five at the very least.

It was a long day, but Sara was pleased to see that Lucian allowed Gregory to take the reins for several stages. Whether that was simple common sense because he knew he should give himself a break from time to time or, as Marguerite thought, a sign of forgiveness, it did at least mean they could keep up a good time. They reached Northampton just after sunset and she let out a sigh of relief when they finally drew in to the yard of the King's Head.

Lucian came to help them down from the chaise while Gregory went inside to secure rooms. 'I told him to bespeak four rooms and a private parlour,' he told his sister as he swung her down on to the cobbles. 'You need to get into practice for the house party.'

'Yes, Lucian,' she said obediently, her docility at odds with the longing look she gave Gregory from under her lashes.

Will Lucian come to my chamber tonight? Sara wondered as they went into the inn. *Or was last night enough for him? Perhaps he has sated his desire and his curiosity.* Although he had seemed to imply a longer relationship in his words when they were dressing that morning. She hoped so, since *her* desire and curiosity were certainly not sated yet.

When they were settled in their rooms, which all led off a small upstairs parlour, Lucian ordered dinner, poured wine and settled at the head of the table. 'We need to get this story straight. Where will we have come from tomorrow?'

'Reading would have been a good place to have broken our journey from Sandbay,' Sara suggested. 'Then we have no need to leave too early tomorrow.'

'Very well. Now then. Marguerite has been unwell—a severe attack of influenza that you could not shake off.' His sister nodded. 'I took her to Sandbay to recuperate and Sara befriended her and invited us to the house party. Just before we left we were joined by Farnsworth, who has been taking a holiday to recover from his injury. That can have happened just as it did, and in Lyons but, shall we say that I was there on business and you had accompanied me?'

'So I have not seen Greg… *Mr Farnsworth*…for some time and I find myself surprised at how shaken I am by his accident,' Marguerite chipped in. 'Lucian has *heaps* of work for him, which is why he must accompany us, but I will keep checking to make sure he is not being overworked while he is still convalescent.'

'And it will not occur to anyone that they need strict chaperonage because they never have before,' Sara suggested, shrugging when Lucian raised his eyebrows at her. 'And before we know where we are they have fallen in love.'

'And so on and so forth,' Lucian said. 'And I will amaze everyone by yielding to my sister's pleas to allow them to marry, even though she is not yet out. The company will think I have lost my mind. As well they might,' he added grimly.

Gregory was fiddling with his eyepatch, presumably prey to nerves, or perhaps embarrassment. The bruise on his chin from Lucian's punch the previous night was darkening.

'How did Gregory acquire that bruise?' Sara asked.

'I am not used to having only one eye and I misjudge distances, Lady Sara. I could have tripped over last night,' he suggested.

'That will have to do,' Lucian said impatiently. 'Now remember, both of you, for the sake of Marguerite's reputation, this has to deceive a number of people, some of whom are probably eagle-eyed matrons on the look-out for the slightest impropriety.'

Sara reminded him of those words when he slipped quietly into her bedchamber several hours later. 'My lord, are you by any chance here to commit some slight impropriety?'

'I sincerely hope so, given that I face at least a week of being on my best behaviour,' Lucian said as he turned the key in the lock. Under-lit by the candle flame, his face had a stark, unearthly quality.

I could look at that face for ever, she thought. *Desire is such a snare. I see him, I want him and I cannot seem to think beyond what is going to happen in this bed tonight.*

Lucian shrugged off his robe and put down the candle, easy in his skin, relaxed about his nakedness. But there was nothing relaxed about the look in his eyes as he watched her waiting for him, nor could she be in any doubt that however long and tiring the day had been this man fully intended to make love to her now—and probably for half of the night.

Chapter Twelve

'Darling!' Lady Eldonstone, looking like a woman half her age, ran down the steps and reached the door of the chaise before the footman. She stood there while the man opened the door and let down the step, then seized Sara in a fierce hug the moment she emerged. 'You look beautiful, darling, and do not take any notice of your father, or of Ashe. They are being ridiculous, the pair of them. You must be Lady Marguerite, welcome to Eldonstone. Have you had a good journey? Come along inside, both of you.'

'*Why* must I take no notice of Papa and Ashe, Mata?' Sara dug in her heels and stopped dead. 'What are they being ridiculous about?'

'Ashe went down to Sandbay to see you. I think he wants to plot a surprise birthday party for your father next month. He got back this morning saying that you were not there and had left mysteriously and that Mr Makepeace told him some cock-and-bull story about being worried because you left town with a Mr Dunton.' She shrugged. 'Well, you know what he and Nicholas are like, so primitive about that sort of thing, which when you consider that your father and I hardly had a conventional courtship and if you can convince me that Ashe was exactly as pure as the driven snow—although I am sure he would die if he heard his mother say so—is most unreasonable of them.'

'Lady Eldonstone.' Marguerite had stopped, too, and was listening, white-faced. 'You have discovered that Sara is helping me to cover up my disgrace and, of course, you do not approve. I apologise, I will tell Lucian that we must leave immediately.'

'Goodness, child, this is not about you at all. My ridiculous menfolk have come over all *male* and protective of Sara. I can only hope that your brother is impervious to insult or we may have a very exciting day in front of us.'

'I believe you will find that the Marquess of Cannock is about as impervious to insult as Papa or Ashe are,' Sara said, looking round. Yes, there they were, grim-faced on the terrace. She picked up her skirts and ran across the gravel to put herself between them and her lover.

'Papa.' She kissed his cheek and received a fierce hug in return. 'Ashe. Where is Phyllida?'

'I asked her to stay inside and distract the other guests,' her brother said, glaring over her shoulder. 'They are all round at the garden front.'

'Distract them from what?' Sara demanded. Out of the corner of her eye she saw that Lucian had handed over the reins of the curricle to a groom and that he and Gregory were walking across to them.

'Us dealing with Cannock.'

'Lucian does not require *dealing with*. He is a guest and my friend, as is his sister, and—Ashe!'

* * *

'Farnsworth, I believe we might be in for a somewhat cool welcome.' Lucian began to stroll across the gravel towards the steps, assessing the two men standing there with Sara in front of them. He was too far away to hear what was being said, but from the rigid set of her shoulders and the vehement hand gestures, he suspected not all was well. Gregory's head turned as he looked for Marguerite. 'Do not react, whatever the provocation,' Lucian added. 'Leave this to me.'

This was Sara's home and he owed her a great deal, too much to cause a rift with her family. Her brother brushed past her, took the steps down two at a time and strode towards them. Instinctively Lucian shifted his stance, but kept his hands down when every ounce of instinct and training told him to lift his fists in the face of the Viscount's evident hostility. Even so, he had expected some preliminaries, some insults at least, not that Clere would aim a right hook squarely at his jaw. He rocked back three paces, riding the punch, but stayed on his feet.

He ran one hand over his chin and contemplated throwing manners, caution and common sense to the wind and taking out the frustrations of the past few months on the man in front of him. Then he saw Sara run across the carriage drive towards them and gave her the faintest shake of his head. She stopped, then walked forward warily to stand beside him, facing her brother. Her loyalties would be torn between them both and he admired her for even attempting the balancing act.

'An unusual welcome,' Lucian drawled, ignoring the pain. *Damn, but the man has a punch like a blacksmith's hammer.* It was a miracle his teeth were not all over the drive. 'Farnsworth, this is Viscount Clere. I suggest you stay out of his way until we establish whether this is his normal greeting to guests or if I am uniquely honoured by a display of pugilism.' He should be diplomatic, soothing, make a joke of it, perhaps. He needed this family's help. But he was not going to act the punching bag for anyone, not even this man whom he had always liked and who was reacting as he strongly suspected he would have himself if he was in Clere's shoes.

'You have seduced my sister,' the other man snarled. 'And—'

'Why not wait until you can find a speaking trumpet, Clere? I am sure there must be one or two of our audience who did not quite catch that announcement. Look, the men scything the grass over there must have missed it.' The truth was, a fight would be welcome. More than welcome. Some mindless violence… His hands curled into fists as Clere took another step forward.

'Stop it, both of you.' Sara managed to wriggle between the two of them when they were almost toe to toe. 'No one has seduced anyone.'

'It was ravishment, then?' her brother snarled.

'It was no such thing and none of your business whatever it was, Ashe Herriard,' Sara snapped. 'I am a grown woman, an independent widow, and you have absolutely no right interfering. And, might I remind you, this is not your house and if Mata is happy to welcome my guests— which she is—what have you to say to it?'

God, she is magnificent. Ashe folded his arms and prepared to leap to Sara's defence if she showed the slightest sign of needing him. At the moment, though, she appeared to have her brother on the back foot.

'Father is not—'

'Good day, Cannock.'

Lucian looked away from the seething Viscount to the tall figure of Sara's father standing behind him. 'Eldonstone.' He inclined his head a trifle, as much courtesy as he was prepared to offer the older man in the midst of this crackling hostility. 'We came at the invitation of Lady Sara. If we are not welcome we will, naturally, remove ourselves.' He locked gazes with Clere again. *Unfinished business*, he promised. *You will not provoke me into a fist fight on your mother's doorstep, but later...*

'Do come in.' The older man regarded him, unsmiling, his grey eyes uncannily like Sara's. 'I feel you and I have matters to discuss.'

One thing, and one thing only, kept him from turning round and driving out of there and that was Marguerite. For her sake he would swallow his pride, shackle his temper and deal with these two angry men. But he was damned if he was explaining himself or discussing his relationship with Sara.

He sent her a quick smile and strolled across the expanse of gravel beside Eldonstone. The colour was up on Sara's cheekbones and she was bristling at her much taller brother like a she-cat confronting a mastiff. As he passed her, Lucian heard her snap, 'Don't you dare,' presumably at her brother. The Marchioness was already leading Marguerite inside, gesticulating with her hands as she talked. It seemed she had prevented his sister from seeing what had just occurred, thank goodness.

'My study.' Eldonstone opened a panelled door at the end of the hallway and gestured for him to enter. 'Have a seat, Cannock. Brandy?'

'Thank you, no.' Not when he was an unwelcome intruder in this place.

'My son went down to Sandbay to visit his sister and found that she had left early that morning, alone with you. And yet you would have us believe that you, and your entourage, have come direct from there. The rumours were already spreading. Something clandestine is going on.'

'Not under your roof,' Lucian said coolly. 'I do not discuss my private affairs with anyone and if you wish to know about Lady Sarisa's, then I suggest you discuss them with her. My sister and I owe her a great deal and, she is, as she pointed out to her brother, an independent woman.'

'She is my daughter and if you have been toying with her affections with no intention of marrying her then your *private affairs* are most definitely my concern.'

'Her affections do not enter into this.' The Marquess's eyes narrowed dangerously. Lucian deliberately poured oil on the flames. *Get it over with.* 'Nor does marriage.'

The big hands that had lain relaxed on the desk curled into fists. 'In my house—'

'In your house I imagine that Lady Sarisa would conduct herself with the greatest respect to your wishes. As would I, were I a guest here.'

'He is playing with words.' The door in the far corner was flung open to reveal Viscount Clere. 'Playing with *us*. Will you or will you not marry my sister?'

Lucian curled a lip at him for the drama and received a glare in return. A bout in the stable yard would be so very satisfying. 'No,' Lucian said baldly, staying where he was and crossing his legs. Marriage was not what their relationship was about. They were lovers. Sara was not ready for marriage to anyone, he could tell that, and as for himself, he had other plans. Long-standing plans that involved the careful and considered choice of the next Marchioness of Cannock.

'No, he will not,' said Sara, emerging from behind the screen in the opposite corner. 'Why should he? Why should *I*, come to that?'

'Give me strength!' The Marquess slammed one fist down on the desk. 'What is this? A French farce? This confounded room has too many doors—and I have two disrespectful offspring. Ashe, sit down. Sara, if this man has seduced you, he must marry you.'

Her colour was up and so was her chin. Under any other circumstances Lucian would have sat back and admired the show, but this was his lover under fire and, magnificent as she was, it was his battle to fight, not hers. He stood up and went to stand at her side, not touching. 'Lady Sarisa makes her own decisions, her own choices. She is an independent woman with enough force of character to withstand seduction. I believe she has made it clear that she does not wish to discuss her personal life. As for my own, I would simply point out that I would not dream of abusing my hostess's hospitality by any behaviour that might cause her distress or embarrassment.' And if they could not interpret that to mean that he and Sara would behave with perfect propriety when under her parents' roof, then he would have to draw them a diagram.

Sara gave him a fleeting smile. 'Lord Cannock is my lover, although he is too discreet to say so in as many words. It was a mutual decision, naturally, as he is a gentleman of honour,' she said, before he could add anything. 'And no seduction was necessary on either side.' She turned to look at her brother. 'And don't grind your teeth, Ashe. You know perfectly well that if one of your friends was having an *affaire* with a widow of his own class you would not turn a hair. In fact, if you hadn't met Phyllida when you did, I expect you would have been dallying with widows yourself.'

'That is irrelevant.'

'Then you are a hypocrite,' she flung back.

'Damn it, you are only twenty-four, Sara. What some older woman about town does is completely irrelevant. You have no experience of rakes and you know it.'

'Lucian is not a rake.'

'How do you know?' That silenced her. As she sought for an answer Ashe spun round to face Lucian. 'You marry my sister or you will meet me.'

This was getting out of hand. Sara had gone white and he suddenly realised why. It was not simply the hostility and her distress at arguing with her father and brother, although that must be affecting her. But she had already lost her husband to a duel and now her brother was not only raking that memory up but making her fear that she could lose her lover, or, far worse, her brother, the same way.

'Actually, I have the priority for a challenge,' he drawled. 'You struck me.'

'Damn it, then challenge me!'

'Lucian.' Sara's voice shook and he felt as though he had hit her.

He glanced down and shook his head in reassurance before meeting her brother's furious gaze. 'Whether I call you out, Clere, or you call me out, I will delope. I will not risk killing Sara's brother. If you do not delope, then you will be meeting me with the intent to kill me. Is that clear enough? And what your sister does when she is not under her parents' roof is her affair, not yours.'

'Exactly.' Sara had the tremor almost under control now. 'Now, are we welcome, *all* of us, or do we leave? Because if Lucian goes, I go.'

'You are always welcome, Sara,' her father said. 'And Lady Marguerite needs our help, from what your mother hinted. So, no, my darling, you do not leave.' He rose and held out his hand to Lucian. 'I am sorry for your reception, but when you have a daughter of your own you will understand. I happen to trust mine and to trust her judgement. You are welcome here for as long as Sara is happy.' For the first time he smiled and Lucian felt he knew what meeting a tiger face to face would be like. 'On the other hand, if you make my daughter unhappy I will not trouble myself with the formality of a challenge.'

'Understood.' Lucian returned the firm pressure of the big hand with its calluses from years of handling reins and weapons. He did not make the mistake of offering his own to Clere, nor would he forget that blow outside just now. There would be a reckoning for that.

The room the footman showed him to was large, luxurious and decorated in an eclectic mix of fine furniture of the previous century and rich, dark, Indian fabrics and embroideries. It felt a little like being inside an exceedingly masculine jewel casket.

'Lady Marguerite's chamber is opposite, my lord,' the footman volunteered when he had checked that hot water had been delivered to the dressing room. 'Lady Eldonstone thought you would prefer her ladyship to be nearby. Mr Farnsworth is just around the corner to the left. An informal luncheon will be served in the Green Dining Room in half an hour.'

Lucian tidied himself up, grimaced in the mirror at the bruise on his chin and went in search of his sister. A maid opened the door to his knock and he found Marguerite happily exploring a room that was swagged in pale silk embroidered with flowers and animals.

'This is lovely, Lucian! It is like being in a garden. Lady Eldonstone is so kind and understanding—Lucian, your chin?'

'I walked into something.' No more than the truth. 'Ready for luncheon?'

'Of course. I am starving.' She dimpled at his grin. 'I know, how unladylike of me. But I am. We must collect Gregory.'

'*Mr Farnsworth* will make his own way down.' He trusted them—up to a point. Showing the little minx the location of her lover's bedchamber was positively begging for trouble. 'Concentrate, Marguerite. This is the first act of a play, remember. Your reputation hangs on its success.'

She nodded with all the confidence of youth and Lucian gave mental thanks once again for Sara's help. 'It will be all right, do not fuss, Lucian.'

'We haven't met the other guests yet,' Lucian said grimly. All they needed were a couple of those eagle-eyed dowagers, able to spot a scandal at twenty paces, and the acting would have to be of a very high order indeed.

When they located the Green Dining Room the first sight of the assembled company was promising, he thought. Everyone there was known to him, at least by sight, although for Marguerite, not yet out, they were all strangers. Lady Eldonstone had organised a casual buffet with several tables scattered through the room and out on the terrace which was accessible through the open full-length windows and the guests were standing about chatting while servants brought in various dishes to set out on the sideboard.

Two young bachelor acquaintances from his clubs came over at once. 'Cannock, this is a surprise. Ma'am,' Toby Peterson said, beaming at Marguerite.

'Marguerite, this is Sir Toby Peterson and Lord Hitchin. Gentlemen, my sister, Lady Marguerite.'

'Delighted, Lady Marguerite.' Sir Toby moderated the smile to something more respectful. Marguerite, Lucian was amused to see, blushed and smiled back. He only hoped that her devotion to Gregory held firm in the face of close encounters with other personable young men or they really were in the soup.

'What's wrong with your face, Cannock?' Hitchin enquired, loudly enough for several heads to turn. 'Nasty bruise coming up on your chin.'

'An unfortunate collision,' Lucian replied. 'I should have been more careful. Is that Fitzhugh I see over there?' He abandoned the inquisitive Hitchin and moved to greet an acquaintance from White's. His wife expressed interest in meeting Marguerite and made her way over to detach her from the baronet.

'She misses her own young sister,' Fitzhugh confided. 'We fired Annabelle off in fine style this Season, but now Marie is like a hen without a chick. She'll keep an eye on your sister with these young bucks around. Her first time out, isn't it?'

'Yes, I thought it sensible to let her try her wings before her Season. It always seems cruel pitching the girls straight from the schoolroom into society and the bear pit of Almack's.' Time, he thought, to change the subject away from Marguerite. 'That racehorse of yours did well at Wincanton.'

Sara came in and began to circulate, her expression when they met decidedly cool and collected. Was she play-acting for her family's benefit or had he upset her in the study? he wondered, schooling his own face. Hell, this could be a long week.

Something white fluttered to his feet as she passed. 'Your handkerchief, Lady Sara.' He stooped to pick it up and, as she took it from him, her fingers curled into his palm for a moment, the nails gently raking the sensitive flesh. 'Stop it, you tease,' he murmured and she chuckled, a low, wicked sound, as she moved on.

Chapter Thirteen

Lucian conjured up thoughts of cold porridge, icicles and Latin verbs. A *very* long week. He looked around for his sister and saw Marguerite was talking to the Dowager Countess of Thale, a notoriously outspoken old besom, and her companion, the bluestocking Miss Croft. He moved across the room so he was within earshot of the conversation.

'Oh, good, poor Mr Farnsworth has come down,' Marguerite said. 'He is my brother's confidential secretary, you know, and he has been in the most horrible accident and it is *so* brave of him to come back to help Lucian even though he is still recovering. I tell my brother he must not work him too hard, but you know what men are like.'

'Indeed I do,' Miss Croft said darkly. 'He looks a scholarly type, though.'

'My brother?' Marguerite asked innocently. Lucian's lips twitched. He must warn her not to overdo the sweet naivety.

'The secretary.'

'Oh, yes, I believe he is. Rather serious, you know,

even though the eyepatch makes him look most piratical.' She laughed and Lucian relaxed. Marguerite would do.

'Lord Cannock.'

He turned and saw a tall brunette by his side, regarding him with wide brown eyes full of curiosity. He recognised her, but had never met her. 'Lady Clere.' An attractive lady and expecting a child, if he was not mistaken. Sara's brother had good taste, he would give him that. The child, he remembered Sara saying, would be their first.

'I suspect I know where that bruise came from,' she murmured. 'Ashe can be exceedingly protective, which is very commendable, but sometimes…infuriating. I must congratulate you on not retaliating. But by the look of her I think you are making Sara happy, so I approve. But if I find you have hurt her I will disembowel you myself, Lord Cannock.' She smiled brightly as if she had just made a joke. He suspected it was not. 'Luncheon is ready, do make yourself at home.'

She passed on to the next group of guests with a warm smile, leaving Lucian wondering just what sort of bloodthirsty family Sara belonged to. She was skilled with a knife, as was, apparently, her mother. Her brother hit first and asked questions afterwards, her father positively exuded controlled menace and her sister-in-law uttered unladylike threats with relish.

He filled a plate with cold meats and salads and went to an unoccupied table on the terrace in the hope of finding some peace to think. He had no sooner settled and sent a footman off for ale than he had to rise as his hostess approached.

'Please, do not stand, Lord Cannock.' Lady Eldonstone settled beside him in a flurry of elegant green skirts and he thought what a truly beautiful woman she was, with her glossy dark brown hair and her gilded skin and those wide, expressive green eyes. She and Eldonstone had created handsome children between them, he thought, eyeing her warily. What threats would she utter? he wondered, knowing he could not bring himself to speak to his hostess as he had to her husband and son if she attacked him.

'You may relax, Lord Cannock, I trust my daughter's judgement,' she said without further preliminaries as she tore a bread roll apart with one quick twist.

'Thank you.' It was a novel experience, to be talking to the mother of a lover, and it went against all his instincts as a gentleman. The ladies with whom he normally formed liaisons were as old as he was, sophisticated widows living independent lives far detached from the bonds of family. Sara was sophisticated enough in her own way, but he had not counted on this close proximity to the rest of the Herriards, her unconventional, exceedingly frank, family.

'And I like your sister, a charming girl. All will be well,' Lady Eldonstone added serenely.

'I sincerely hope so.' Lucian had the distinct impression that if anything was *not* well, she would give it a severe talking-to.

'Now, tell me your impressions of Sandbay,' she said as two more guests, a middle-aged couple, approached their table. 'Dr Galway, Mrs Galway, do join us.' She made the introductions when she discovered they knew each other only by sight and, when they had settled, told them that Lord Cannock and his sister had been staying at the resort where they had met Sara.

'It sounds a charming place,' Mrs Galway remarked eagerly. 'I keep telling my husband we should go and stay. What is your impression of it, Lord Cannock? One would hope for rational entertainment without the sort of thing one hears about at Brighton.' She lowered her voice. 'Immorality and vice. Shocking. One shudders to think what the tone of society will be once That Man becomes king.'

'I certainly did not observe any immorality,' Lucian said. Which was true enough. The only immorality he was aware of had been perpetuated by him and he had hardly *observed* it. His body stirred at the memory of it though and he focused resolutely on Mrs Galway's earnest face. 'It is a small town still, but exceedingly pleasant. It was just what my sister, who has been un-well, needed. Good air, relaxation, some unexceptional diversions.'

He continued to talk platitudes and eat cold ham under the amused gaze of his hostess. Lucian gritted his teeth. If this polite boredom was the price of making all secure for Marguerite, then he would pay it.

Sara, meanwhile, was deep in conversation with Gregory who was doing an excellent job of not look-ing at Marguerite who had escaped Lady Fitzhugh and had been rejoined by Peterson and Hitchin. Lucian knew he should probably show some disapproval of his sis-ter sitting with two lively young gentlemen. They had found her a table and were plying her with refreshments, squabbling in the most flattering manner over which of them would fetch her lemonade. But if they were guests here they would be trustworthy and it seemed to him they were too young to be any danger to her affections for Farnsworth. Besides, a little flirtation with them would divert attention from any attention she paid to her brother's secretary.

Peals of laughter made him glance across the terrace to where four young ladies, barely older than Marguerite, were clustered around a table, heads together as they chattered. Their charmingly fashionable, obviously expensive, morning dresses marked them as being out, probably part of this Season's crop of young ladies launched on to the Marriage Mart.

Lord, but they are young, he thought as he watched them giggle and tease and cast lingering glances at the two young men who were talking to Marguerite. He had always managed to avoid the innocents, he realised. His London social life revolved around his clubs and invitations to dinner parties, balls, receptions and entertainments where he could mingle with men his own age or older, married couples, the dashing widows—anyone, in fact, rather than the pastel-clad girls so fiercely chaperoned by their anxious and ambitious mamas.

And these were the young ladies from whom he would choose his bride. His *wife*. He looked at the pretty faces unmarked by life's experiences—or even much thought, he suspected. How did you choose, how could you know which would mature into a woman of character and intelligence, a woman he would want to spend the rest of his life with, the mother of his children?

A ripple of rich, amused laughter reached him through the chatter. He found he was smiling as he looked across at Sara, who was still talking to Farnsworth. What his somewhat solemn secretary had said to her to make her laugh he could not guess, but as Lucian watched Farnsworth said something else and she was immediately serious, listening with her chin cupped in her hand.

Intelligent, complicated, loyal, beautiful and, as he now knew only too well, sensual and desirable. Why the devil was he even contemplating marriage to one of those unformed little chits when he could marry this woman? She was eminently suitable by birth, Marguerite liked and trusted her—

'We saw very little of you in London this Season, Lord Cannock,' Lady Eldonstone remarked, jerking Lucian back from thoughts which were fast running away from him.

'No, unfortunately I had business on the Continent. Brussels, then France,' he replied, wondering why she had raised what Sara's letter would already have told her.

'And France was where young Mr Farnsworth suffered his dreadful injury?'

Ah, so she was setting the scene in front of two of the guests. Lucian did his bit. 'Yes, Lyons. He had the misfortune to pass a house just as a heavy tile fell from the roof. It was a miracle he was not killed. I was not certain I should let him back to work so soon, and my sister tells me I am a cruel slave driver for doing so, but he seems to be coping.'

It gave him an excuse to look back to the table where Sara sat. She would be perfect. The shop would have to go, of course, but once they were married surely any desire to behave unconventionally would leave her...

He half-rose as the Galways got up to go, caught the eye of one of the four young ladies and produced his best brotherly smile when she simpered at him. She looked a trifle daunted.

'Poor little birds in their gilded cage,' Lady Eldonstone remarked as he sat again. It seemed she had noticed the direction of his gaze. 'They cannot stretch their wings, all they may do is flutter from one perch to another, displaying their pretty plumage and singing their banal songs.'

'You do not approve of the way young women are brought out into society?'

'I was brought up in an Indian princely court. In many ways the restrictions on a young woman were as great, but no one would have dreamed of telling me to appear ignorant or feeble and helpless.'

'You certainly did not raise your own daughter to be any of those things.'

'No. Sara is independent and her standards are high, many would call them unconventional. She married for love to a scholar, the last man I would have expected my fierce little hawk to fall for, but perhaps she needed sanctuary in this strange new world she found herself in. And they were happy, until he let those primitive instincts you men are so prone to overwhelm him.' She tossed her table napkin down beside her plate and made to get up. Lucian stood and held her chair for her. 'Thank you.' She put her hand over his as it lay on the chair back. 'It is not easy to forgive someone you love when they kill themselves for your sake and even harder to forgive yourself for feeling that way.' She hesitated, then turned back to him. 'We can only do our best for those we love. Flagellating ourselves with guilt when we were wrong, or could not do the impossible, helps no one.'

Had that parting shot been meant for him? Lucian wondered if Sara had found time to tell her mother more about Marguerite than her letter could convey and whether Lady Eldonstone guessed at his own feelings of guilt. Probably she had—he was half-convinced the woman was a mind-reader.

Lucian stopped by Sara's table and she smiled up at him, a perfectly friendly smile that she might have given any of the male guests. Yet deep in those grey eyes there was another secret smile just for him. Was he mad to think of marriage and this woman? He had been raised to regard a wife as a responsibility to be guarded, protected, shielded from the slightest puff of cold air, yet Sara wanted none of that, seemed to regard his protective instincts as some kind of patronising patriarchal domination. Did she share her mother's view that those unmarried girls were simply birds in gilded cages? Did she regard marriage as yet another cage?

Her husband's death had been a tragedy, but he could not but see it as an inevitable risk. As a gentleman, Harcourt had had no choice when his wife was insulted. He himself had no choice but to forbid the match when Marguerite had fallen for an unsuitable man when she was far too young. He could accept that he had handled the situation badly, but that did not negate the principle. Nor could he blame Eldonstone and Clere for their hostility to himself, even as he resented it.

Sara would expect him to let her fight her own battles and she would be constantly fearful that he would meet his death on a field at dawn for some slight. For himself, he would be always on edge, convinced that she was hiding things from him that might trigger that imperative to protect.

'Impossible,' he said and only realised he had spoken out loud when both Sara and Farnsworth stared at him.

'My lord?' Farnsworth got to his feet. 'I apologise, I have lingered here far too long. I should be working.'

'Nonsense. I mean, you have not lingered too long. All I meant was that it is impossible to relax and enjoy myself when there is such a press of work. If you have finished and Lady Sara will excuse us, we can discuss priorities in the garden.'

The last thing he wanted was company, but he could hardly justify bringing his secretary to a house party unless he showed some evidence of needing him to work.

'I will fetch my notebook, my lord, and will be back directly.' Farnsworth excused himself and went out.

'Sit with me while you wait for him,' Sara said.

Reluctantly Lucian took Farnsworth's chair. He did not want to be with Sara, not until he could work out what he wanted to be to her—lover or husband. Somehow there did not seem to be any other options.

Around them the room was emptying. Some guests were drifting out to the terrace to enjoy the afternoon warmth, others were talking of resting, letter-writing, a visit to the gunroom with their host.

Lucian leaned back, distancing himself from her to prevent any impression of intimacy. 'A delightful meal. Your mother has the knack of entertaining, I think.'

'Oh, yes. And wait until she has one of her picnics,' Sara said.

Lucian repressed a start as her foot nudged his and then rose to slide up his leg until her extended toes just brushed the inside of his thigh.

'It really is not fair to tease me with delightful possibilities, Lady Sara.'

Icicles, cold porridge, Latin verbs...

Sara's teeth closed on her lower lip as she hid her smile. 'Oh, a picnic is not merely a possibility, the weather is set to remain fair, I believe. Or was there some other activity you were thinking of? Something delightful...'

'I might think all I wish, but I am under your parents' roof,' he said, low-voiced. 'And you agreed with me that discretion was necessary.'

'I know.' That provoking toe-tip continued its exploration. 'But they do not own the sky and, as I said, the weather is set fair.'

'I am their guest,' he said firmly as he reached under the table, seized her foot and set about establishing whether Sara was ticklish. 'Misbehaving in the grounds is not acceptable either.'

'We could explore the gardens together without committing the slightest improper—oh, stop it!' she gasped as he slid one finger into her kid shoe and caressed her instep. 'That is so unfair. *Let me go!*'

'If you promise to behave.' When she nodded, lips compressed on her giggles, he released the foot and Sara sat up very straight.

'Gardens? Surely you can give Gregory some work to be getting on with and then be free for me to show you the lily pond and the rose garden and the herbery.'

'You want to torture me, in other words.'

'A medieval knight would regard it as a test of his devotion to his lady to put himself constantly in her way and yet resist the temptation to steal so much as a touch.'

'More fool him.' It sounded like a recipe for a permanent state of frustrated arousal to Lucian.

'It was romantic.' She regarded him, head on one side. 'You are not at all romantic, are you, Lucian?'

'Not in the slightest.' Romance got a man into foolish entanglements and led to imprudent marriages. To his relief, because he could not tell whether he was being teased or had gravely disappointed Sara, Farnsworth came back into the dining room, deserted now except for the two of them at the table and the servants clearing the buffet.

'I am ready, my lord. Lady Marguerite is playing battledore with the other young ladies and some of the gentlemen on the front lawn.'

'Thank you. We will stroll to the lily pond, I think, if Lady Sara would be good enough to direct us. I do not expect it will take long, unless you have some knotty problems in the correspondence folder.'

'Just the one about boundaries on the shooting-lodge lands, my lord.'

'Walk straight across the terrace, down the steps, turn left and follow the slope of the lawn down,' Sara directed them. 'Do enjoy the dragonflies.'

So, her lover was not at all romantic. Sara sighed as she stood in the window, watching the two men strolling down the grassy slope to the hidden valley. Out of sight of the house the stream had been dammed to make a lily pond before making its way out over an artificial waterfall to join the main lake.

Michael had been romantic, given to quoting Shakespearean sonnets in the moonlight, or laying single roses on her pillow. He would come home, apparently preoccupied with his current problem in a Greek translation and surprise her with one perfect peach or a pretty silk handkerchief that he had seen in a shop window and thought she would like.

And in turn she would like to surprise him with little gifts tucked into his papers or by greeting him wearing nothing but a scandalous negligee when he got home and luring him upstairs.

Lucian was passionate and tender and exciting in bed,

but he probably thought that romance was for foolish youngsters like Marguerite and Gregory and had nothing to do with the real world.

He was quite right to resist her teasing about making love out of doors. She would not misbehave here, inside or out, but a little flirtation, a few stolen kisses, were hardly outrageous and a week of frustration could only give their eventual lovemaking a passionate urgency.

How long to give the two men for their discussion? Surely the trickiest of boundary problems would not take more than half an hour. She would wander round to see how the battledore match was progressing and then go and admire the dragonflies herself.

Chapter Fourteen

Marguerite was sitting on a rug watching when Sara arrived. 'Running around after a shuttlecock is rather tiring,' she explained. 'I thought I had best stop when I became breathless, because it will be no good for our plan if I am laid up in bed again.'

'Very sensible. But no doubt the young men will want to take you for a stroll through the grounds soon. It might be best not to venture out of sight—the maze and the shrubbery are best explored in a group.'

'Oh, quite.' Marguerite laughed. 'It is very flattering that they want to talk and flirt, but the young ones are so very young and the older ones are not a patch on my Gregory, so you need not worry that I might do anything imprudent.'

'Of course not. Still, a little very mild flirtation will help divert suspicion when you and Gregory suddenly fall in love.'

'It is lovely, isn't it?' Marguerite gave a happy little shiver and wrapped her arms around her knees. 'Being in love. And I am so happy about you and Lucian.'

'About…? Marguerite, I am *not* in love with your

brother. I did explain about not getting married.' What a disaster that would be! The moment they got out of bed they would be disagreeing about something and when those shutters came down behind his eyes she felt as though she was on the other side of a pane of glass, a moth fluttering helplessly against a barrier she could not see and did not understand.

'Oh.' The younger woman rested her cheek on her crossed arms and looked at Sara. 'I am sorry. I know what you said, but every time I see you together I think that you and he are falling in love.'

'There is desire,' Sara said cautiously. 'But not love.'

'So you *really* aren't going to marry him, then?'

'No. I am sorry if that shocks you.'

'Not *shocks*.' Marguerite lifted her head and watched the flight of the shuttlecock, pursued by two laughing young women. 'I am disappointed. I had hoped for a sister.'

'That would have been lovely. We could have formed an alliance against older brothers,' Sara said, trying for a lightness she did not feel. She was very fond of Marguerite and the thought of her as a sister made her eyes swim with sudden, unexpected tears. 'But I have been married once, very happily, and I do not think that Lucian and I would suit.'

'He watches you, you know. All the time when he thinks you aren't noticing. You watch him, too.'

'Goodness.' *I watch him? I suppose I do. But he watches me, too?* She should be worried, but the thought was dangerously welcome. 'I do hope we are not as obvious as that.'

'It is only noticeable to someone who loves you both. Oh, they have finished the game. It looks as though they are going down to the lake, so I will join them. I feel quite rested now.'

Sara remained on the rug as the group of young people wandered away. There were several of the married ladies down by the lakeside sketching, quite adequate for chaperonage, so she felt no compulsion to stir and certainly none to join Lucian with his sister's words still reverberating in her head. *Thought you were falling in love…he watches you, you know…*

It was desire, surely? That was why she looked at him, because he was very easy to look at, very desirable to daydream about. That was all. That was not *love*. Love was wanting to spend your life with someone.

She looked up to see Gregory Farnsworth walking back to the house, his head bent over his notebook. He was no doubt laden with notes and instructions to write memoranda or draft letters. Poor man, stuck inside when his love was down by the lake, laughing in the sunshine.

Lucian had not followed him. She got to her feet and shook the wrinkles out of her muslin skirts, then made her way down the lawn towards the secret dell with its circle of still water.

Sara found him sitting on a rustic bench, his elbows on his knees, his chin on his clasped hands. He smiled when he saw her, but did not move his position and she felt strangely warmed by the fact that he was so easy with her that he neglected the gesture of immediately getting to his feet.

'The boundaries are all sorted out?' she asked as she sat beside him and leaned in so their shoulders touched companionably.

'I need more information on that. I have given Farnsworth just enough work to make Marguerite's complaints that I am a slave driver convincing.'

'She is very happy, you know. It means a lot to her that you are finally reconciled to this.'

'It isn't what I wanted for her, this match, but I must settle for her being safe and happy.' Lucian spoke briskly, setting the subject firmly aside, she assumed. 'Look, there's a dragonfly, a monster.'

Sara followed his pointing finger and exclaimed over the insect, but she could feel the tension in him, just from that small point of contact where her shoulder touched his. Marguerite was never going to be the wife of a high-ranking man of fashion, never be as rich as her brother's ambitions for her. She might be happy, but he was going to have to learn to forgive himself for allowing the relationship in the first place and then for driving the young couple to near-tragedy. She sighed a little and let her head rest on his shoulder, relaxing at the contact, even with his body so tense. She knew all about guilt, about the difficulty of self-forgiveness.

'Tell me about your husband,' Lucian said abruptly.

'I did tell you.' This was too close to her thoughts, as though he had divined her anxieties that she had not been a good wife.

'Tell me about how you met, how you fell in love, what it was about Harcourt.'

'I did not enjoy my first Season very much,' she confessed, feeling that this was almost a *Once Upon a Time* story. 'That makes me sound shy, or perhaps bored or difficult to please, I suppose. Oh, the gowns were lovely and I went to so many truly wonderful balls and receptions and theatrical performances. It was all new and strange and interesting, such a change from India. And yet, somehow I never felt I was really a part of that world.'

Lucian made a sound, an encouraging one, so she pressed on, wondering if he could possibly understand. The London *ton* was *his* world, the one he was born and bred to, and she was an outsider. 'We caused rather a sensation—Papa having been out of the country for so long and Mama, of course, so beautiful and so exotic. Some high-sticklers were cold because of Mama's parentage, but she simply dealt with them without turning a hair. And Ashe is very good looking and he had led a very adventurous life in India, at my uncle's court, so he was accepted by all the gentlemen, and the ladies all flirted, and he met Phyllida and settled right in.'

'And you are not good looking? Not beautiful?' Lucian's tone was teasing.

'I am…different. I was a young lady and young ladies, just out, are expected to conform. My skin is never going to be milk white with roses in my cheeks, nor have I the dark hair and eyes that might make me look glamorously Italian or Spanish. I just looked wrong in white muslin and pastels.'

'I can see that. Jewel colours suit you best.' He shifted against the bench until he was sitting in the angle made by the back and the arm, with one foot on the seat. 'Come here.' He pulled her gently back until she was sitting with her shoulders against his chest, his arm steadying her.

Sara let her head fall back against his shoulder and wriggled until she was comfortable. 'And I had been brought up to be as well educated as my brother, to have my opinion listened to, to take part in discussions, to read what I liked.'

'And to do a man damage with a sharp knife.'

'Yes, that, too.' She felt his chuckle and smiled. 'And suddenly I must have no opinions, I must pretend to be ignorant and sweet and demure. I must pretend to know nothing about the relations between the sexes. I had to learn to be a ninny.'

'Surely your parents did not want that?'

'No, but they also wanted me to fit in. My father was the Marquess and we had no choice but to live here, to live within this society. They wanted me to be happy, but it was obvious that somewhere compromises would have to be made, either by me or in society's expectations of me.'

'You had no beaux? Surely you were courted.'

'Oh, yes. But you see because I was *exotic* many of the men thought I was also…loose. And I was a virgin and I did not want to behave in the way they expected. So I spent a lot of time snubbing gentlemen or sticking hatpins in them. It was all very tiring.'

'And your father and brother did not do anything?' Lucian sounded outraged.

'I made very sure they did not know. Can you imagine the trail of challenges and duels if those two had guessed?'

'It would only have taken one for the point to be taken.'

'At what risk? Anyway, I soon became good at repelling advances, but I did not see anyone I could feel the slightest *tendre* for. They all seemed so alien.'

'Do I seem alien?'

'Of course.' She dropped her hand to his thigh and squeezed it in apology for her words. 'And then, one night at Lady Lanchester's ball, I slipped into an alcove shielded by palms to sit out a dance in peace and found there was someone already there. He was reading a book.'

'Michael Harcourt.'

'*Dr* Michael Harcourt, if you please. Spectacles on the end of his nose, totally engrossed. So I sat down and pretended to ignore him and he must have reached the end of a chapter because he looked up and saw me and shot to his feet, sending the book flying. By the time we had rescued it from under a chair and found three scattered bookmarks and flattened the bumped corners we were firm friends.'

'And he was at Cambridge? A don?'

'Yes. Classical languages and philology. I knew enough Latin and a little Greek to understand what he was talking about and I speak several Indic languages, which interested him. And he *listened* to me and he would argue things out with me. It was so refreshing. Before long we were firm friends and then, gradually, more. He had come to London to keep his mother from fretting at him about finding a wife and settling down, but he wasn't enjoying the Season much either.'

'Was he good looking?'

Was that a slight overtone of masculine rivalry there? Sara smiled and closed her eyes, strangely comfortable with this intimate confession as she half-lay against Lucian's broad chest. 'No. He was not ugly, you understand, or even plain. He was almost as tall as you, but of a more slender build. His hair was mousy and his eyes grey and his nose not particularly distinguished, but his chin was firm. His face was a little too long for good looks and his ears stuck out, just a little, but perhaps that was because he was always jamming pens behind them. It was a kind face and an intelligent face and… Michael's face.' She found that tears were running down her cheeks. Tears of recollection and regret, but not desperate tears. She let them flow, strangely comforted by them.

'And one day,' she said, clearing her throat because it was a little husky, 'we were in Hatchard's bookshop. We both stretched up for the same book and bumped elbows and the next thing I knew I was in his arms and he was kissing me in the corner of the Greek and Latin translation section. Fortunately, it is not a popular area.'

Lucian's grunt of amusement made her smile, too, and suddenly Sara realised that she was smiling over a memory of Michael for the first time since his death. Smiling out of amusement and affection, not the sad smile of memories and regret.

How strange that it was this man, her lover, who had given her that humour back.

'So what happened next?' Lucian prompted when she had fallen silent for several minutes.

'Michael dropped three different translations of Homer that he was carrying and the shop assistant came and he had to end up buying two of them because the corners were bent.'

'Not with the books, with your romance,' Lucian said in her ear. 'Women! Never can tell a story.'

Laughing—how did that happen when she was crying, too?—she nudged him in the ribs with her elbow. 'So Michael took himself off to see Papa, all very proper and formal, and Papa was really very good about it. I don't think he had ever come across someone like Michael because he had not gone to university himself, but straight into the East India Company army, so intellectuals were a strange breed to him.'

'And I should imagine he was a terrifying prospect for a quiet scholar.' Lucian shifted a little and managed to link his arms around her.

'Oh, no. Michael could stand up for himself. He was quiet, certainly, but exceedingly intelligent, so he could play Papa like a fisherman with a trout, long before Papa realised he was being manipulated. And he had courage. He loved me and he wanted me, so he was going to stand up and ask for me. He was not a poor man. Not rich, but he could keep us in very respectable comfort. And Papa, bless him, did listen and talk to both of us and then it was agreed. Before the Season was over I had married and moved to Cambridge and I was learning an entirely new culture.'

'You liked life in a university town?'

'Yes. I made a lot of friends amongst intellectual women—bluestockings, I suppose you would say—and I began to learn Greek in earnest and I taught Michael the languages I knew and we were friends as well as lovers. We were so happy.' *I was safe.*

'Are you weeping?' Lucian murmured, close to her ear.

'Just a little, and smiling, too,' she admitted and he kissed her in the soft hollow behind her ear. 'I could not cry much, before. I was too angry.'

'With his friend, the one he challenged?'

'No, with Michael. I have to learn to forgive him for wanting to protect me that way.' *And with myself. If I had been a better wife this would never have happened.*

'Perhaps the need to protect our womenfolk is as deep in a man as the need to protect a child is in a woman,' Lucian suggested. 'I had never thought of it like that before, but it does not seem to me to be something one learns, or has impressed upon you. For me, certainly, it feels like instinct.'

'Perhaps,' she agreed, reluctantly impressed by the comparison. 'But the man should talk it over with the woman first. I don't mean if there is a physical attack, it would be foolish to stand about debating when someone is brandishing a cudgel. But if it is a case of an insult, then definitely.'

'You would let an insult pass?'

'There are more ways of getting even than getting up before dawn and shivering in a damp field with the chance of getting killed at the end of it. A woman would apply her mind to finding a poetic form of revenge. Itching powder in a rake's silk breeches at a Court presentation, a mouse in a spiteful gossip's reticule...'

'Itching powder? Remind me never to upset you.'

His breath was warm on the side of her throat. Was he going to kiss her there? She arched her neck in invitation and was rewarded by the pressure of his lips, the slight friction of stubble. Lucian was going to have to shave before dinner.

All too quickly the caress stopped. 'What do you miss most about being married?' he asked.

Sara thought about it for a while and he did not press her, simply held her while she lay back in his arms, watching the wildlife around the pond come out, reassured by their stillness. A dabchick bobbed across the surface, fish rose and dived, the dragonflies buzzed.

Strange that her lover should be so interested in her marriage. Most men would have wanted to ignore the subject, pretend her husband had not existed. Some would have jealously probed for a flattering comparison—was he more handsome, taller, better endowed, a better lover? But Lucian's questions did not seem like that, more as though he was genuinely interested in her past, wanted to understand and sympathise with her loss.

'Miss?' she said at last. 'I miss *him*, of course, as a person, because he was my friend. And I miss the companionship of marriage and being able to say what I was thinking without having to censor it in any way. I miss discussing things. I miss…missed, the lovemaking. I miss the intellectual stimulation of trying to keep up with him mentally and the community of friends we had.'

'You were not tempted to stay there, in Cambridge?'

'No. That would have felt like second best, somehow. Michael was why I was there and without him… No, I wanted to do something different, something for myself.' *Somewhere new to run away to while you tried to find the real you,* the niggling little voice of her conscience murmured.

'Someone is coming.' Lucian had heard the voices raised in laughter before she had. He pushed her gently upright so she could slide along the seat and let him get both feet on the ground. 'Heading this way, by the sound of it. Shall we make a bolt for it or be found earnestly studying pond life?'

'Bolt. This way.' She took him by the hand and ran round the head of the pond and into the stand of willows fringing it. 'Now, if we make our way along the path I think we will come out by the lake, which is where they have come from.'

'You think? Don't you know?'

'I did not grow up here, so I have not discovered all the secret ways that a child would have found. Yes, here we are, just behind the boathouse. Can you punt?'

'Yes,' Lucian said immediately, and then, with a shrug, 'badly. I am usually well co-ordinated, but I am a shambles with a punt pole. But this is too deep, surely?'

'There is a sunken causeway going to the island in the middle with deep water either side. It used to be a track before the lake was made larger. If we punt half-way, then I can finish my tale and no one will disturb us and yet we will be sitting out in full view in perfect respectability.'

'You will risk us going round and round in circles?' Lucian eyed the punt tied up to the side of the boat-house dubiously.

'No, I will punt, you recline and look decorative.'

'That is my line.' But to her surprise he got in with-out protest and sat down, not even insisting on handing her in or untying the rope.

Sara lifted the long pole, got her balance and pushed off. The punt glided out in a straight line, much to her satisfaction, and she took them to halfway between shore and island before she jammed the pole upright in the mud and tied the rope around it.

'You looked very elegant doing that.' Lucian was lying back on the cushions, his hands behind his head, and she was reminded of her great-uncle's court and how the Rajah would have himself rowed out into the great lake with its pleasure pavilion in the centre. Lucian would not look out of place here if there was a marble summer house on the island, filled with beautiful women all ready to pleasure him. She kept the thought to herself as she settled down on the cushions at her end of the punt.

'There is no middle way, I find, with punting. Either it goes well and you look elegant or it doesn't and then you most definitely do not! I fell in four times when Michael was teaching me.'

She could see his face now and studied it for any reaction to her husband's name, but could see none. A part of her, one she should be ashamed of, was a little piqued. Shouldn't her lover be just a little touchy about any men who had been before him? Probably he did not care enough.

Chapter Fifteen

'You were telling me about your decision to leave Cambridge,' Lucian reminded her.

Sara drew a deep breath and tried to explain. 'I wanted to get away from all of it, the places that reminded me of my marriage, the love and concern my family were wrapping me in. I ran away to the coast and found Sandbay. When I wanted to do some drawing I looked for a shop selling equipment and found the one I now own. That was all it did, artists' equipment, and it was a poor affair. The owner was selling up and, on a whim almost, I bought it. And that was the beginning of Aphrodite's Seashell. I made no secret of who I was and I found people were wonderfully discreet. I think they enjoyed the cachet of having a marquess's daughter at their resort when they would have expected me to go to Weymouth. I kept my daytime and my evening personas apart and it worked.'

'And you are happy in Sandbay, shopkeeper by day, lady by night?'

'Yes. But…'

'But?' Lucian lounged there, all long legs and heavy-lidded eyes, temptation personified. Sara wanted to stop talking about herself, stop thinking about difficult things and pole over to the island and—

'When you look at me like that I am tempted to try punting again,' he said. 'That island looks wickedly inviting, but I will behave like a gentleman if you tell me about the *but*.'

'*But*...the shop is successful now. I have succeeded, proved that I can create and run a business, make a profit. Soon Sandbay will start to grow beyond the point where I can hide in plain sight. I need to find a new direction, but I have no idea what it might be. Certainly I have no intention of becoming yet another merry widow with an ambiguous position in society and a succession of lovers.'

Lucian sat up, his forearms resting on his raised knees, and seemed to be finding something on the bottom boards of great interest. Then he looked up. 'Why not marry me?'

'*Marry* you?' Sara sat bolt upright and stared at him. 'Marry *you*? But why? You wanted an *affaire*, right from the beginning, I could tell. You realised I was a widow, recognised that I was a lady, and so suitable for a dalliance for a limited time. A little mutual pleasure, no unseemly demands on either side. That was what you were looking for, wasn't it? Can you deny it?'

'No, of course not. And there was mutual attraction, mutual desire—can *you* deny that?' He was frowning now.

'No. So that is what we have. An affair. We are lovers. Lovers interrupted, maybe, but lovers none the less. You told my father, very definitely, that you had no intention of marrying me. And next Season you intended to

launch Marguerite—you probably still will as Gregory
has yet to find his feet in society—and you would have
been looking for a nice young thing to marry. Marguerite thinks you have already decided on one. After all,
it is about time you married and set up your nursery.
Deny *that*.' Something was building inside her chest, a
pressure that she did not stop to examine because she
feared it was anger.

'I do not… And you are a *nice young thing,* are you
not? You are simply slightly older than the fluffy little
misses that Marguerite is making friends with. And she
is wrong, I have fixed my interest with no one. This
would be so logical, Sara, such a sensible step for both
of us.'

Logical? Sensible? Yes, that *was* anger building inside her. And hurt, but she couldn't probe that now because she rather feared she would cry if she did. 'Of
course, I am the daughter of a marquess, even if my
family on my mother's side is a trifle unusual, and I am
still young enough to give you an heir and I have all my
own teeth and you have tried me out in bed.'

Lucian straightened up and seemed, for the first time,
to realise that she was angry, not simply taken by surprise. 'Well, yes, although I certainly would not have
put it like that. Sara, I can see that you are annoyed for
some reason and I realise that this must have taken you
unawares, but—'

'But you really cannot see what I have to be annoyed
about? I agree, it is most unreasonable of me to take exception to your charming *logical* offer, accompanied
as it was by protestations of devotion and regard. And
how unreasonable of me to conclude that it has only just

struck you how much time and trouble it would save you
if you married me.'

How very irritating it was not to be able to stride up
and down as she ranted. 'This way you do not have to
go through some wearisome courtship. There will be no
having to endure the rigours of Almack's, no having to
do the pretty or fight off predatory mamas. You simply
speak to my father, who would be delighted to secure a
marquess for a son-in-law, and regularise our relationship in one blow, and there you are.'

'Do you want me to make a declaration of love? Is
that what this is about? Are you back to accusing me of
not being romantic?' He seemed mildly baffled by her
reaction and also patiently willing to humour her, which
was even more inflaming.

'No, I do not want some false declaration. Do you
think I want you to lie to me? I thought you understood
me, I thought you were listening just now while I was
telling you about Michael and our marriage, and all the
time you were fitting me nicely into the compartment
marked *suitable wife, needs looking after, poor thing,
young enough to breed from.*'

'Sara, that is not at all how I think of you.' Lucian
stood up and made to move towards her, his hand held
out.

'Yes, you do. I need a man to protect me, fight duels
on my behalf, make sure I do not do unconventional
things like running a shop or wearing male clothing.
Why else would you offer for me out of the blue like
this? You do not love me, you have already slept with
me, you do not need to give me a reason to chaperon
Marguerite—it can only be for your convenience and

because your male arrogance thinks I would be better off in your charge.'

She found she was on her feet, too, one of the battered old cushions clutched in her right hand. Had she meant to throw it at him or was she simply gesticulating so wildly that she let it go? Whichever it was, Lucian had not been expecting it. It hit him squarely in the face, he clawed at it, staggered and then, with awful inevitability, the punt tipped sideways and they both fell into the lake.

Her skirts were only light muslin, her undergarments no more hampering. Sara surfaced within seconds, spluttering, and kicked the few strokes that enabled her to grab hold of the side of the upturned punt.

'*Sara.*' Lucian was right beside her, his shoulders just out of the water, and she realised that he must be standing on the submerged causeway. 'Hell, are you all right? I thought I was going to have to dive for you.'

'Yes. I can swim perfectly well, thank you.' She swiped at a weed that was dangling from her hair and realised that the ducking had done nothing to cool her anger. 'I do not think that trying to turn the punt back over is going to be easy.'

'No, and unsafe, considering that you are out of your depth. I will carry you back to shore.'

'I told you, I can swim.'

'But you have no need to.' Lucian got one arm behind her shoulders, dislodging her grip on the punt. She flailed as she tried to get hold of it again, her legs floated up and he slid the other arm under her knees. 'There. I have you safe.'

There was nothing she could do but submit to being carried ashore like some helpless shipwrecked maiden. Struggling was undignified and would only put them both under the surface again. Then she heard the shrieks and cries from the shore.

'You have an audience for your gallantry,' she said between gritted teeth as Lucian began to walk. 'It appears that the entire house party is assembled on the shore to view the rescue.' Her mama must have decided to have tea served on the lawn under the great cedar tree where there was an excellent view of the lake. 'How gratifying. They presumably saw me hit you with the cushion as well.'

Lucian grunted. The effort of walking through water that rose almost to his collarbone while carrying a woman in his arms must be considerable and, despite her feelings about him, there was an undeniable thrill in being carried like this. Which just went to show that even the most rational and independent woman could be turned into a quivering blancmange by a display of masculine muscle. And that realisation did nothing to cool her temper either.

Sara focused on the shore through wet eyelashes and strands of soaking hair. Most of the female guests were at the water's edge, shrieking encouragement, although one of the young ladies had managed to faint strategically into a gentleman's arms. Her mother was still seated at the table calmly pouring tea and her father and brother stood on the boathouse jetty, apparently poised to carry out a full-scale rescue by rowing boat if necessary. Ashe was scowling, her father had the bland expression that meant he was controlling laughter, the beast.

As Lucian reached the shallows within a few yards of the shore and began to emerge from the water Ashe took off his coat and ran back along the jetty to meet them.

'Put this on.' He flung it around her shoulders as soon

as Lucian lowered her to the fringe of shingle. 'That muslin is glued to you. What the hell were you playing at?' That was directed at Lucian. 'Sara could have been drowned.'

'I can swim, as you know perfectly well.' That was comprehensively ignored. Sara turned her back on the bristling male aggression and began to squelch uphill towards the tea table while the female guests surrounded her like a flock of agitated chickens.

She finally arrived in front of her mother who handed her a large rug and gestured to a chair. 'It is rattan, the water will not harm it and it is perfectly warm out here in the sun. Have a cup of tea, dear, and let us watch the men…er…analysing the situation.'

Sara discarded Ashe's coat, huddled into the rug and accepted the tea gratefully.

'Whatever happened?' someone asked.

'Did you not see?'

''We were all looking at this wonderful cake that Cook sent out because it is Miss Henderson's birthday and no one noticed until the splash,' her mother said. 'More tea, dear?'

Sara had a strong suspicion that her mother had seen everything. When she was a child she had been convinced that Mata had eyes in the back of her head and, although she now realised that she simply kept a very sharp eye on all the members of her family without seeming to do so, it still felt like witchcraft sometimes.

'It was my fault. I stood up suddenly,' Sara explained, more to quell the chattering than anything.

'Entirely my fault, I stood up suddenly.' Lucian's voice rose clearly to them as he strode up the hill, flanked by her father and brother.

'You *both* stood up suddenly?' Lady Thale exclaimed.

'We saw a Marsh Harrier,' Sara said.

'—an otter,' Lucian explained at the same moment.

'Incredible,' Mata remarked. 'Presumably the bird of prey had the otter in its talons as it flew over? Your Cousin Ernest will be so interested to hear that, he is a keen naturalist, I believe.'

'The otter was swimming in one direction, the harrier flying in another,' Lucian said. He was tight-lipped, presumably disapproving of the Herriards' habit of levity.

Even Ashe was grinning. 'Ah, that explains why the punt overbalanced.'

The ridiculousness of the whole episode was beginning to dawn on Sara. 'I think I must go back to the house and change,' she said, not quite managing to quell the unsteadiness in her voice. 'I feel a trifle, um, shaken.'

'Hardly surprising.' Lucian strode forward, showering the assembled onlookers with lake water, much like a large gun-dog. He bent and scooped her out of the chair. 'You must rest.'

'Lucian!'

He was already several strides away from the tea table. 'Did you want to stay there dripping gently while we made a mess of our stories and dug ourselves even deeper into the mud?'

'No, but I can walk.' Although it really was delicious being carried like this. Sara reminded herself that she was angry with him and could not quite recall why. His shoulders were shaking, she realised, and not with the effort of carrying her. 'Lucian, are you *laughing?*'

'Of course I am.' He twisted to check that they were out of sight, then sat down on the edge of the terrace, Sara still in his arms. 'And so are you.'

She made an effort to sit up, found that he was holding her too tightly and gave up. It was far too pleasant to lie there and share the joke, held against the wet heat of his body, the pair of them smelling of mud and lake water. 'When Mata said that about the otter and the harrier, I nearly spluttered into my tea. And your face— I couldn't decide whether you had a mouthful of pond beetles or were trying not to laugh.'

'It was laugh or weep,' Lucian said wryly. 'I have hardly appeared in a very impressive light since I got here, have I? Almost floored by your brother on the drive, being raked over the coals by your father for my immoral behaviour with his daughter, making an utter mull of a marriage proposal and then emerging from the lake dripping with pond weed for the amusement of the entire house party.'

Sara managed to lever herself upright and twisted to look into his face. It was exceedingly unfair that he managed to look so good even soaking wet when she imagined she looked as though she had just emerged from a close encounter with a ducking stool.

'Is that really how you think you appeared? Let me tell you that your restraint in not punching Ashe straight back was admirable, you stood up to Papa with great dignity and courtesy and I have to admit to an utterly shameful pleasure at being carried around by such a strong man.' Lucian began to grin, so she added, 'But I agree, that was an appalling proposal.'

'I know. I will try again when we are both dry.'

He will? Did she want Lucian to propose? For a moment Sara seriously considered it, then she realised what she was doing. She did not want to marry a man who did not love her, whom she did not love—and it did not matter how good he was in bed, or how good looking or how eligible.

'Lucian—'

'You look enchanting wet through, you know. I feel as if I had fished out a water nymph.' He gathered her in again and kissed her, open-mouthed, possessive, very certain.

The weak, primitive female part of her kissed him back, tongues tangling, her body arching to get as tight to his body as she could, and all the time the sensible part argued that this was wrong, that she was encouraging the ridiculous notion that they might marry.

Lucian released her far too soon for the primitive part. Too soon for the sensible part, if she was honest with herself. 'That was skating rather too close to behaviour I gave my word not to indulge in while we were here. And you will catch a chill in those wet clothes. See— you are shivering.'

She was shivering from reaction, not the wet clothes, but Sara did not contradict him. 'Yes, you are quite right.' She got to her feet. 'I will order baths for both of us and I will see you later, before dinner. Prepare yourself to be teased or interrogated by everyone though. I suspect the joke may be too good for the company to resist.' He had laughed at the lake, but would his sense of humour stand teasing? Most marquesses held themselves very high and such a loss of dignity would affront all of them—except Papa, of course. She hadn't seen much evidence of a light-hearted side to Lucian before, but then his worry about Marguerite would explain that, no doubt.

* * *

Lucian watched Sara's progress to the terrace steps and then into the house and wondered at the emotion stirring in his chest. She should have looked amusing, her skirts bedraggled and clinging to her legs, muddy water dripping, her hair in rats' tails. And yet he felt no temptation to laugh, only to smile. The feeling, the warmth in his chest, must be affection, he supposed, although it was very different from the affection he felt for his sister.

Lord, but he had made a fool of himself, making that proposal as though it were nothing more important than an offer to take her for a drive in the park—and one made on the spur of the moment, at that.

He had misjudged the moment, her emotions and, he supposed, his own. But, strangely, it did not make him any less determined to try again. Sara had been pleased that he had found some humour in the situation, he re-alised as he got to his feet and grimaced at the state of his breeches and his Hessians. She must have thought him very dour and intense all the time she had known him and he suspected that humour was important to her.

Lucian made his way round to the garden door and found an old settle to sit on while he pried off his sod-den boots and stockings before he sullied the polished floors. He was met by the butler in the hallway who ushered him upstairs with the air of a man to whom half-drowned marquesses dripping on the marble were an everyday occurrence. Lucian managed to keep the straight face that his dignity was obviously supposed to require until he was inside his room and then gave way to mirth.

Lord knows what I'm laughing about, he thought as he

began to wrestle with the knot of his neckcloth. *My sister isn't out of the woods by a long chalk and when she is I've got to find some way of advancing Farnsworth's career. I have just made a complete fool of myself in front of a highly select company who will doubtless spread the tale all round town as soon as they can get pen to paper. I've thrown my perfectly rational plan for finding a wife out of the window and I have made a pig's ear of a proposal to my mistress. Who, at the moment, is not my mistress but my host's daughter.*

'My lord?' Charles, the footman who had been delegated to act as his valet, came out of the dressing room, his arms full of towels. Pitkin, his real valet who was enjoying a much-deserved holiday in Sandbay, would have simply ignored his master's behaviour, but this young man was obviously uncertain.

Lucian grinned at him and threw his arms wide, an invitation to view the wreckage.

The footman's lips twitched. 'Your…your bath is ready, my lord. I will consult with Mr Rathbone, his lordship's man, and seek his advice on restoring your boots and garments.'

'Thank you, but do not spend too much effort on them, I fear they are beyond redemption.'

'Mr Rathbone works miracles,' the young footman assured Lucian in awed tones, almost setting him off again. His host's valet was obviously far more awe-inspiring than any marquess, especially a sodden one.

He dismissed Charles, stripped, and wallowed in hot, pine-scented water and thought. When was the last time he had laughed out loud? Not a laugh at some single joke, but uninhibitedly at something ridiculous, at himself. Laughed for the joy of it, because he was happy.

But what had he to be happy about here? Marguerite's situation was still to untangle, his dignity was in tatters, his proposal of marriage had been rejected. There was no prospect of lovemaking until they left Eldonstone. And yet… It was Sara, of course. She made him happy and even when she was angry with him his heart lifted at the sight of her, at the sound of her voice. He enjoyed her courage and her common sense and her intelligence and her passionate defence of Marguerite and Gregory. She made love like an angel. A *wicked* angel, he corrected. And…

The thought trailed away unfinished, leaving him staring at the picture hanging on the wall opposite. A still life of exotic fruit and foliage was absolutely no help in focusing his disordered thoughts. *And… And I love her?*

Chapter Sixteen

I love Sara? No, impossible. Love, from what he had heard of it, involved a great deal of mooning about sighing, the urge to write poetry to the lady's eyebrows and an inability to focus on anything but the beloved object and her perfections.

There was nothing, from what he had ever heard, about brooding on the beloved object's *imperfections* and she certainly had those. Sara was independent to a fault, argumentative, worryingly apt to produce weapons when thwarted and had no hesitation in telling him that she disagreed with him on the subject of masculine honour and a man's responsibilities to his womenfolk.

And she had made a love match before, had felt her husband had been a friend. Lucian scrubbed his back and tried to fit that kind of relationship into his model of a *ton* marriage. It did not fit, however much he twisted and turned it.

So why did he want to marry her? Because he desired her? But they were already lovers. Because she was so good to Marguerite? But they could remain friends whether sisters-in-law or not.

He slid right under the water and came up again with a sudden flash of insight. He felt alive when he was with Sara in a way he did in no other company, or his own, come to that. She made him feel happy.

Lucian climbed out of the bath and began to towel his back, then, swathed toga-style in a pair of large bath sheets, strolled into the bedchamber to find Charles laying out evening wear.

'What do you think about happiness, Charles?'

'My lord?' The young man eyed him warily. Nobs were obviously not expected to come out with questions like that, but he answered readily enough. 'I'm all for it, my lord.'

'So what makes you happy, Charles? Not just cheerful for the moment, but happy.'

Charles pondered while he smoothed out a shirt. 'Having a good place, like this, where they're fair and there's opportunities. And being with my girl.' He shot Lucian a sideways glance, obviously assessing his views of staff 'walking out'. 'If I make second footman then we could get married, because she's head dairymaid now and I reckon her ladyship will let us have one of the little sets of rooms over the dairy. Anyway, I'm happy when I'm with Miriam. And going home to see my old mum and her being proud of me, like she is. Plain black silk stockings, my lord? Or the ones with the stripe in them?'

'Oh, striped, I think. Let us be frivolous today, Charles.'

Sara was in the drawing room before dinner, in the midst of a group of the younger guests, when Lucian came down looking immaculate and not at all like a man who had been pitched into a muddy lake. He took a chair opposite her and smiled when the other men chaffed him about his misadventure.

'Most inelegant, I know. The word will get around town and I'll be cut by all the swells,' he said easily. 'I trust you not to spread the word, gentlemen, or I'll be lampooned in the press as the Marquess of Duckweed.'

'You're a good sport to take it like that, Cannock,' Lord Tothill remarked. 'Me, I would have been contemplating putting an end to my existence.'

'Oh, I was utterly cast down for a while,' Lucian agreed. 'Actually fingering the edge of my razor. But then I had a most uplifting conversation about happiness with my temporary valet, a young man named Charles, and now I am positively cheerful about the whole thing. After all, I have the satisfaction of making you gentlemen all feel superior, of entertaining the ladies and of having the opportunity of holding Lady Sara in my arms for minutes on end.'

'That, naturally, is worth any amount of pondweed,' Philip Greaves agreed, with a gallant bow to Sara.

When the laughter died down she studied Lucian, trying to decide what was different about him this evening. He seemed far more relaxed, she realised, which was strange considering he had proposed and been turned down and had ended up in the lake.

'What did Charles say about happiness?' she asked.

'That for him it is being in a position where he feels he can do well and advance, he is making his old mum proud of him and he has a young woman he hopes to marry. It made me think and it seems to me that is not a bad definition—be doing something we enjoy to the best of our ability, make those whose opinion we value proud of us and have the prospect of a happy marriage before us.'

'I think that is truly inspiring, Lord Cannock,' Miss Eversleigh, the most sensible of the young ladies, said. 'I shall write that in my commonplace book so I do not forget it.'

'Sounds a bit serious to me.' Johnny, her brother, pulled a face. 'What about fun, I'd like to know?'

'Nothing wrong with adding champagne, race horses, a good hand of cards and a dance with a pretty girl to the recipe,' Lucian said and the other men laughed.

'Are you looking for that special young lady yourself, Lord Cannock?' Miss Hopely, definitely *not* one of the more sensible girls, enquired with a flutter of long lashes.

'What single gentleman with any sense is not, Miss Hopely?' Lucian countered.

'And what young lady is not looking for a handsome gentleman with some sense?' Marguerite came up and perched on the arm of Lucian's chair. 'It works both ways, brother dear. And I am come to scold you for overworking poor Mr Farnsworth. You must remember he has only one eye now. I have been helping him sort those dreadfully dull estate papers you have heaped on him.'

'That is very thoughtful of you,' Lucian said absently. Sara thought she caught just the flicker of an eyelid in her direction. 'But there is a great deal I need him to do.'

Marguerite pouted in a most convincing manner and Sara got up and went to find Porrett, the butler. 'Can you place Mr Farnsworth next to Lady Marguerite tonight please, Porrett?'

'That is just as her ladyship made out the seating plan, Lady Sara. It did not appear to accord with precedence, but her ladyship said that she would like to create an informal atmosphere.'

'Excellent.' The plan was working out perfectly. By the end of the week Gregory and Marguerite would appear inseparable, Lucian, in this strangely mellow new mood, would bow to the force of young love and all would be well.

But what on earth was the matter with him? First he proposed to her, out of the blue, now he was talking about happiness and marriage in a way far removed from the starchy man she had first met. Very strange. This Lucian she could almost…

Mata was already working her way around the drawing room, chatting to the guests and pairing people up for dinner. 'Lord Cannock, will you take Sara in, please?' she said. 'Mr Eversleigh, Miss Hopely. Lord Brendon? Now, where has he got to…?'

Gradually everyone sorted themselves out and began the walk to the dining room. 'It is going well with Marguerite and Gregory, I think,' Sara murmured as she laid her white-gloved hand on his sleeve. 'We must draw him out a little, make sure the more influential ladies have an opportunity to discover what a nice young man he is.'

'Yes.' Lucian sounded vague, although Sara had the distinct impression that he was anything but, this evening. 'I would like to talk to you later.'

'That might be as well,' she agreed, evenly. 'We need to clear the air, I think. I promise not to get you soaking wet this time.'

'You think I had a brainstorm this afternoon, don't you?' He held her chair and then pushed it in as she sat and began to remove her gloves.

'Didn't you?' She did wish he would stop alluding to

that proposal. Even thinking about it made her feel confused and flustered and she hated feeling like that—had not felt that way for an age, not since Michael had kissed her in the bookshop and she'd realised—

'Oh, no. *No.*'

'I am sorry, my lady. Would you prefer the white wine?' The footman at her elbow was looking at her in a way that made her realise she had spoken aloud.

'Oh, Thomas, I'm sorry. The champagne will be perfect, thank you.'

No, I am not *falling in love with Lucian Avery. I refuse to. I... He... We...*

'The library, do you think?' Lucian suggested. 'It always seems deserted in the evenings.'

'Yes, yes of course.' *I must stop gibbering, I sound a complete ninny.* 'Papa is threatening to put together a cricket match later this week. Will you play?'

'I would enjoy that,' Lucian said politely. 'But are there enough men to make up two teams?'

'He has an Eldonstone Eleven already made up of staff and tenants and they play regularly with other village and estate teams all through the summer. With him and Ashe, and if all the male guests play, then we will have two teams.'

The meal passed in a blur. On one level Sara made unexceptional conversation first to Lucian on one side, then to the vicar who had been invited for the evening, on the other. Both men were interested in cricket, so it was easy to engage harmlessly with that. On the other level she was wrestling with her feelings for the man sitting so near that she could feel his familiar heat all down her right side.

All she could think about as dinner wended its way through what seemed like interminable courses was that she must sit down with Lucian, quietly, calmly—*without touching*—and ask him why he had proposed marriage. He had said he would propose again when they were both dry and this time she hoped that he would explain just why he thought it even likely, let alone a good idea.

He watches you, Marguerite had said. *And you watch him.*

Finally, her mother stood up and led the ladies out to the drawing room where the doors were open to the terrace and the warm evening air. The men joined them after half an hour and people began to stroll outside or break up into small conversational groups around the drawing room.

Sara joined Lucian as he stood looking at a picture in one corner. 'I think we can safely escape now.'

They did so by the simple expedient of going out on to the terrace, then ducking into the dining room and out again into the deserted hall. 'I like your parents' approach to a house party,' Lucian said as they walked slowly along to the far door that led into the library. 'Very relaxed.'

'I would have thought you would disapprove and expect something more…starched-up.'

'I do not know where you get the impression that I am starched-up,' Lucian remarked. He turned to face her and bent to snatch a kiss. 'I would not have thought my behaviour merited that epitaph.' When she did not answer immediately he asked, 'Do you think me a hypocrite? I was very strict with Marguerite because she is young and not out. And I strongly disapprove of adultery and of seducing single girls.'

'I am glad to hear it. No, I do not think you a hypocrite and it was unfair to say that about being starched-up. I suppose it is your attitude to duelling. I live in dread of finding that you have called Ashe out over that punch when we arrived.'

'He was within his rights to resent me and to want to protect you.' Lucian shrugged. 'I may well return the favour should we find ourselves in the stable yard with no ladies around, but that is different.'

'Yes, I suppose it is. You would thump each other black and blue and emerge firm friends, I suppose. The masculine mind never ceases to amaze me.' She was still shaking her head and laughing as Lucian opened the door into the study for her to step inside.

The room was unlit, except for the two lamps left burning on the side tables, but the curtains were still drawn open and there was more than enough light for Sara to see the young man who started up from the comfortable old leather sofa that stood with its back to the door.

He had obviously been lying on the sofa and what he was doing there was all too obvious from his open shirt, missing neckcloth and tousled hair. *Gregory?*

There was a muffled shriek and Marguerite sat up beside him, clutching the bodice of her gown to her half-exposed bosom. Behind Sara Lucian said, 'What is wrong?' She could feel him pressing close as he tried to see past her as she blocked the way.

Sara was about to close the door on them and at least allow them to get themselves decent before Lucian got his hands around Gregory's throat when there was the sound of footsteps.

'I am sure Eldonstone has a good globe or an atlas in

the library. I can show you exactly where my nephew Alfred is posted in India, Marjorie dear.'

Lady Thale. Sara whirled around, pulled the door to and leaned back against it, giving the panels a painful warning thump with her elbow while she was about it. If those two inside had not managed to escape through the window by now they would have to take their chances.

'Kiss me.'

'What? Here? Now?'

'Kiss me. This is an emergency.' She could not wait for any further protests—or to worry about what happened next—the two ladies would come around the corner at any moment. Sara threw her arms around Lucian's neck, pulled his head down and kissed him with fierce determination.

From behind them as they stood embracing there was a shriek, then, 'Lady Sara! *Lord Cannock?*'

Sara untangled herself from Lucian as slowly as possible, 'Lady Thale, Mrs Montrum—oh, my!' She managed a flustered, fluttering gesture that was only partly play-acting. What had she done? 'Oh, you must be shocked, but believe me, you are the first to know our secret.' She beamed at them and kicked Lucian on the ankle as she clutched his arm. 'Lucian… Lord Cannock, I should say, is just on his way to speak to Papa.' Under her hand she felt his muscles tense like iron.

'A betrothal!' Mrs Montrum advanced on them, hands outstretched. 'What a marvellous union, *so* suitable in every way. Now, you are a very naughty fellow, Lord Cannock, but one cannot be too critical of a young man in love, can one? Not when he has such honourable intentions.'

'You may rely on us to look suitably surprised and delighted when the news is announced,' Lady Thale added, nodding approval. 'Come along, Marjorie, we will go and consult the atlas while we recover from the excitement. It would not do to return to the drawing room and betray this little secret, now would it?'

'So kind,' Lucian murmured, opening the door for them.

Sara held her breath, but there was no shriek of horror, so Gregory and Marguerite must have made their escape and managed not to leave any incriminating items of clothing behind them in the process.

'What was that about?' Lucian demanded, towing her none too gently back along the corridor and into the empty dining room. 'Why did you kiss me—and kick me? And why the sudden change of mind about marriage? Not that I am not delighted that you have come to see it as I do—'

'I have not changed my mind, but it was the only thing I could think of on the spur of the moment.' *Could I have done something different? Fainted? Have I only created an even worse problem?* 'Gregory and Marguerite were in the library.'

She apparently did not need to draw him a diagram. 'How bad was it?' Lucian demanded.

'Bad enough. They still had *some* clothes on.'

'I will kill him, I swear it.' His fists were clenched and Sara could well believe it. 'We go to all this trouble, impose on your parents, gatecrash a party and the *blo*—confounded fool can't keep his breeches buttoned for a week.'

'Killing him is not going to help and you know it.' Sara kept her back to the door, even so. 'I strongly suspect Marguerite is leading him about by the…er…nose, as it were, and he is almost as young, and, I suspect, as inexperienced, as she is. I am sorry about telling Mrs Montrum and Lady Thale that we were betrothed, but I do draw the line at ruining my own reputation with two of the biggest gossips of the *ton*. We can always decide we do not suit after a week or so.'

'Why should we do that?' Lucian enquired. He rested one hip against the sideboard and folded his arms. At least, she thought, he was not bent on murder any longer. 'If we had got inside the library just now, I fully intended asking you to marry me again and doing it properly this time.'

'And I fully intended asking you why you would ever think of such a thing,' Sara retorted. 'One minute you are more than happy for us to be lovers, the next you are proposing to marry me.'

'It occurred to me that I would be driven to drink by some sweet little innocent no older than my sister and with probably even less sense. You, on the other hand, have a great deal of sense and would make a very suitable wife.'

How very flattening. It was wonderful to find a man who valued sense, flattering that he attributed some to her, but even so, the most practical young lady wanted something rather less prosaic and more passionate in a proposal. Sara did not point that out: she did not need him spouting romantic nonsense he did not believe.

'We would drive each other mad within days. I need my freedom, Lucian, and that includes the freedom to do things that you will not find suitable for your wife. I know what a good marriage is like and I do not want to settle for second best.' That was probably not the most tactful way to put it and Sara realised it as soon as the words were out of her mouth. 'I mean, the marriage would be second-best, not that you would be.'

'So I am good enough to sleep with, but not to marry?' Lucian enquired coldly.

Chapter Seventeen

'It is not a question of *good enough*, you exasperating man! Being lovers and being husband and wife are two very different things.'

'A married couple cannot be lovers? I suspect that you are thinking with your emotions, Sara, not working this through and considering the benefits.'

'Of all the patronising things to say, Lucian Avery.' She pushed away from the door and took one furious step towards him before caution stopped her where she was. Too close and they might well end up kissing again and that simply turned her brain to pottage. He had made it very clear that he wanted marriage for three reasons—one, he desired her, two, she was *suitable* and, finally, by needing no courtship she would save him a great deal of trouble and effort. 'Marriage *should* involve emotions. I do not want some coldly calculated suitable match, I want a marriage of friends, of lovers, of shared interests and passions. Of equals.'

'Men and women can never be equal, we are different.' He straightened up, too, and came to stand in front of her, reached for her and drew her, stiff but unresisting, into his arms. 'Delightfully different.'

'I had noticed.'

Sara resisted the temptation to rest her forehead on his chest. Just because marriage to Lucian would be a disaster it did not stop her wanting him, stop her wishing it could work.

She tried to explain. 'Men are usually larger and stronger, women have different anatomies with all the consequences of that, but everything else is simply differences we allow to exist or which society imposes. Gentlemen normally get a better education, so of course you are often better informed and have a firmer grasp of many subjects. Men are allowed freedoms that women are not, so you can become fitter, more adventurous, can travel more widely, have a say in political affairs. But…' She paused to draw breath. At least he hadn't begun arguing yet.

'I have a good education, thanks to my parents' enlightened views, and I have built on that. I know that as a woman there are limits on what I can do in public, I know I have no vote and no power. But I do have a brain and I do have opinions and I must and will decide how I live my life. If I married you we would constantly be at odds. You would want to decide everything, you would be mortified if I behaved unconventionally, you would never believe I could stand up for myself if I was attacked, physically or verbally.'

'Marriage is a compromise, I imagine. Your experience of that is greater than mine.'

'Yes,' Sara agreed cautiously. She had expected a flat rejection of what she had said, not talk of compromise.

'Yes, even when you believe you are in accord, there are still compromises to be made.'

'If I promised equal decision-making in all aspects of our life together, promised to discuss everything fully with you and to take your opinions seriously, would you compromise by being at least as conventional a marchioness as your mother is and allowing me to leap to your defence whenever you are threatened or slighted? If we could agree on that, would that help you to decide? You are a woman of courage, Sara. Take a risk, follow your instincts.'

I love him, I desire him, I like him. Is that enough to risk the rest of my life on? Marrying Michael was so... safe. No doubts, no real compromises, an escape from a world that was alien and where I did not fit in. Now...I could cope with that world. Was I timorous before when I thought I was brave and bold? What are my instincts telling me? If I say yes, this is for the rest of our lives.

Lucian took half a step back as though to reassure her that he was not pressuring her. 'Stop biting that beautiful lower lip of yours,' he chided. 'Or I will have to kiss it better.'

She came up on tiptoe and leaned in to press her lips to his. *I love you. Is that enough?* It felt right. Right but frightening. 'Yes.'

'Yes?' Lucian caught her up, whirled her round and spun down the length of the room with her laughing, clutching at his shoulders.

This was such a different man from the one she had first met. *He is happy*, she realised. *The thought of marrying me makes him happy.* He set her on her feet at last, both of them laughing. Sara felt slightly weak at the knees, perhaps from the spinning, perhaps from the decision she had made.

'I must go and find your father before those two old hens cannot resist cackling their secret. But first, I need to find Marguerite and knock some sense into the pair of them.'

Not literally, she sincerely hoped. He would never lift a finger to his sister, but Gregory was battered enough. 'If you go and find Papa, I will locate Marguerite and give them both a trimming. I know I have no standing yet—but perhaps as your betrothed I might be allowed to help with this?'

'With my abiding gratitude,' Lucian said. 'Tell Farnsworth he is within an inch of a horsewhipping now and if he steps out of line one more time I will not hold back.'

Sara ran upstairs. She had no great hope of finding Marguerite in her bedchamber and was not disappointed when the room was empty. Nor was there anyone in Gregory's bedchamber. Cursing that she was going to have to search the entire house for them, and then probably find they had taken refuge in the summerhouse, Sara went to her own suite to repair the damage that Lucian's kisses had doubtless created. When she pushed open the door to her sitting room the two young lovers were there, one each side of the cold hearth as though a respectable distance might make things better.

Sara closed the door and advanced on them. 'Thank goodness I have found you. What did you think you were about? Gregory, you know perfectly well that this is our one chance to safeguard Marguerite's reputation and have your early marriage accepted without gossip. Have you any idea how close you came to being discovered by two of society's most avid tattlemongers?'

'It was my fault,' Marguerite admitted, waving aside Gregory's protests. 'I suggested we discuss tactics and we were, honestly, Sara. Just talking. Gregory had been working in the library earlier and we decided that if he pretended to go back after dinner I could discover him and be shocked and lecture Lucian about it in public and everyone would see that I was becoming emotionally involved with Gregory and then he would come in and I would fly to his side and he would take my hand and...' She shrugged. 'We would play it by ear, but I think by the time we had finished Lucian would have had to take us both away to discuss Gregory's intentions and everything would be perfect.'

'And I kissed her because it was such a good idea and to give her courage before she went back to the drawing room for the big scene. And it got out of hand,' Gregory confessed, looking as hang-dog as a young man with a piratical scar and eyepatch could.

Was I ever this young? Sara wondered. And yet these two had conceived a child together and had survived weeks on the Continent and, if it had not been for the accident, might well have begun married life in a respectable, if humble, manner.

'I do not think tonight would be a good night for the plan, but you might try it, say, the day after tomorrow. Another day of being seen to fret over Gregory's well-being and "helping" him would make it more convincing,' Sara suggested. 'And let us pray it succeeds, because I, for one, cannot stand the strain on my nerves much longer.' And the guests would think that Lucian's happiness over his own betrothal had made him softhearted towards the young lovers if he gave his consent once her own betrothal was known.

'Marguerite, I suggest you go back down to the drawing room. Gregory, a strategic retreat to your bedchamber is in order and I advise you to avoid being alone with Lord Cannock tomorrow—he was muttering about horsewhips when I last saw him.'

Lucian gave his appearance a hasty check in the hall mirror, ran a hand through his hair and straightened his neckcloth under the interested gaze of a passing footman before braving the drawing room again. His heart was thumping and he realised he had not felt this nervous since he was a raw youth. Sara had agreed to marry him. He should be delighted. He *was* delighted—she was everything he needed, had hoped for, in a wife. But there was a nagging doubt now where before there had simply been certainty. Did she need more than he could give her? Could he live up to the expectations of this complicated woman? Marriage was for life and it would change their lives for ever.

Lucian gave himself a brisk mental shake. He knew what he wanted and Sara was no green girl who did not know her own mind. He strode into the drawing room and found his quarry was standing, one foot on the fender, glass of port in his hand, arguing the rival merits of snipe, woodcock and grouse as game birds with a group of the male guests.

Lucian waited for a lull in the conversation. 'Might I have a word, Eldonstone?'

Sara's father turned, one grizzled eyebrow raised. 'Of course. My study?'

'If you don't mind, sir.'

When they were alone Sara's father waved Lucian to a chair. 'Port? Brandy?'

'Brandy, if you please.' There was no cause to feel that knot in his gut. He was an excellent match for Sara and there was, surely, no reason to fear her father's approval would be withheld. Not that he needed it with a widow who was of age, but it would distress her immeasurably if her family were hostile.

'I have come to ask your blessing,' he said as the older man handed him the glass. 'I have asked Sara to marry me and she has very graciously consented.'

'Have you, by God?' Eldonstone sat down. His expression was impossible to read.

'Yes. I am aware that this visit did not get off to a good beginning because we had chosen to anticipate this decision,' he began. He was damned if he was going to be defensive about becoming Sara's lover, but an acknowledgement of Eldonstone's feelings was certainly in order.

'You've changed your tune. Marriage was *out of the question*, I seem to recall.'

'Certainly it was while we were unsure that our feelings would endure. Neither of us wants this marriage to be less than happy.'

'You've a glib tongue, Cannock.'

'I have an honest one, sir. I thought I would be looking at the cream of the crop of next year's Marriage Mart, some well-bred little chit scarce out of the schoolroom. Observing some at close quarters and in proximity to Sara has shown me that what I would truly value in a wife is a woman of character and intelligence.'

'And you are telling me that my daughter, who you quite rightly say is a woman of character and intelligence, has agreed to marry you?'

A nasty dig, that. This was a man who had fought

his way round the Indian sub-Continent and then taught himself how to be a marquess in middle age. He was never going to be a soft touch.

'I am almost as surprised as you are,' Lucian agreed, refusing to let Eldonstone rile him.

'Hah!' It was a bark of laughter. 'I trust Sara and she, it seems, trusts you. But if she is wrong you'll have her brother to deal with and I will be standing right behind him to finish off anything that is left breathing.'

'As I would expect. You forget, perhaps, that I have a sister. I share your sentiments about men who betray the trust of a lady.'

'Is that why you refrained from retaliating when Ashe hit you? I was most impressed.' Eldonstone lifted his brandy glass in an ironic salute.

'Brawling on my hosts' doorstep when Clere was merely being protective seemed unlikely to endear me to Sara.' Lucian returned the salute and took a mouthful of the dark liquid. 'My compliments to your wine merchant.'

'Good, isn't it?' They sipped in comfortable silence for a while. 'Doubtless brothers-in-law would enjoy sparring a little.'

'Oh, yes.' And there was no need to wait until he was Ashe Herriard's brother-in-law. Just as soon as they found themselves outside and safely out of sight of the ladies he intended returning that punch with interest. 'You will want to discuss settlements. I'll have my secretary assemble some figures for you.'

'You can discuss that with Sara and she will ask me if she needs advice. I presume I have no need to worry about your ability to keep her in the manner I would wish for her?'

'None at all.'

'Then I suggest we take our brandy back to the drawing room and rejoin the other guests. When do you want to announce this?'

'Tomorrow night before dinner?' Lucian suggested. Now they just had to get Marguerite's love life choreographed to climax at the most advantageous moment and all would be well.

They strolled back to the drawing room as the clocks struck eleven. It seemed incredible that so much had happened in so short a time—that his life had turned around so completely.

Sara was with a somewhat subdued Marguerite, talking to her mother and some of the older ladies, and he went to drop a kiss on his sister's cheek. 'Staying up late, Puss?'

'I shall go to bed shortly,' she said, then adopted a chiding tone. 'Poor Mr Farnsworth is probably still labouring over all that paperwork you gave him and you are not worried about him.'

'You are very protective of young Farnsworth,' Lucian observed with a tolerant smile. 'I hope you are not flirting with him and distracting him from his work.'

'I wouldn't dream of flirting with him,' Marguerite said indignantly. 'He is far too serious to take any notice if I did. I admire him greatly,' she added, verging towards Mrs Siddons at her most tragic.

And you are a loss to the stage, my dear.

He smiled across at Sara and she smiled back, with a little gesture of her head towards her mother. Whispered confidences had been exchanged, he assumed. He met the Marchioness's beautiful green gaze and was rewarded with a smile, as lovely as her daughter's, but holding years' more experience and guile. This was the woman who had taught her daughter to defend herself with a knife and to ride astride and he had asked of Sara that she was *at least* as conventional a marchioness as her mother.

A month ago all he had asked of life was to have his sister back well and happy and to find a wife of the utmost, highly conventional, suitability. *And now...* He met Sara's smile again. *And now what could possibly go wrong?*

'I would like to see your stables, Clere. Any objections?' For the first time Lucian found himself alone with Sara's brother. The ladies of the party, Sara and Marguerite amongst them, were either sketching on the back lawn or admiring the artists. The other men had accompanied the Marquess to see his improvements at the Home Farm and Lucian had taken the opportunity to come across Ashe Herriard on his way to the front door, dressed for riding.

'None at all. Care to ride?' The Viscount nodded thanks to the footman who opened the double doors for them and led the way diagonally across the circle of the carriage drive to where a clock tower appeared above a screening shrubbery.

'I would certainly enjoy some exercise,' Lucian agreed, truthfully.

'I gather you are marrying my sister,' Clere said as they emerged from the shrubbery on to a rather trampled area just outside the arch into the imposing stable block. 'You had better make her happy,' he added with a charming smile that entirely failed to hide the threat behind it.

'Oh, I intend to.' Lucian smiled back. 'We don't know each other very well, do we? I keep my word, I take my duty to look after my family very seriously and I never, ever, forget a debt.'

The right hook was perfect. Solid, powerful, right on the point of Clere's chin. The bruise on his own chin ached in sympathy. And he had taken the other man totally by surprise.

Ashe Herriard levered himself up on his elbows in the dust and grinned. 'Point taken. Give me a hand, will you?'

He held out his right hand and Lucian took it, was jerked forward and on to a booted foot that rose to catch him squarely in the stomach. He let himself go with the move, over the top of Clere and into a rolling somersault. Lucian came to his feet and stripped off his coat to find Clere doing the same thing.

'Come on.' He lifted both hands, open, beckoning Lucian to advance. 'I am going to enjoy this. Who do you spar with?'

'The Gentleman, of course.' Lucian tossed aside his neckcloth and squared up to the other man. 'I've seen you there, but I've never seen you fight.'

'Thought I'd come across you at his saloon. Jackson's a good teacher, even if he does live up to his soubriquet.'

Gentleman. That is a polite warning that this pupil will be anything but gentlemanly, Lucian guessed. And Ashe Herriard had grown up in India, learning any number of exotic tricks, he had no doubt.

As he closed with him the other man's left foot shot out, aiming a high kick at his elbow. Lucian spun away, untouched and landed a punch on Clere's ribs. *Oh, yes, this is going to be fun.*

* * *

'Darling, can you see if you can find that album of prints of Calcutta? Mrs Galway was interested and although I left them on the side table in the Chinese Salon they aren't there now. I cannot think where they have got to.'

'Of course, Mata.' Sara made for the library first, glad of an excuse to escape the knowing looks and whisperings of Lady Thale and Mrs Montrum. It seemed the logical place for an over-tidy housemaid to have put it and she took a shortcut from the side terrace where the ladies had been sitting out of the direct sun and through the rear corridor that led from the gardens into the flower room, the boot room and down to the basement.

A glance through the glazed back garden door as she hurried past brought her skidding to a halt on the worn old flagstones. Two men were coming across the gravel from the direction of the stables. *Staggering* across, holding each other up. Ashe and Lucian.

Chapter Eighteen

Sara wrenched open the door and ran to them, nightmare visions of riding accidents blurring her vision. When she came to a panting halt in front of them they straightened up a little and she could take in their injuries and their clothing.

'You've been fighting—look at the pair of you!' Both had grazed and bloody knuckles, Ashe was sporting a split lip, a promising black left eye, a ripped shirt and seemed to be limping. Lucian's right eye was bruised, the side seam of his breeches was gaping, there was a nasty graze on his left cheek and a footprint on his shirt over his ribs.

'Sparring, that's all,' her brother said and winced.

'Bare-knuckled without gloves? In your decent breeches? Kicking? You've been fighting, you horrible creatures. How could you? You are going to be brothers-in-law, for goodness sake.' Oh, she could have wept, if she wasn't saving all her energies for thumping the pair of them just as soon as she was sure neither had any serious injuries. 'Come inside, quickly, before any of the ladies see you and faint dead away. Into the flower room, at least there is water in there and good light.'

'Good light for what?' Lucian asked as the two of them resumed their unsteady progress towards the house.

'Checking you over and patching you up, of course, you pair of savages. Peter!' One of the footmen came out of the door with a vase of drooping flowers in his hands. 'Put those down for now and go and fetch me the bandages and salves. Hurry now.'

She got them into the flower room and sitting on benches. 'Take those coats off, strip to the waist. Oh, let me help—have you broken ribs?' she demanded as Lucian struggled out of his coat and began to tug at his shirt.

'Doubt it. Just bruised.' He squinted down at himself as Sara tossed the shirt aside and prodded the discoloured foot-shaped area. '*Hell's teeth*. Yes, just bruised, possibly a crack.'

'And you.' She whirled round to her brother. 'Why are you limping?'

'Twisted my knee when I went down. And, no, I am not going to take my breeches off.'

Peter came in with the hamper full of salves and bandages. 'Shall I stay, Lady Sara?'

'No, thank you. Fetch hot water and some small bowls, would you please?' She waited until he was out of earshot. 'How could you both? Papa and Mata are happy for me—couldn't you be, too, Ashe?'

'I am. Cannock's a perfectly decent fellow.' Her brother shrugged, swore in Hindi under his breath and managed a lopsided grin at Lucian. 'Can't fight worth a spit, but otherwise, I approve.'

'Can't fight, you cheating excuse for a viscount?' Lucian lobbed a wadded-up neckcloth at Ashe. 'I had you down as many times as you floored me and you know it.'

Sara glared at them both. 'Oh, I see. This is that ridiculous male thing where you have to knock seven bells out of each other and then you're friends for life, is that it? Never mind that Mata has a houseful of guests, or that Lucian's sister might be upset at the sight of him in this mess or I might be, come to that. And do not roll your eyes at me, Ashe Herriard!'

'Are you certain you want to marry her?' Ashe enquired, reaching for a wad of lint and dipping it in the cold water before he applied it gingerly to his eye. 'She's grown into a shocking nag.'

Lucian looked at her, his face as innocent as any young urchin explaining how it wasn't his fault he'd come home bloodied, dirty and with split breeches. 'I've got to,' he said, sounding resigned but noble. 'A gentleman doesn't jilt a lady even if she turns out to be a virago and he was expecting a ministering angel.'

'Well, the virago can jilt the gentleman,' Sara retorted and put down the pot of calendula salve with a bang. 'And you can minister to each other as you are such good friends now.'

She swept out and off to the library where the volume of prints was sitting in the middle of the table, which did something to soothe her. By the time she came across Porrett in the hallway she was calm enough to ask him to send Ashe's valet down to the flower room. If anyone could make them halfway respectable in time for dinner it was Gorridge.

She delivered the album to Mrs Galway and plumped down on a fat cushion next to her mother. 'Those wretched men have been fighting.' When Mata raised an interrogative eyebrow she explained, 'Lucian and Ashe.

They are black and blue, limping and look as though they have been in a street brawl.'

'Oh, bless them. That is a relief. I was so worried about Ashe refusing to accept Lucian.'

'Mata, they look as though they were trying to kill each other and now they are apparently the best of friends.'

'That is men for you.' Her mother shrugged. 'They are like dogs and need to establish their order in the pack. Lucian outranks Ashe, but Ashe is your brother. It sounds as though they were evenly matched when they fought, so they have settled for equality, with each respecting the other.' She fell silent for a while as Sara sat and fumed quietly. 'Michael didn't fight, did he?'

'Certainly not, he was far too civilised for that.'

'A pity, because they let so much aggression go that way. If Michael and Francis had been used to that sort of rough-and-tumble way of settling matters, then possibly Michael would have punched him, not challenged him.'

She laid her hand on Sara's head and began to smooth her hair absently, as she might have stroked a cat. Sara let herself relax back against the rattan chair and absorb her mother's words.

'It isn't that I object to fighting if it is necessary,' she said, as much to herself as to her mother. 'You taught me to defend myself and sparring wearing gloves seems to be very good exercise for men, but that fight must have been brutal.'

'Are either of them seriously hurt?'

'No,' she admitted reluctantly.

'Then they were deliberately making sure it did not become dangerous. Ashe is trained to kill and if Lucian was holding his own with him then he knows how to fight seriously, too.'

So Lucian's instinct to fight to protect his sister and now, she supposed, her, was actually part of a strictly controlled repertoire of responses and if Michael had allowed himself to be just a bit more uncivilised he would not be dead now? It was an indigestible thought and part of what made it so hard to accept was the nagging fear that her own expressed opinions on what constituted civilised, rational behaviour might have contributed to Michael's reluctance to simply let fly when his friend was so foolish.

Sara was too preoccupied with her thoughts about Michael and the duel to have any room for anxieties about the evening's announcement, other than to think that if Lucian and Ashe were too obviously battered, then Papa would simply postpone mentioning the betrothal. But she dressed in her best evening gown, a pale straw-coloured silk sheath embroidered with crystals around the low neckline and the hem. She put her hair up with strings of crystals woven into it and wore no other gems. The image in the mirror was elegant and ethereal and renewed her flagging confidence in everything from her basic beliefs to her decision to marry Lucian.

It was a reaction, she told herself. Meeting Lucian had turned her world on its head just when she was beginning to feel unsettled in Sandbay, thinking about what she should do with the rest of her life, how she wanted to live it.

Perhaps this disquiet about Michael was simply a stage in the mourning process, a belated upwelling of unhappiness at his loss. But marriage to Lucian was a

very big step away from everything she had thought that
she wanted. Just how well did she know him?

I know him quite well enough in bed, she thought ruefully as she descended the staircase towards the hum of
conversation in the drawing room. Even though they
had only slept together twice she knew her betrothed
was skilled, thoughtful, demanding and understood to
a certainty how to pleasure a lady. *But how well do I
know him as a future husband?*

'That is a very charming blush on your cheeks.'
Lucian appeared at her elbow as she entered the room
and handed her a glass of champagne. 'Who has been
flirting with you on the stairs?'

'The second footman,' she said with a smile of thanks
for the wine. It would never do to let him guess she had
been thinking about him, let alone his performance in
bed. 'Ashe's valet has done wonders, I must say. You look
as though you have actually been indulging in a proper
sparring match with padded gloves, not some primitive
free-for-all. Does Ashe look as respectable?' She wanted
to brush the hair away from his brow where it fell over
a discreet patch of sticking plaster, wanted to run her
hands all over his body and check him for injury. If truth
be told, she was feeling possessive and wanted to fuss.
'And how are the ribs?'

'Your brother is pretending not to limp, although I
suspect Phyllida has kicked the other leg, so it is more
of a pained hobble. And my ribs are merely bruised. It
doesn't hurt at all unless I laugh.'

'I will promise not to say anything amusing.' They
moved until they were shielded by the partly open door
and Sara slipped her hand between his coat and waistcoat
to cup it around his ribs. 'I really do not blame Phyllida.'

'But you forgive me?' He was smiling down at her and under her hand his body was warm and solid.

'I might as well forgive you for being male,' Sara said and leaned in until she could rest her forehead against his lapel.

'I cannot do much about that state of affairs, whether you forgive me for it or not—and if I wasn't male I wouldn't find you half as beautiful when I looked at you. Tonight you are exquisite, a creature of fairyland, Sara.'

She looked up as he bent his head to kiss her and his breath feathered over her lips, blurring her mind and her fears.

'Stop it, the pair of you.' Ashe was resting one hand on the edge of the door, a screen between them and the room. 'If the old biddies see you before the announcement they will very correctly conclude that this is not a well-regulated, carefully contrived dynastic marriage and that the two of you actually care for each other. Bad enough Phyllida and me making a love match, but both of us being so unsophisticated? Shocking.'

He glanced back over his shoulder as Lucian gave a snort of laughter that ended in a sharp intake of breath. Sara drew in her breath sharply. *A love match?* But Lucian had not seemed to notice the implications of what Ashe had just said. 'Everyone's down now and Father is about to make the announcement. You had both better make your way to his side and look suitably bashful.'

Surprisingly, given that she had been married before and was both older and more experienced than the last time this had happened, Sara found that she did, indeed, feel bashful. It was probably the fact that she and Lucian had anticipated their vows.

Her father did a very good imitation of a proud parent. Perhaps now he knew Lucian did intend to marry her he was genuinely content with the match. His speech was short, warm, and had several of the ladies sniffing into their lace handkerchiefs.

Lucian responded with a few dignified words about how fortunate he was to have secured such a beautiful and intelligent bride and kissed his future mother-in-law and then Sara—both chastely on the cheek. Everyone applauded warmly and then clustered round to congratulate Lucian and kiss Sara.

The hubbub had almost died down when Marguerite appeared at Lucian's side, her hand on Gregory's arm. 'Lucian, we must speak to you.'

'You must?' He gave her a quizzical look.

'*I* must, my lord.' Farnsworth's scarred face was pink with embarrassment, but he kept his head up and looked Lucian squarely in the eye.

Lucian looked from one to the other, then turned to Sara. 'If you'll excuse me for a moment, my dear.'

She watched him lead the two lovers out of the drawing room and was immediately in the midst of a buzz of speculation as all the ladies began to wonder out loud just what was going on.

'I suspect we have another romance here tonight,' she said with a smile. 'Lady Marguerite has been spending much time assisting Mr Farnsworth. I did think that I detected a growing attachment and I believe they have just realised that they have fallen in love. He is such a worthy, intelligent and diligent young man, the son of a clergyman, I understand. Lord Cannock believes he will go far.'

'She is very young, is she not?' Lady Fitzhugh queried. 'And it is a somewhat unequal match.'

'One such as I made and I was very happy indeed, for the short while it lasted.'

That gave all the ladies pause. Sara could see their minds working—she was a marquess's daughter, she had married a commoner and a scholar, but she had remained a lady. Perhaps it was not so shocking after all…

Lucian came back, spoke with her father and then raised his voice for attention. 'My friends, this is an evening for good news. I am delighted to say that my sister Marguerite is now betrothed to Mr Gregory Farnsworth.'

Gregory was white with nerves, Marguerite was pink with happiness and Lucian was smiling with what looked like genuine pleasure, but was probably simply relief that they had pulled off the deception. Sara found she was dabbing sentimental tears from her eyes with her handkerchief without even realising that she had taken it out of her reticule.

When Lucian returned to her side he took her hand and squeezed it. 'Thank you, Sara. If it had not been for you this would never have ended well.'

'Anyone would have wanted to help them, despite their errors and adventures, and I am very fond of Marguerite. Lucian, we are going to have to plan wedding dates.'

'I know.' He looked faintly harassed, which Sara found rather endearing. Lucian was not a man given to being harassed, she suspected. He would make up his mind about something and then ensure it happened. 'You and I must marry first and as soon as possible, then we can establish ourselves in the London house and Marguerite can be married from there.' He looked down at her. 'Is that rushing you? I do not want you to feel our marriage is simply a convenience for establishing Marguerite and I confess I have no idea how long you would want to plan everything.'

'I need to go down to Sandbay to close down Aphrodite's Seashell.' Lucian managed to cover his relief about that really quite well, she thought. 'There is a lady in the town who comes to our group and who I think might well like to buy me out, but I must speak to her and of course pay Dot and make certain that she does not suffer for this. If you came with me we could make our plans at the same time.' She watched him think that through. 'Marguerite could stay here with Mama as chaperon, I am sure she would love to have her stay on.'

'And I could send Farnsworth to open up the London house and you and I—'

'—would be alone again.'

'A pre-emptive honeymoon?' Lucian suggested, his voice suddenly husky.

'Is that very wicked of me?'

'Oh, I hope so, my Aphrodite. I do hope so.'

Chapter Nineteen

'Chaises and postilions are fast compared to carriages with a driver, but they have one major disadvantage.' Lucian observed as they rolled away from Eldonstone three days later.

'The springing? It is very bouncy, but neither of us gets travelsick, it seems.' Sara stretched out her toes and wriggled back into the soft upholstery. Much as she loved her family it was a relief to be away from the house party and the guests' constant curiosity and probing.

'There is too much glass,' Lucian said darkly, gesturing towards the window at the front that allowed them to look out over the horses and postilions. 'How can I make love to you? It would be like being in a conservatory.'

Sara stamped firmly on erotic thoughts about making love in a moving carriage and tried to be practical. 'We can make it in the day, can't we? The weather is dry, the roads are turnpiked almost all the way. If we pick up food to eat as we go and stop only for changes it would take us twelve or thirteen hours.'

'You will be exhausted when we get to Sandbay.'

'Not if we sleep along the way.' Sara rested her head on his shoulder. 'We can take it in turns being the pillow.'

'I do not sleep when I am travelling and certainly not with a lady. What if we were held up?'

'And what if we were in a closed carriage making love and a highwayman held us up?' she teased. 'What would you do then? Wave your weapon at him?'

'You shock me, Lady Sarisa. My *weapon*, indeed.'

She felt his suppressed laugh shake his body and smiled. 'I suppose the answer is not to make love while going across Hounslow Heath and similar locations. Road books could have special symbols on them to designate dangerous areas.'

'A cupid in red, perhaps to indicate stretches of road where lovemaking might be inadvisable? We could expand on that—the guide could have inns with dreadful food marked with a red leg of beef and ones with damp beds with a rain cloud. If we lose all our money we could go into the publishing business.'

'Idiot,' she said and kissed him, regardless of the fact that they were bowling along the main street of Bricket Wood and the local inhabitants were going about their early morning business.

I fell in love with him without even being certain whether he had a sense of humour or not. Thank goodness he has.

It occurred to her as they rattled through the countryside that Michael had not had much of a sense of humour, or at least, not much of a sense of fun or the ridiculous. He hadn't been dour or humourless, but she could not imagine him entering into her silly little fantasy about road books marked up with warnings to lovers. He had been a good companion, but, she supposed, a serious one.

Not that Lucian could not be serious, she thought,

shifting so she was in the corner and could look at him as he sat relaxed, watching the road ahead. He was serious about family, about honour, about Marguerite's feelings, even when he had been exasperated with his sister. He had been serious about her own feelings, too, about her memories of Michael, even though he had not understood her opposition to duelling.

He still doesn't understand why I do not feel glad that Michael cared so much about honour as to fight for it, she thought. *It shocks him that I see it as a weakness that Michael did not find some other way to deal with Francis's drunken ramblings.*

A cold shiver went down her spine as she wondered, yet again, what exactly Francis had said. Had Michael gone to his death believing that she had betrayed him with his best friend? And many people would say that she had, she supposed, even though nothing had gone beyond a light, fleeting kiss.

Somewhere after Basingstoke, when they were, all being well, halfway back to Sandbay, Sara slept. It was two o'clock in the afternoon and they had just finished half a roast chicken, some soft bread rolls with fresh butter and a jug of ale.

It was the ale that had put her to sleep, Lucian thought, smiling at the crumbs on her skirts and the greasy smudge on one cheek from the chicken leg. Not one for standing on her dignity, his future Marchioness. He put an arm around her shoulders and tugged gently until she was cradled against his side and was amused to find that his other hand rested on the butt of one of the horse pistols he had pushed into the side pocket next to the seat.

She made him feel very protective, he realised, even more than was normal for him. *Was* this love? He supposed it was, although there were none of the symptoms he had expected. Or feared, to be honest. Her brother had said something about love matches—not that she had reacted to that in any way—so what had Clere seen? Lucian did not feel himself to be in a daze, or to have lost his judgement. He was not attempting to compose sonnets to Sara's eyebrows, fine though they were, and he had no desire whatsoever to put her on a pedestal.

Far from it. His desires towards her were decidedly earthy and the only pedestals that appealed were ones of a suitable height to perch her on, or bend her over, while he had his wicked way with her.

He had felt desire like that for other women, so why did the mere thought of this one vanishing from his life leave a hollowness inside that he suspected might be fear? Now *that* he had definitely never felt about any other woman.

But why? Yes, she was desirable and very lovely, intelligent, loyal, courageous, honest. Passionate. All of those things and yet…he suspected that it was none of them that made him feel like this when he was with her, but some indefinable quality that combined them all in a way that spoke to his heart and his soul. Was this love?

Honest, outspoken—and she had said nothing about loving him. He had not said he loved her, Lucian acknowledged, but it was a difficult thing for a man to admit to, even to himself. Surely Sara would have told him if she loved him? He began to wonder why she had agreed to marry him at all. They had moved from an expedient to distract attention from Marguerite and Gregory's indiscretion to discussing compromise in marriage, he realised, and then she had accepted him and he had not thought to ask the obvious question—*why?*

Perhaps it was because she had become his lover and then realised that she had made a mistake in having a sexual relationship outside marriage. Yet she had stood up to her father and brother's disapproval with no sign of either repentance or of changing her mind and expecting marriage. Unless she was too honest to want to trap him and it was not until he proposed that she allowed herself to agree.

That line of reasoning was making the hollow feeling considerably worse. Lucian closed his eyes. *Hell, but this falling in love business is a miserable thing, not at all what it is puffed up to be.*

His confidence was seeping away, he felt sick and he very much feared it was fear itself that caused it. He was out of his depth here. No wonder men went mad for love, shot themselves in despair. Where was all the sunshine and roses that were supposed to go with love? The songbirds tweeting, the bloody cupids flying...

'Lucian! Wake up, you are having a nightmare.' Someone was shaking him.

He blinked, opened his eyes and found himself nose to nose with Sara who was, predictably, laughing at him. 'What?' he asked, disorientated, his hand clenched around the pistol which was half out of its holster.

'You were muttering about Cupid doing something that I suspect is anatomically impossible, especially for someone with wings. You were quite correct when you said that you are not a romantic, weren't you?'

He jammed the pistol back, hoping Sara had not noticed that reflexive movement. 'I could try,' he suggested, imbuing as much confidence as possible into his voice. What did being romantic involve, anyway? Courtship seemed to be fairly straightforward—squire the lady about, bring her flowers, pay attention to what she wore, pay her compliments—he had felt no qualms about the prospect of doing all that once he had identified his potential bride next Season.

His previous lovers hadn't expected romance, only the best lovemaking he could give them, and he had certainly done his level best to please Sara in that way, with, from her reaction, excellent results. But she had mentioned romance twice, which made him think it was important to her.

'Men!' She laughed and rolled up her eyes, making a joke of it that he suspected was not a joke at all. 'If you have to try, then it is not romantic, you see. Do not worry about it, we have agreed to a perfectly rational marriage, haven't we?'

But why have we? Lucian asked himself. *Or, rather, why have you?* And realised that he did not want to ask that question because not only might she think hard about it and decide she did not want to marry him after all or, just as bad, she might think he was trying to hint that he hoped she would decide just that. No gentleman could jilt a lady, it was up to her to end an engagement if she changed her mind, and the thought that she might lose faith in the sincerity of his proposal appalled him.

'Of course we have,' he said and that time it sounded as though he meant it. He would not say the word *love* to her, admit what he felt, because then she would feel he was pressuring her to admit the same and she obviously did not feel it or she would have said so when she accepted him. She wanted a *perfectly rational marriage* so, as he loved her, that was what he would give her. It was what he had always thought he wanted, after all.

'We have arrived.'

Sara surfaced from jumbled, bumpy dreams as the chaise began the descent towards the centre of Sandbay. It was dark and the lights from the Assembly Rooms made a constellation of stars on the surface of the sea.

Home. And yet it would not be for much longer. Home would be somewhere unknown, somewhere with Lucian. Lucian's homes would be the shells around an entirely new life, the kind of life she had run from when she had married Michael.

'Sara?'

'Sorry... I must have been wool-gathering. Oh, the men have stopped for directions.' She let down the window and called instructions to the postilions, then sat back in the gloom of the chaise's interior and stared blankly out at the dark, familiar streets.

Run from... Is that what I was doing? Running away from an alien, difficult world, not running to *the man I loved? But I did love him. I did. He was my friend and he was so safe and he gave me the* entrée *to a whole intellectual world that fascinated me.*

He was my friend... She had loved Michael, she realised, but not as she loved Lucian. She had loved him as friend who was also a lover and that, she realised, was a very different thing from what she felt now for Lucian. For Lucian she was prepared to take risks, take a step into a frightening unknown. With Michael she had taken what she wanted and needed. If she had felt this for him then she would never have— No, she would not think about Francis, about that foolishness that had

had such a terrible result. Foolishness on her part, on Francis's part—and, fatally, on Michael's.

It had not been her fault, she had told herself over and over again. But it had. Michael had loved her in a way that she had never been able to return and that was why he had challenged Francis. That was why he was dead.

'Sara? Are you well? We have arrived at your house and you seem to be in a dream.'

Lucian, here and now. 'Yes, I am well, just not properly awake, that is all.'

'There is light down in the area. Wait here and I will go and knock.'

He did so and the door opened after perhaps half a minute, sending light spilling out down the steps and across the façade of the house as Walter held up a lantern. On the very edge of the light a shadow moved, a swift movement back into the darkness. A footpad waiting for an unwary passer-by or a beggar, perhaps, looking for an unlocked gate to slip inside and find warm shelter for the night. And yet there had been something familiar and unsettling about the way the figure moved.

Sara gave herself a shake. She was imagining things, seeing ghosts. It was because she was tired and had let herself dwell on the past, on Cambridge.

Lucian helped her down while Walter and one of the postilions sorted out her baggage from his. They made a very decorous goodnight, out in the open on the street. She did not ask him in, he lifted her hand and kissed her fingers lightly. The shadows stayed shadows, unmoving.

'I will call in the morning.'

'I must go to the shop. Could you meet me there?'

'For Mrs Farwell's cake? Certainly.' A bow and he was back inside the chaise and driving off.

'Is all well?' she asked as she followed Walter inside. He locked and bolted the door as Maude came running down and moved the valises to the foot of the stair.

'Yes, my lady,' Maude said. 'Mrs Farwell came round and left some money and I locked it away with your jewel case as the safest place. She said to tell you that everything was quite as it should be. Your post is on your desk and I opened the ones that looked like invitations and sent messages that you were away this week.'

'No callers?'

My imagination or a footpad, that was all it was. Who would be waiting for me out there in the dark?

'No, my lady, very quiet it has been.'

'Excellent, although I hope you were not too bored. I think I will go up and wash and change into my nightgown and just have a cup of tea before I go to sleep. It was a long journey from near St Albans in Hertfordshire.'

She waited until Maude was brushing out her hair to tell her the news.

'Oh, my lady! You will be a marchioness, just like your mama. Oh, how grand.'

'And I hope you will stay on with me, Maude. It will mean moving to London for much of the time and wherever Lord Cannock's various country houses are.'

How little I know about him. I must check the Peerage.

'Oh, yes, please, my lady. Oh, just think—London for weeks at a time and grand balls and dinners. The gowns—'

'You will be busy indeed, Maude. You will be my dresser and have a maid of your own and be the highest-ranking female member of staff in the household after the housekeeper.'

At least someone had stars in their eyes about the future and no worries or doubts, Sara thought as she settled down in bed with a cup of tea and the hope that sleep would come soon.

In some distant corner of her mind she knew she was dreaming, knew that she should make an effort to drag her eyes open and wake up and yet she was powerless. Michael's voice was speaking the words that she had only ever seen written on the letter he had left that morning when he had gone out to meet Francis in the dewy early light. Michael's face showed vague and misty as though seen through a shifting fog bank, his mouth speaking the words.

> *Francis said things that I could not let go unchallenged—implied that when I was at the college in the evenings, at night, he would not be keeping you company having dinner, as I believed he would, but making love to you. He would not deny it, would not confirm it.*
>
> *Of course I know it is all lies, that you would not so much as flirt with my friend, but he said such things... My friend no longer.*
>
> *Duels have always seemed to me to be archaic, violent. Now I see that sometimes there are slurs too great, betrayals too vile, to leave unpunished. I will defend your honour and mine and if I do not come back then remember that I love you and do not believe his lies for one moment.*
> *Your husband*
> *Michael*

And the fog swirled around her, choking her, muddling the words in her ears as she sank, drowning into the whiteness.

It was only flirtation, she tried to say to him. *I was bored. I was lonely. All those long evenings you were in college at those interminable meetings and dinners. Francis was there—he was fun, amusing, a friend. I never loved him, Michael, only you. Only you.*

Then there were three voices in that fog, like some devilish part-song. Michael's, hers, and one she had not heard for two years. Francis Walton's.

'Just a kiss goodnight, Sara dearest. Where's the harm? Just a kiss for an old friend...'

Sara woke sweating and crying, the sheets tangled around her legs, her hair in her face, clinging like the tendrils of the dream fog.

'But I can't have loved you, Michael,' she said out loud. 'Not enough, not as I should, or I would never have flirted with fire like that.'

Now Michael was dead and Francis an exile and she had been rewarded with a man she loved and desired and did not deserve.

Chapter Twenty

The tendrils of fear and shame still seemed to wrap her round next morning. As Sara made her way down the hill towards Aphrodite's Seashell the air itself was misty with tendrils of sea fret swirling in, chill from the ocean. It was as if her dream had moved with her into the real world, even though her rational mind told her it was only to be expected at this time of year and was the first warning that autumn was on its way.

Dot was already in the shop, dusting, when Sara slid her key into the lock. 'There you are, home safe and sound.' She cocked her head to one side as though knowing full well there was a tale to tell.

'Safe and sound,' Sara agreed. 'And Lady Marguerite is safe, too, and will be married to her Mr Farnsworth without a breath of scandal or gossip.'

'Now that's good news, bless her. A sweet girl from all I could see, even if she's still got a lot of growing up to do.'

'And I am selling this shop and I will be marrying the Marquess of Cannock,' Sara said, delivering all her news in a rush. She saw Dot's jaw drop. 'It is all right, Dot, I will make sure you do not lose by it.'

But it was apparently not the sale of the shop that astounded the other woman. 'The Marquess of Cannock?'

'Yes?' drawled a deep voice as the shop door closed on a tinkle of bells. 'You wanted me?'

'Mr Dunton? *You* are the Marquess of Cannock?'

'Dunton is a family name,' Lucian said smoothly.

'Good,' Dot stated. 'So long as you do right by her.' She stomped off to the back room. 'I'll put the kettle on.'

They stood there alone and Sara watched Lucian's gaze wander over the shop and its contents. Was he already wondering whether she could put this behind her, become the sort of Marchioness he thought he needed?

'We'll have tea, shall we? Then I must talk to Dot and then go and see if I can find Mrs Ingram, who might be interested in taking over the shop. I can always lease it if she doesn't want to buy.'

'I'll take it,' Dot said, coming through the curtains with a vast tea tray borne in front of her. 'Have to rent it, mind, don't have the sort of money to put down to buy it.'

'You, Dot? But you've never taken any interest in the money side, or the orders.' In fact, Sara was not certain just how literate the ex-dipper was beyond basic reading and writing.

'Oh, not the bookkeeping and ordering. And not the things you do out the front, but I can carry on looking after the teas and keeping the place in order. But I've got a niece, well, the daughter of a cousin really. Nice lass, well brought up, her father's a farmer and could afford an education for her. Went as a governess and was doing all right, by all accounts. Then the grown-up son of the house made a nuisance of himself, the slimy little…

worm, she slapped his face—and she got the boot, with no references neither. She'd make a good job of this, I reckon, and all she's doing at the moment is moping at home in Dorchester helping her ma.'

The temptation to simply hand the keys over was considerable. Sara owed Dot a great deal and she trusted her judgement—if she said this young woman would do well, then she probably would. But Dot's pride would never allow her to take a gift of that size, not for herself or for her young relative. Sara would have to be more subtle.

'We'll form a partnership,' she said. 'I will be a sleeping partner and you and your niece will be the active partners. I will get my man of business to draw up an agreement and if your niece can come down from Dorchester in the next few days I can show her everything she will need to do.'

Dot dumped the tea tray down on the table and took off her apron. 'Oh, bless you! She's been that much of a worry to me, I can't tell you. I'll go down to the receiving office and get a message sent up to her by the next post. I'll miss you, Sara love, but it'll be a joy to be able to do something for our Laura, bless her.'

'Why not make her a present of it?' Lucian asked when they were alone.

'Because Dot would not accept it, it would hurt her pride. This way I can gradually ease back and let them take over, but they will feel they are working for it.' She shrugged. 'Which they will be. But that is a weight off my mind. The shop is popular with residents as well as visitors and I would not have liked taking that away from them.' She poured tea and nudged the cake plate towards Lucian. Despite having picked at her breakfast she was not at all hungry.

'What is wrong, Sara?' Lucian's voice was gentle as he pushed the cakes aside and lifted his hand to lay the back of it against her cheek. The gesture was so tender that she closed her eyes against the sudden urge to weep. 'You are pale, there are dark shadows beneath your eyes and you do not look as though you slept. Surely you were tired enough?'

'It is just a reaction, I suppose,' she said with a smile and let her cheek press against his fingers. 'I did sleep, but I had bad dreams, very confusing and full of fog.'

'You are not having second thoughts?' It seemed the question was dragged out of him and, just for a moment, she wondered if he wanted her to say *yes* and call this off and free him.

Have faith, Sara told herself. *Trust Lucian, trust yourself. We can make this marriage work.* 'Absolutely not,' she said and twisted to catch his caressing hand in her own and kiss it.

'Sara, how long will it take Dot to get to the receiving office and back here?'

'Half an hour, I would guess, because she will need to write the message and that will not be quick for her. Then there will be any amount of discussion about how long it will take and how reliable the post boy is, to say nothing of talking to anyone she encounters along the way.'

'Excellent.' Lucian got to his feet, turned the key in the front door, flipped over the *Open, Please Enter* sign to *Closed* and went to the door to the balcony. 'Come along.'

'Lucian, you can't mean—not out here?' But she was

already feeling pleasantly flustered and warm in all the right places and when he banged the door closed behind her and turned that key, she did not protest beyond murmuring, 'Outside in the open?'

'No one can see us unless they are out to sea directly in front of us and even then they would need a telescope to see anything untoward.' He unfastened his falls and sat down in a rattan chair with no arms. 'And all they would see is you sitting on my lap, after all.' His eyes were alive with wicked intent and unfastening his breeches had released the evidence of considerable desire.

She was wet for him already, and hot, and so, so ready. Sara lifted her skirts primly, settled astride his knees and then, with a bold rummage amidst the petticoats, took hold of him in a manner that was most definitely not prim. She gasped with the pleasure of touching him, so strong, so male, so aroused by her, for her, and he growled, deep in his chest, and strained up, pushing within her circling grasp. Sara wriggled, the leather of his breeches rubbing, coarse and exciting, against the bare skin of her legs above her gartered stocking. The space was tight and her hands tangled with skirts and the flap of the falls and the tails of his shirt and she growled in her turn with desire and frustration and need until she had placed the hot, smooth head just where she wanted him.

They both went still, looking deep into each other's eyes, holding their breath, holding the moment until, unable to bear it any longer, Sara sank down, taking him, enveloping him, hard and almost, perfectly, too much.

'Ahh.'

Almost too much, almost too big, too male, too…

Lucian. And perfectly so. She held still, letting her body adjust, soften around him, embrace him, while she leaned forward and lay against his chest and let him hold her safely on the perilous brink of bliss.

Then she began to move, slowly upwards, rapidly down, making him gasp and throw back his head, his face a mask of intensely controlled pleasure on the brink of pain. Riding astride had given her thigh muscles that let her rise and fall to pleasure them both, forcing the urgent rhythm. Lucian let her lead until suddenly he caught her around the waist with both hands and held her still as he surged up, taking control, wringing gasping cries from between her lips as her vison began to blur.

'We don't have to be careful now,' Lucian ground out.

'No.' She clung on as the pleasure mounted, twisted and broke over her like a breaker on the rocks below as he pulled her to him and shouted his release against her lips.

Lucian came to himself to find Sara limp on his chest, her head nestled against his shoulder, her lips tracing teasing patterns on his neck. Faintly the sound of voices and laughter drifted down to them.

'Lucian, it is people on the library balcony we can hear—do you think they could have heard us?' She sounded almost too sleepy to care.

'Seagulls,' he murmured, kissing her ear, which was all he could reach. 'They will think it was seagulls.'

'I'm glad the gulls are having such a nice time,' she said, making him laugh. 'Oh, listen, Dot is back and banging around, rather. We had better unlock the door.'

Sara simply had to shake out her skirts, Lucian had to wrestle with shirt tails and breeches and Sara's attack of the giggles. 'You look as disarrayed as Gregory did when I found them in the library.'

'Your Mrs Farwell is about as terrifying as an enraged brother on the warpath,' he grumbled, giving up on his neckcloth. He tied a rapid, plain knot and jammed the loose ends into his waistcoat.

'Nonsense. She approves of you, she did right from the beginning. Mind you, it is probably the perfection of your profile and the width of your shoulders that she admires rather than your moral character.' Lucian pretended to preen and they were both laughing when they opened the door and found Dot clearing the table.

'You let your tea get cold,' she said, fixing Lucian with a severe stare. He returned it with his best Marquess-on-his-dignity look and was rewarded with a twitch of the woman's lips. Dot Farwell would have done well as the retainer who rode behind Caesar in his triumphal chariot, whispering, 'Remember you are mortal...' in his ear.

'The word is spreading already,' she reported. 'It was all over the receiving office by the time I left. Hope you don't mind, but that silly noggin Makepeace overheard me dictating the message and I put him in his place by telling him about his lordship here. And Lady Wharton is having vapours because her daughter danced with you, my lord, all unknowing that you were a marquess and if only she had worn her primrose silk you would have been so smitten you would have fallen for her and not Mrs Harcourt.'

'Am I in everyone's black books for not announcing who I really was?' Lucian enquired. For himself he couldn't care less, but he did not want to make Sara the target for jealousy on top of the gossip.

'Only with Lady Wharton and no one takes any notice of her, what with all her airs and graces despite her husband being knighted for all the money he made in boot blacking,' Dot announced with snobbery equal to any dowager duchess. 'And that Mr Winstanley at the hotel is wringing his hands because he put you in the second-best suite and now he doesn't know whether to move all your things before you get back or wait and grovel all over you and see what you think of the best rooms.'

'It is a perfectly adequate suite that I am in. I suppose I had better go down and reassure him before he is too distracted to pay any attention to all his other guests.' This was the last time he went anywhere incognito. Marguerite was always reading romances with dukes in masks and princelings of improbable European principalities roaming around in disguise and winning the hearts of poor but virtuous maidens before revealing their true selves. He had tried it and Sara had him spotted as a marquess within hours and everyone else was in far more of a taking about it than if they had known from the start.

He looked at her and saw to his relief that the colour was back in her cheeks and her eyes were bright. His conscience was troubling him over dragging her about the country on one long journey after another, but that glorious bout of lovemaking had restored her. As for him, he was fully prepared to do it all over again now. Perhaps the hire of one of the hotel's bathing machines and a chilly swim was in order.

The door opened and three ladies came in, all hardly able to disguise their excitement.

'Mrs Harcourt, I will leave you now, I am sure you must have much to do. Perhaps you would give me the pleasure of dining with me tonight at the hotel?' He kept his tone formal.

'Certainly, thank you.' She was just as proper as he in her response. 'It is ball night at the Rooms and I would appreciate your escort, Lord Cannock.'

'Delighted.' He bowed, the ladies sighed gustily and Lucian took himself off down the hill, amused despite himself. At least this was likely to do wonders for the profits at Aphrodite's Seashell because all of the curious ladies would have to buy something to justify their snooping.

Chapter Twenty-One

Conscious of Sara's reputation, Lucian ordered dinner to be served in the hotel's dining room, not in his suite. Mr Winstanley assured him that the chef was giving it his most personal attention, sent up four different menus for approval and a request to decide between the best table in the room in the bay window or the discretion of the screened corner. As Lucian had no intention of appearing to have anything to hide, that was an easy choice, but he nearly lost all patience when offered the choice between roses and a mixed floral arrangement for the table. Could his lordship tell him the colour of Lady Sara's evening gown so they could co-ordinate the flowers, perhaps? No, his lordship had no idea.

His lordship, if truth be known, would rather like to dine with Lady Sara wearing no clothes at all and with a menu consisting of oysters and strawberries and cream. An afternoon swim, which apparently was quite outside the normal hours for such activity, although he was assured that the tide was perfect, had done little to cool his physical need for her. In fact, he suspected that the exercise had merely sharpened it.

Sara arrived, was ushered into the dining room with huge ceremony, which from the unusually serious expression on her face was making her want to laugh. She did chuckle quietly when they were finally left alone at their window table to drink their soup.

'Was it very bad?' she asked sympathetically.

'I was about to ask you the same thing. Remind me, when I am complaining about the work involved when we hold our first ball, that it cannot be as bad as this. I escaped eventually and went for a swim.'

'This afternoon? My goodness, you must have thrown the entire town into a tizzy. I am amazed no one came to tell me. No one, but *no one*, swims in the afternoon.'

'I will start a fashion in that case. It certainly cost me a pretty penny—double the usual rate and I had to pay for a dipper whose services I entirely dispensed with.'

Sara was wide-eyed. 'You mean you really did *swim*? You didn't just lurk under the awning of the bathing machine and duck yourself? Oh, my, every telescope in the town must have been trained on you.'

'Certainly I swam. Out and around the point into the next bay.' He gave her a significant look which made her blush deliciously. 'I find I have a great deal of surplus energy to get rid of.'

'I wish I could have swum with you,' she murmured. 'There are some coves along the coast where no one goes because the paths down are steep. If the weather is fine tomorrow—'

She broke off suddenly, the colour draining from her face as she stared out of the window at the promenade, lit by the hotel's lights and a string of lanterns swaying in the light breeze.

'Sara? What is it? You look as though you have seen

a ghost.' Lucian twisted in his seat, trying to see what she had seen, but all there was to be seen was the cavalcade of beach donkeys being led back to their stable, a gig drawn by a single horse vanishing into the distance and a few strolling couples.

'I…' She made a visible effort to compose herself. 'I think I probably did. See a ghost, that is.' Her laugh was utterly unconvincing.

'A ghost? You mean your husband?' Had their betrothal stirred up memories and feelings she had buried?

'No.' She shook her head. 'No, not Michael. Not the ghost of anyone dead, at least, I hope not. It was nothing.' She stared at the salt cellar as though it held some vital significance, then took a deep breath and shook her head. 'I am not going to be brave and independent about this. That would be foolish. Now we are betrothed I should tell you what worries me, share with you as I hope you would with me if something was wrong.'

Despite her words she stayed silent, not meeting his eyes. Lucian waited, forcing himself to patience until Sara took a shuddering breath and spoke. 'I thought someone was watching the house last night when we arrived. It was a fleeting impression and I put it down to being half-asleep. But just now, the man driving that gig…his face was shadowed by his hat, but he was staring at us so intently…'

'So is just about everyone else who passes by. It is someone being nosy, that is all,' he said with relief, although the thought that someone was skulking near her house was concerning. He would deal with that later. 'We are the talk of Sandbay and this bay window is well lit. I am sorry you find it intrusive, but I did not want to appear to be hole-and-corner about our being here together. Where's that waiter? I will have the table moved.'

'No, you don't understand, Lucian. I thought it was someone I knew, I thought it was Francis.'

'Francis?'

'Francis Walton, Michael's friend. The man who killed him in the duel.'

'Hell.' Lucian was halfway to his feet, a soup spoon went clattering to the floor and every head in the dining room turned. Lucian made a half-bow to the other diners and sat down. 'My apologies,' he said, raising his voice to carry. 'Hot soup.'

'He will be long gone.' Sara held up her hand to stop the waiter who had started towards them, napkin at the ready. 'Whoever it was. It is only my imagination. It must be,' she added with what sounded like desperation to her own ears. 'Francis fled abroad immediately afterwards. The coroner's court gave a verdict of unlawful killing, so he cannot come back to England without risking trial.'

'So how has he been supporting himself?' Lucian paused while the waiter cleared the plates and brought a lobster in aspic. 'Is he a wealthy man?'

'No, he is the son of a prosperous squire. I think his family send money abroad to him.' She shivered. 'I have no idea why I should suddenly start imagining that I see him now.'

'Has it ever happened before?' Lucian seemed to realise that people were still staring so he began to serve the lobster. 'Laugh, pretend nothing untoward is being discussed.'

Obediently Sara gave a trill of laughter and pointed

to something outside on the promenade and heads turned back again. 'No, never,' she said, the artificial smile feeling as though it had been glued on to her lips. 'Lucian—' *How to say this?* 'I do not think that becoming betrothed to you is the reason I am imagining this.' *If I am imagining it...* 'But I have thought more deeply about my first marriage, I must confess.' She wondered if that offended him, but she was determined to be truthful.

'It would be remarkable if becoming betrothed again did not prompt those kinds of thoughts.' They ate their lobster in silence for a while, then Lucian said, 'I have no intention of trying to replace Michael, Sara. I am a very different man, I think.'

'Yes. You most definitely are.' Sara pushed a tiny shrimp, trapped in a pearl of aspic, around her plate. 'I was not ready for you before, when I was younger. I could not have coped with you, I think.'

'Coped?' His eyebrows lifted.

'You are… You have responsibilities that Michael did not have and that gives you a maturity, an assurance. He was like a student in many ways and I suspect always would have been.' And perhaps they would have grown apart as he became more immersed in his work, in the academic world. Looking back now, she could see it had already begun to happen. 'He let me into his world, but he could not truly share it. Now, I think, I can move in yours fully.'

'I am certain that you can.' His smile was sudden, as warm as a hug. 'But why not before?'

'I was running away. This was a strange country, one where I was different. Ashe and my mother adapted to it, my father made himself into an English marquess by sheer force of will, but I saw only so many rules, so many traps and snares, so many disdainful smiles because I was not quite *one of you*.'

'And now you are?' The smile became teasing.

'No, and I never will be. But now, you see, I do not care because I know who I am. I will be different and you do not mind, and I do not mind, and that is all that matters.'

'I will drink to that.' Lucian raised his glass as the waiters came to reset the table. 'I thought we would not want a heavy meat course and so I ordered fruit and ices next. But say if you would like something else, won't you?'

A month ago, Sara thought, she would have felt belittled by not having her opinion asked first. But now she realised that she did not have to be defensive. If she did not like his choice she would simply say so and Lucian would not be offended, would simply call the waiter over for her to order.

And if he was offended, why, then I would tease him for it, she thought, *and he would smile that slow, lazy smile and I would fall even deeper in love with the man.*

'Fruit and ices would be delightful,' she said and meant it.

'To the Marchioness of Cannock,' Lucian said, lifting his glass. 'My perfect Marchioness.'

'My perfect Marquess.' She toasted him back and felt the familiar cold finger of apprehension trail down her spine. She was not perfect, she knew that only too well, was coming to realise just how flawed she was. She had done nothing to displease Lucian yet, she realised. Right from the beginning of their relationship she had done the things that he wanted—helped Marguerite, become his lover, agreed to marry him. What would happen when, inevitably, she did not please him over something? He wanted a perfect wife, a perfect marchioness, it seemed, but she did not want to pretend to be perfect, or expect him to be.

I love you just as you are, she thought, watching him peel a pear for her. *If only you could come to love me the same way.*

'Chin up, shoulders back, smile in place,' Lucian whispered as they stepped into the ballroom of the Assembly Rooms. The level of noise rose immediately, then dropped as people stopped their own conversations and watched the latest sensation, the greatest Sandbay had ever had—their Lady Sara and the Mystery Marquess. As Sara had visited the cloakroom to leave her cloak some of the more romantic young ladies had come up, flushed with excitement, and congratulated her on catching this elusive creature and she had been hard put not to box their ears, the silly chits.

She glanced up at Lucian, who was perfectly composed and dealing with all the attention as to the manner born and had the wicked desire to disrupt that calm. It seemed her earlier qualms about being an *im*perfect marchioness had subsided a little. 'The young ladies call you the Mystery Marquess, you know,' she whispered. 'That was how I first thought of you once I discovered your secret. I think that is *so* romantic.'

'Codswallop,' Lucian retorted inelegantly, making the Master of Ceremonies shy like a startled horse. 'They have air between their ears, the lot of them.'

'Oh, look, there is Miss Wharton, wearing her primrose silk. You must ask her to dance, Lucian, it will make up for not falling in love with her at first sight, which you would have been bound to do, if you recall her mother's words.'

'Introduce me then and I will do my duty.' He let her steer him across the room to where Lady Wharton was fanning herself furiously and nudging the blushing Miss Wharton.

'Lord Cannock, may I make known to you Lady Wharton and her daughter Miss Wharton? Lady Wharton, allow me to introduce the Marquess of Cannock as a suitable dance partner for your daughter.'

'And it is a waltz!' Lady Wharton was almost beside herself with joy as Lucian led her daughter on to the dance floor for the set that was just forming. 'All the young gentlemen will see how favoured she is and all the other mothers will be beside themselves with envy. I do thank you, Lady Sara, for your gracious introduction.' She sank down in a billow of purple silk and flapped her fan.

Sara bit the insides of her cheeks to control her smile and strolled slowly around the room, pausing to exchange words with acquaintances, most of whom managed to keep their rampant curiosity in check. She had no desire to dance yet and managed to avoid being asked with some strategic dodging, until she found herself by the doors on to the terrace.

That was where she and Lucian had exchanged their first kiss. She smiled at herself for being such a romantic as to begin treasuring landmarks like that and was about to move on when a movement outside caught her attention.

'*Sara.*' The whisper stopped her in her tracks. 'Sara, out here. I must speak with you.'

No... No, this is my nightmare again.

Despite herself she stepped outside and closed the door behind her as a hand caught her wrist and pulled her behind one of the potted palms that flanked the entrance. 'Francis. It *was* you.' Not a nightmare, or, rather, not a bad dream. She stared at him blankly, all feeling and all ability to move deserting her.

This is the man who killed Michael, a voice in her head stated, as though giving a lecture. But it was also Michael's friend. Her friend. She had never believed he intended Michael harm and she could not feel fear now, or hatred, only a numb sort of shock.

'I have to talk to you,' he said urgently, his voice low. 'I had to see you before you heard that I had returned in any other way.'

He was thinner, she thought. Still handsome, although all the vibrancy that had made him so attractive to be with had gone, leaving his face serious and drawn. 'Heard… How can you be back?' she managed.

'I have been cleared of any ill intent towards Michael. My godfather used his influence to get the inquest reopened. No, do not say it—he did not use any influence to change the *verdict*, only to allow the evidence to be heard properly, but—'

Behind them, in another world, the music stopped and reality rushed back and with it, her voice. 'We cannot talk now, here. Anyone might come out at any minute. Go to my house and knock. Give this to Maude, my maid, she will let you wait in the drawing room.' She took a card from her reticule and scribbled a few words. 'You know where I live, don't you? You were there last night.'

'I know. I saw you come back, but you looked so tired, I didn't have the heart to approach you then.'

'Go. Please, just go.' She gave him a little push. 'I cannot be seen with you.'

'No, of course—I hardly fit in, dressed like this.' He smiled wryly and waved a hand to encompass his breeches and boots and somewhat dusty coat.

That was not what Sara meant, but she nodded and turned back to the ballroom before Francis had even vanished around the corner of the building.

'Are you well?' Lucian was at her side, his broad shoulders shielding her from the crowded room. 'I saw you go outside—is it too hot for you?'

'I—'

I should tell him, ask him to come home with me and then talk to Francis with Lucian at my side. But would he understand?

Inevitably, the reason for the duel would come up. Would Lucian think less of her? It was cowardly to fear the truth, but she could not help it. And Francis was no threat to her. That was the one thing she was certain of. Whether she was a threat to him remained to be seen.

Michael...

'It *is* hot, isn't it? But I am well.' She went up on tiptoe and whispered in his ear, 'But too jealous to watch you succumbing to the charms of Miss Wharton in her primrose silk.'

'It is a close call to choose between you both,' Lucian said, straight-faced. 'But as I have fallen deeply for your mother I can make the decision based on a comparison of mothers-in-law and there is no contest in that case.'

'Wretch.' Sara poked one finger into his flat stomach, surprising a grunt from him. 'Dance with me so I can make all the other ladies jealous.'

'They must be already,' Lucian murmured, caressing one long finger down her cheek, then cupping her face tenderly. 'You are the most beautiful, the most accomplished, the most elegant lady here.'

'And you, my lord, are the most arrant flirt!' If she didn't think about Francis until she got home she could do this, appear natural and relaxed and happy—and deceive Lucian.

'May I come in?' he asked as he gave her his hand to help her from the sedan chair and walked her to her door. 'This morning was bliss, but very quick bliss. I would very much like to spend the night making up for that…slowly. I will come round to the back gate so no one will see me go in. That would be more discreet.'

'Lucian—I am sorry, but not tonight. Do you mind very much? I had such a bad night last night. Tomorrow—come for luncheon and then you need not leave at all.'

'Of course.' His kiss was quick as they stood in the shadows, then he took her latch key and waited until she was inside before murmuring, 'Good night and sweet dreams, Sara.'

'I will try and dream of you,' she promised as she shut the door.

Maude came out into the hall at the sound of the door closing, but Sara held up her hand for silence, leaning back against the panels until the sound of Lucian's footsteps faded away down the street.

'Did a gentleman call, Maude?' she said at last.

'Yes, my lady. He showed me your card and I put him

in the drawing room. I gave him a light supper, my lady, and the decanters. I hope I did right?'

'Yes, thank you, Maude. He is an old friend from Cambridge.' Which did not explain receiving him at night. She took a deep breath. 'Maude, that is the man who fought the duel with my husband.'

Chapter Twenty-Two

'My lady! Shall I call the constable?' Her maid caught at her hand, tried to pull her towards the front door.

'No, he is quite safe to be with.' Sara freed herself and patted the other woman's hand in reassurance. 'It was an accident, Maude, a horrible accident. But I need to speak with him before all of society knows that he is back. I would like you to sit in the dining room, if you would, and we will leave both doors ajar. I am quite confident that will be adequate, but I would not like Lord Cannock to think I was unchaperoned.' Lord Cannock was probably going to resemble one of Congreve's military rockets going off when he found out about this, but she would deal with that when she had to.

'Yes, my lady,' Maude said dubiously as she took herself off to the dining room, leaving the door wide open.

Sara did not give herself time to get any more nervous than she already was. She tossed her evening cloak and reticule on to the hall chair and went straight in.

Francis got to his feet, a brandy glass clenched in one hand. 'Sara. Thank you for receiving me. I would not blame you if you never wanted to see me again.'

'I do not know how I feel.' She sat down before her shaking knees betrayed her and forced herself to look at him. 'I just want to hear what you have to say and then, I think, I will ask you to leave.'

'Of course.' He sat down again. 'We were both drunk that evening, you know,' he began abruptly. 'I could not believe it at first when he challenged me, Michael had always been so scathing about men who fought duels. But I had been such an idiot, I knew it as soon as I opened my mouth and all that nonsense came out, I could hardly blame him. I was too proud to apologise, can you imagine? If he was too proud to back down, I was far worse.

'But I knew I had to delope, whatever he intended, whatever he did to me. It was all my fault that it had come to such a pass and besides, I couldn't hit a barn door with a pistol if I threw the thing at it. That was the trouble, I suppose, my utter hopelessness with a gun—' He broke off, scrubbed his hands over his face, then swallowed hard as though forcing his stumbling words to come out in some order. 'I aimed wide, as I intended. The white handkerchief dropped, Michael deloped, fired into the ground, and I twitched, I think, at the noise and with nerves and I stumbled and the gun went off. And...'

'And he was dead, shot through the heart,' she finished when his voice gave out. Strange that she could say it so steadily, but there seemed to be a cold emptiness where her own heart should be.

'Yes. And George Harper, my second, said he had to get me away, off to the Continent, because the coroner could bring it in as murder, or unlawful killing at the very best, and I could hang. The doctor had already made a bolt for it, there was nothing he could do and who can blame him, he didn't want to be an accessory.

Jimmy Philips, Michael's second, said he didn't think I had done it deliberately, but he agreed with George that it wasn't safe to chance it, so I ran.'

Sara could imagine him, white-faced, stark with the horror of what he had done, driving at breakneck speed through the early morning light. *While Michael lay still and cold in the dew in a Cambridge meadow.*

When she did not speak he picked up the story again, his voice a monotone. 'I went home, confessed to my parents, packed my bags, took all the cash that was in the house. They promised to send me money regularly when I found somewhere safe. My father suggested Brussels, my mother was crying too much to say anything. I tried to write to you before I left, but what could I say? I am sorry? Much good that would have done.'

'I wanted to kill you—and yet I wanted to hold you and tell you that I knew it must all have been a horrible mistake. I wanted to believe that. I wanted to know that you were all right, but no one would speak of you to me.'

Francis ran his hand over his mouth as though to control the words on his lips. Eventually he said, 'I went to Ghent in the end. It was not so full of people who would know me as Brussels was. I called myself Mr Smith and found a small apartment to rent. My parents sent money and I settled down to a life full of nothing except the knowledge that I had broken their hearts, killed my best friend and made you a widow. I thought about putting a bullet in my brain more than once, but that would have finished my mother.'

'So what happened to change everything?'

He shrugged. 'Good fortune. My godfather knows the Lord Chancellor and he started chipping away at him about the inquest. The original coroner was dead set against duelling, especially in a university city because of encouraging students to fight. Apparently he refused to take any evidence about how we had both deloped—or, rather that I had tried to. Finally, Lord Eldon agreed to a new inquest and both the seconds spoke out, and Michael's groom who had been driving his gig and saw it all did, too. It was brought in as death by misadventure and the time I had spent in exile was taken into consideration.' He seemed to run out of words, then added, 'So I have come back.'

'What will you do now?' Sara felt sick with reaction, but at least she felt something. Nausea was better than that cold hollowness inside. Why had the seconds not told her what had happened? Why hadn't Jed, the groom, told her? Because she had not been there, she supposed. Her family had swept her up, taken her away, cocooned her in love.

'I will go home to Haddon, stay away from London and learn to manage the estate, take some of the burden off my father and try to make it up, somehow, to my mother. There's a girl she wants me to marry, who'll likely have me, it seems. I'll do my best to make her a good husband, raise children. I'll soon be forgotten outside a ten-mile radius, with any luck.'

The words were bitter, but his voice was not. Francis was home from exile, his name was cleared and he could begin to build a new life, even if he would never, Sara suspected, be able to forget Michael's death or forgive himself for it. Could she? Face to face with this handsome, likeable man, could she forgive herself for what had happened to cause it all?

'I flirted with you.' The words seemed to come from very far away and her lips were numb. 'When Michael was away, out for the evening or late working and you would call round, I flirted. I enjoyed your company, I was flattered by your friendship and your interest in me and I was lonely. That is no excuse,' she admitted, more to herself than to him. 'It was my fault you said those things to him when you were drunk.'

'*No*. No, you never overstepped the bounds of what was honourable. You never treated me as anything but Michael's friend, your friend.' He sprang out of his chair, knelt at her feet, ungainly in his urgency, and caught her hands in his. 'Yes, you teased a little, but only a rake or a fool would have thought you meant anything by it. But I was that fool.' He looked up, into her eyes, his own startlingly blue in his haggard face. 'I was fool enough to fall in love with you.'

'Francis, *no*.' She had no idea he felt anything for her beyond friendship. Had she been so very blind or had she not chosen to see what was under her nose?

'I would never have said anything to you, never have touched you, never have betrayed him like that. But I kept it bottled up and it grew and grew and that night he said something about what a lucky fellow he was and it all just came pouring out, what I felt about you.'

There were tears in his eyes and a pain too terrible to look on, so she gathered him to her and he laid his face on her lap and sobbed as she held him and finally feeling flooded back—pain and regret and loss and a desperate pity.

'I love you.' He lifted his face. 'I always will.'

'Oh, Francis.' Sara bent her head until their foreheads touched and held him tightly.

'*I love you, Sara.*'

'How very touching.' The voice from the doorway

dripped sarcasm. 'My dear Sara, might I suggest that if you are going to run two lovers at the same time that you learn to keep the back door locked?'

Sara twisted round in the chair, Francis fell back sprawling on the carpet. Lucian stood looking down at them with pure murder in his eyes.

'However did you get in?' Sara demanded, shock and fear giving an edge to her voice.

'You left your fan in the sedan chair. I walked back with it and caught a glimpse of a male silhouette against the drawing-room blinds. It seemed prudent to enter from the back if I could get in, and the back door was, very carelessly, on the latch. I was rushing to your rescue, my dear, thinking to protect you from the man who was giving you nightmares. Apparently that was not what was disturbing your sleep.'

'I can explain,' Francis said urgently. 'I mean Lady Sara no harm. I came to explain what happened when her husband died and my feelings overwhelmed me. She was comforting me, that is all.' He started to stand up.

'Stay down if you know what is good for you.' Lucian's voice was a snarl.

To his credit Francis got to his feet regardless. 'Cannock, isn't it? What business is this of yours—and what right have you to speak to Mrs Harcourt in that way?'

'And you are Walton, I presume. The friend of the family,' Lucian said, his lip curling. 'Mrs Harcourt is betrothed to me.' He glanced down at Sara who registered the present tense, as no doubt she was meant to.

'Lady Sara has done nothing wrong. I am entirely to blame both for the duel that led to Michael's death and for placing her in this present position. I love her and I am all too aware that the sentiment is not returned, but she is a compassionate woman and, I had hoped, able to forgive me. At least, she allowed me to explain what had happened.'

'You are not lovers, then?' Lucian regarded Sara with an expression that seemed to hold nothing but simple curiosity. She was not deceived.

'No.' They both spoke at once.

'Never,' she added. 'I have never been with anyone but my husband and with you.'

'And yet you put your hands on her, Walton. On my fiancée. You blubber on to her bosom, you pour sentimental twaddle about love into her ears, you follow her about making her fearful. I think you had better apologise, Walton, and assure us both that you are taking yourself off to whichever Continental bolthole you have been skulking in before the law catches up with you.'

'The inquest verdict has been overturned and Harcourt's death found as accidental. I have returned to England and I intend to stay. As for apologising to Sara—' Francis smiled at her '—I will gladly apologise for all the distress I have caused her. Apologise for seeking her out to tell her the truth about what happened? No. And as for apologising for loving her, I might as well apologise for living.'

'Then perhaps we should do something about that. I challenge you to meet me, Walton. As neither of us have friends here on whom we can call, I suggest we fix a date when we may both be in London.'

'Certainly, my lord. I will await word from your second. My club will find me.' He reached into his breast pocket and handed a card to Lucian.

'Stop it, both of you!' Sara found herself on her feet, her hands upheld as though to keep the two men apart, even though neither had moved. 'What earthly *point* is there in this? I am not hurt, or frightened of anything but what the pair of you might do. I have already lost my husband—do you think I want to lose my betrothed, or my friend?'

'I killed Michael, even if it was by accident,' Francis said, his face white and set. 'This is only justice. If I had kept my mouth shut, if I'd had the guts to go away and leave you it would never have happened.'

'Rubbish, you cannot go through life yearning for what-ifs. The past is past and you told me yourself the verdict had been overturned. Think what it will do to your parents if you are killed now. Think if there is another accident and you kill Lucian. Nothing would save you if that happened.'

She ignored Lucian's scornful snort of disbelief, but she could not ignore his baleful presence. He had settled his shoulder against the door frame, crossed his arms and was watching them from under hooded lids.

'I cannot refuse a challenge, not and retain my honour,' Francis stated. 'And I will not say I do not love you, because that would be a lie.'

'Is it? I do not think you love me, I think you have talked yourself into it to justify what happened with Michael. We flirted, you and I. Indiscreetly, but innocently, and you talked yourself into making that some kind of noble, unspoken love. The more I think about it, the less I believe in it—I could tell if a man loved me, surely?'

Francis broke into speech, stuttered to a halt and looked at her, aghast.

Lucian cleared his throat and Sara turned. 'I know *you* do not love me,' she said, stating plain facts. 'If you did, you would have told me, shown me.' At least whatever it was that Lucian felt for her, it was not made infinitely more complex by love. 'You have never pretended to feel like that. That was never what our agreement to marry was about.'

'I think perhaps your belief in your ability to tell a man's deepest feelings may be misplaced,' Lucian said, that infuriating, mocking smile on his lips, his eyes bleak in a way she had never seen them before. 'We may not wear our hearts on our sleeves as you seem to think. You believe that men want to give a hostage to fortune in that way, by admitting to love when they do not think it will be returned?

'I told you, when we first met, that I protect the women in my care—and that includes my betrothed. To do other is dishonourable.'

'There is a very simple solution to that, one that will get us out of this hateful, dangerous situation we seem to be in, one that should stop the pair of you carrying on like fighting cocks in the cockpit. I thank you for your flattering offer of marriage, my lord, but I find on further reflection that we will not suit. Please consider our betrothal at an end.'

Lucian was white around the mouth, but his eyes were hard and his voice icy. 'You would have me understand that you place the life of the man who killed your husband above our marriage?'

'Of course I do! I would place the life of any decent human being above my own happiness, my dreams, my hopes of...'

'You are serious about this?' He seemed incredulous.

'Of course I am. Do you think I could jest about it? Our betrothal is at an end. I will take full responsibility for that, your precious honour will have not a smudge upon it and people will tell each other that you had a lucky escape from the eccentric and wilful Lady Sara.'

Lucian turned a baleful stare on Francis. 'And you—'

'I never want to see him again and I very much doubt, once he has thought it through, if he will want to see me. You have no reason whatsoever to call him out on my behalf, my lord. You have no rights over me and no responsibility for me. If my honour is offended, then I have a father and a brother to turn to. To force a duel would be dishonourable and you know it.' She was arguing like a nit-picking lawyer, weaving the threads of honour and the tradition of the duel into a net from which Lucian could not escape. And neither would she. This was the man she loved, the man she was giving up for the sake of her conscience. She could not make him a murderer.

'You had better go. And, Francis, you must leave, too. Go home to your parents, to the young woman who is willing to marry you and learn to love her, and don't talk yourself into emotions that are not true. The real ones hurt too much—and what hurts you is the way you betrayed Michael's friendship, not unrequited love for me. Please go. I wish you well, I truly do, my friend. But I never want to see you again.'

Lucian stood aside to let Francis past and he stumbled into the hall like a man emerging from a dream, or thick fog. There was a murmur of voices, the front door opened and closed and she was alone with Lucian.

Chapter Twenty-Three

'You had better leave, too.' Sara stood up.

'There is no need for this, Sara. I lost my temper just now. If you tell me that there is nothing between you and Walton, then of course I accept that. It is him I am angry with, never you.' Lucian came fully into the room, gestured towards the chair that Francis had occupied. 'May I sit down?'

'If you must, but there is nothing to stay for. Are you concerned about Marguerite? My mother will look after her, just as she promised she would. She will be quite safe until you are ready for her to join you in London.' She sat down again and concentrated on keeping her head up, the polite, frosty little smile on her lips. Her heart was breaking, but that was no reason to give in to floods of tears, she told herself. 'People will understand that under the circumstances she should marry earlier now there is no reason to wait for our wedding.'

'Forget Marguerite,' he snapped, the loss of control so uncharacteristic that for a moment she gaped at him. 'I told you I will not fight Walton, that there is no reason for me to do so. For a second I doubted you, I am sorry for that, but I cannot see why that should mean the end of our betrothal.'

'I… You want to pretend this has not happened? Lucian, that is impossible. What would happen the next time you became suspicious of something—and we are married?'

'You think it possible that I will find you alone at night with a man in your arms professing his love for you?'

'Of course not. I mean that your reaction to any threat to me, or to your possession of me, is unacceptably primitive. Over-emotional.'

'*Emotional?* I would have thought rather that you would have thrown the formality and the codification of duelling at my head, not tell me it is emotional,' he said bitterly.

'It allows you to hide your emotions,' Sara said wearily. 'But why are we speaking of such things? We agreed to marry because it seemed rational. We were suited, we were attracted.'

'What will you do now? Remain here?'

'No. My life here has ended and I have promised the shop to Dot and her cousin. I will hand it over and… go.' *Somewhere.*

'Where? And to do what?' Lucian demanded.

'I do not know and, just at the moment, I do not care. Something different. I will decide sooner or later.'

'In that case I will go and let you decide,' he said with awful politeness as he stood up. 'Just tell me one thing before I leave. You told me I was not a romantic. I know what that means in terms of literature, in respect of the landscape and art, but what do *you* mean by romance, Sara?'

Taken unawares, she reacted without thinking. 'I mean the emotions of love. I mean wanting to feel deep emotions when you are with someone you love, or to show the emotional side of your feelings when you react to something the loved one says or does, how they feel. It means opening yourself up to the hurt as well as the joy. And it means being moved to tears by a raindrop on a leaf or a touch between two old people who have been together for a long time or a perfect line of verse. You do not have to be in love to be a romantic, but I do not understand how anyone who is in love cannot be so.'

She could feel the tears coming now and she was too proud to let him see them, risk him interpreting them as what they were, so she turned her shoulder. 'You should go now, Lucian.'

'Of course. Goodbye, Sara.' The door closed behind him gently but with a firm click that seemed to her to be the sound of finality, the sound of the man she loved leaving for ever.

Lucian strode down the hill to the seafront, blind to everything but the thick black fog that seemed to swirl around him. He was finally brought to a standstill by the railing around the promenade edge. The tide was right out, he could hear it far down the beach where the moonlight caught the breakers.

Beautiful, he thought bleakly. *Probably romantic, but how the hell would I know?* He loved her and he had lost her. Probably he had never had the part of her that he yearned for, the heart of her. Sara *was* romantic and she had probably agreed to marry him so that no longer would she be at risk of being hurt, of having to feel those emotions she spoke of. Her marriage had ended in terrible pain, she would not want to risk that again and yet, when it came to it, she could not bring herself to marry him, the man who could offer her a rational, sensible marriage with no messy emotions.

That water looked attractive. Cold, impersonal and uncaring. It would receive him and make him work hard, stretch his muscles, push him until, perhaps, he would be able to sleep. He worked it out and, yes, the tide was coming in. He was not such a fool as to swim on a falling tide on an unfamiliar stretch of coast.

The town was quiet now. It was past midnight. The Assembly Rooms were closed. No one was visible. Lucian ducked under the rail, dropped down to the beach below and walked to the jetty. He stripped rapidly and piled the clothes on the upturned boat that Sara had sat on to brush the sand from her legs. The night air was cool on his skin, but the sea would be warm. He strode down to the water's edge and straight in to mid-thigh, then dived and struck out into the moonlight.

She would never sleep. Sara let Maude help her undress, then just stood in the middle of her bedchamber, nightgown in hand. 'I am going to swim.'

'What, now, my lady? It is dark.'

'There is a moon, the tide is coming in and I am far too restless to sleep. Find me my swimming clothes, please, Maude.'

Most ladies used a flannel 'case', a shapeless flannel shift, to be dunked in. But that was useless for swimming. Maude fetched her the light calico trousers and simple shirt that she used. It was thick enough fabric not to cling and become transparent in the water, but light enough and free enough for her to swim strongly. She pulled on shoes to protect her feet on the way down, threw a cloak around her shoulders and hung a door key around her neck on a cord.

'Don't wait up for me, Maude. You deserve some sleep after tonight's disturbances.'

It was a beautiful night. Sara leaned on the promenade rail and watched the moonlight on the water and wondered why she could not weep now that she was alone. Perhaps the loss was too deep for tears.

She made her way to the upturned boat to leave her clothes, puzzled by the bump on its usually smooth silhouette. Then she saw it was clothes. As she held them up she recognised the gleam of jet buttons on the waistcoat, the silver buckles in the shape of snakes on his evening shoes. Lucian's clothes.

The panic lasted long enough for her to find she was sitting on the boat, clutching his shirt and staring out to sea, a cry of horror on her lips. Then she got it under control. Lucian was not a man to walk out into the sea and drown himself because of a broken engagement. He did not care that much and he had responsibilities he would never abandon. No, like her, he had not been able to sleep and the sea had tempted him.

She should turn back, she thought, but stayed where she was. The shirt held the scent of Lucian in its folds, a subtle counterpoint to the salt smell on the breeze. Why had he tried to persuade her to marry him regardless of that awful scene? Now she thought about it she was puzzled when before she had simply been too upset to wonder.

Could it be possessiveness, desire or a reluctance to be seen to have been jilted? No, Lucian was not a man to condemn himself to an unhappy marriage for the sake of his pride and what people might say.

What was it that he had said when she had stated with such assurance that she would know when a man was in love with her?

'Your belief in your ability to tell a man's deepest feelings may be misplaced. We may not wear our hearts on our sleeves... You believe that men want to give a hostage to fortune in that way, by admitting to love when they do not think it will be returned?'

Surely that did not mean that he loved her? Why ask her about romance? Was he trying to read her deeper feelings?

His shirt slipped out of her grasp as she stood up. *He loves me?* Perhaps he did, or perhaps she was indulging in the worst kind of wishful thinking. Lucian had never said one word about love, but then neither had she. *Coward*, she chided herself. *You did not dare to risk rejection so you settled for what was safe, what was easy.*

I must tell him.

Even if he did not love her, even if it was far too late for them, she would be honest. She scanned the calm, moonlit sea, but could see nothing breaking the surface of the gentle swell. From what he had said before he was a strong swimmer so he could be either east or west. But he had found the next bay last time, perhaps he had returned there. Sara kicked off her shoes, tossed her cloak on to the pile of Lucian's clothes and ran down the beach.

The water was like silk, cool and slick over her skin. Sara put her head down and struck out strongly for the headland she had walked around with Marguerite, now jutting out into deep water. The very act of swimming was soothing and helped her think. That first, abrupt proposal in the punt—that had not been the considered act of a rational man and Lucian was not insensitive or unfeeling. No, he had realised something suddenly, that he wanted to marry her for reasons that were not rational, not considered, and he had spoken his thoughts aloud before he had time to consider them.

And I gave him no encouragement to speak about his feelings, she realised as she trod water to check her bearings, then angled in towards the beach in the little bay. Their lovemaking had come from a mutual physical attraction, not because they had fallen in love first which meant—

'Ugh!' She collided with something very solid, coming towards her. For a moment she was gripped by alarm, then, as hands met hers and her flailing arms hit warm, sleek muscle, she realised what she had collided with. 'Lucian!'

'Sara?'

They clung together in the water, rocked by the swell, then his arms were tight around her and his mouth was on hers and the kiss was hot and demanding and a possession that she returned as fiercely. She was drowning in him, sinking into him, and came back to herself to find that Lucian was hauling her to the surface.

'Damn it, we nearly drowned. Back to the beach.' He turned, waiting for her.

'I thought it was just your kisses,' she told him, and he laughed and her heart sang.

Side by side they swam to the little beach and splashed ashore before sinking on to the edge of the dry sand. Lucian put his arm around her and pulled her tight. 'We should have gone back to the main beach, you'll catch your death.'

'Just for a few moments. We need to talk. Lucian, you still wanted to marry me? Why?' When he hesitated she murmured, 'I did not think you would be afraid of anything, even of wearing your heart on your sleeve.'

'Perhaps I am a coward when it comes to risking something I fear losing so much.'

'Your heart?'

'Your love. If I have it. I have lost my heart many days past. I love you, Sara, but I thought you did not love me. I thought that you were so frank, so open, that you would have told me if you did.'

'And I thought you would be repelled by that emotion, by the demands that love makes.'

'It does?'

'If it is not returned. You felt it, too, or you would have told me how you felt. I love you, Lucian. I didn't want to, I thought you were so wrong for me, that I would be impossible for you.'

'After this evening do you not fear I would be impossible to live with?' he asked and the lightness of his tone could not mask the urgency of the question.

'And me. Can you live with me? I get into scrapes, led there by my feelings, not my sense of what is proper,' she confessed.

'We can compromise as long as we can talk. Talk and make love.'

She realised that he was leaning back, that in a second they would be flat on the beach. 'Lucian, darling man, have you ever made love on a beach before?'

'No. How do I get you out of this shirt?'

'Sand. Sand gets *everywhere*. We need a... *Oh...*'

'Rug?' he asked from somewhere under her shirt.

'Ah, I see, it just pulls up and over. And these trousers, two buttons. Lift, wriggle.'

'Lucian, I think I am sitting on a crab! Oh, yes, that is…perfect.' He picked her up and moved her astride him as he knelt in the soft sand. 'Love me, Lucian.'

'I will…I do.' He bit gently on her neck as he lifted her, lowered her, took her in one slow, strong thrust that had her shuddering into an instant orgasm. 'I can't… Oh, God, Sara.'

He fell back, taking her with him, and thrust once, twice before he shouted aloud and she collapsed forward on to his chest, gasping with reaction and surprise.

'Lucian,' Sara murmured in his ear. 'My feet are wet, the tide is coming in.'

'How long have we been here?' he asked, almost nose to nose with her. His face was in moonshadow, but she could see the whiteness of his smile.

'I do not have the brainpower to work it out. What on earth happened just then?'

'An explosion of joy, of relief, of love?' he suggested. 'I confess to needing to do it all over again, very slowly, on a bed.' He shifted under her. 'Without sand.'

'The swim will rinse most of it off,' she promised, rolling over and searching for her shirt and trousers. 'For an awful moment when I found your clothes on the boat I thought…'

'That I had walked out into the waves and oblivion?' Lucian stood up, silvered by the moonlight, more beautiful than a man had any right to be. 'How could I leave a world that has you in it?' He held out his hand and she put hers into it and walked with him into the sea, too moved for words.

* * *

'Admit it, you are feeling all soft and sentimental and romantic,' the Marchioness of Cannock whispered into the ear of the Marquess of Cannock who was sitting next to her in the front pew of St George's, Hanover Square.

Before them, at the altar, Gregory Farnsworth was reverently kissing Marguerite, his new bride, and the sound of happy sighs and sniffles rose from every pew where a lady was sitting.

'I will admit to sentimental and romantic, Lady Cannock,' Lucian murmured in return, making her shiver as his breath teased her ear. 'But soft, no. Anything but. It makes me think of our wedding day and that makes me—'

'Shh!' She nudged him in the ribs with her elbow. 'I am on my best behaviour as The Perfect Marchioness today.'

'I have plans for that,' her husband muttered as the happy couple turned and began to walk down the aisle.

'Marguerite looks so poised and beautiful and Gregory looks so happy. It was good of you to find him that post at the Foreign Office, I think he will do very well there.'

'I think so, too. And my little sister has grown up faster than I can imagine with the prospect of married life and his career to support.'

Sara looked up at her husband, loving the pride in his voice, on his face, as he looked at Marguerite and Gregory. She followed him out of the pew and took his arm as they led the guests out on to the steps of the church so that everyone could throw rose petals. Marguerite stood up in the open carriage and tossed her bouquet straight into the arms of her oldest bridesmaid and then sat down with a bump and fell laughing into Gregory's arms as the carriage set off for the wedding breakfast at the family town house in Cavendish Square.

'Oh, that makes me feel so middle aged and sensible,' Sara said, clinging to Lucian's arm as the jostling to find carriages began.

'I have a cure for that.' He guided her down the steps and round the corner. 'Here is our carriage.' He stopped and looked up to the driver. 'Pearson, I want you to take us back to Cavendish Square the long way round, if you understand me. There's no hurry,' he said as he helped Sara into the carriage and reached to draw down the blinds. 'It will be an age before everyone gets there.'

'Lucian, what are you *doing*?' The last word came out as a squeak as he tossed aside his hat and gloves and began to struggle out of his coat.

'I never did get to make love to you in a closed carriage, if you recall. I had such a vivid image of it when we were in that confounded chaise and now...'

'Now I am all dressed up and wearing the famous Cannock yellow diamonds and the world's tightest corset and—ooh!'

Lucian vanished under the froth of her skirts. 'And some very wicked garters, I am happy to discover.' His long, clever fingers were already doing sinful things and his lips and tongue were not far behind. He knew her so well now, after only a month of marriage. He knew her body and her responses and he knew her emotions and feelings, too, and used them to keep her almost constantly either at a pitch of arousal or totally sated, it seemed to Sara as she locked her fingers into his beautifully barbered hair and wrecked a very fine Brutus.

Sara pulled off her new lemon-kid gloves and bit

down on them so her cries of pleasure did not escape as Lucian sent her tumbling into bliss. When she recovered her senses he was kissing her lips, her bodice was around her waist and she could not, frustratingly get his shirt out of his trousers—at which point the carriage lurched against the kerb and they both fell off the seat and on to the floor with Sara underneath.

'Are you all right?' Lucian peered down at her, his neckcloth askew, his hair rumpled. He looked, to her, perfect, wild, sinful and on the edge of out of control.

'Absolutely.' And even more perfect when, with a wriggle of his hips and a tug at her skirts, he was inside her. 'I am making a careful note of the date,' she gasped against the damp heat of his mouth. 'If our firstborn arrives as a result of this I shall call him Barouche.'

'Better still, we could call him Hansom,' Lucian said with a chuckle that became a gasp when Sara lifted her hips to meet him. 'I never thought I could make love to a woman who fills me with such delight and can make me laugh at the same time. But then I never imagined falling in love and marrying a deliciously Imperfect Marchioness.'

They fell over the edge together, laughing and kissing and came to themselves to find the carriage at a standstill. Lucian struggled up on to the seat and pulled Sara up beside him.

'Oh, my goodness, look at us!' she gasped. 'There are over a hundred people waiting for us to make an entrance in there.'

Lucian cracked open the window. 'Once more round the square, Pearson. Slowly. Come on, my delightfully unconventional Marchioness, we have about five minutes to return ourselves to perfect order. Do you have a comb in the reticule I have just trodden on, my love?'

They descended the steps of the carriage in *almost* perfect order, although Sara found an earring dangling in the folds of Lucian's neckcloth and tweaked it out just in time. He took it from her and fixed it in her earlobe with perfect solemnity in front of an intrigued audience. Then he caught her up in his arms, kissed her right on the lips and twirled her round before setting her on her feet again.

'My apologies for keeping you waiting, ladies and gentlemen,' he said with an elegant bow. 'But when a man loves his wife as much as I love mine, occasionally he has to show it. And now, let us proceed to celebrate another happy marriage in the making.'

Amidst laughter, and some tears, they led the way into the great dining room. As Lucian pulled out a chair to seat her at Gregory's side she turned and whispered, 'Love me always?'

'For always and a day,' he whispered back. 'Always, until the tides cease to flow. Always, until the moon no longer shines on the waves.'

'You have become a romantic.'

'You made me one, my love. Only you could.'

* * * * *

*If you enjoyed this story,
you won't want to miss the daring*
LORDS OF DISGRACE *quartet
from Louise Allen*

*HIS HOUSEKEEPER'S CHRISTMAS WISH
HIS CHRISTMAS COUNTESS
THE MANY SINS OF CRIS DE FEAUX
THE UNEXPECTED MARRIAGE OF
GABRIEL STONE*

Her old romantic dreams burst forth. Why hold back?
Dell's kiss was even more than she could have imagined.
Why not give herself to it?

She pulled off her bonnet and threw her arms around
his neck, answering the press of his lips with eagerness.
He urged her mouth open and she readily complied,
surprised and delighted that his warm tongue touched
hers.

He tasted wonderful.

She plunged her fingers into his hair, loving its softness
and its curls. She liked his hair best when it looked tousled
by a breeze. Or mussed by her hands.

He pressed her body against his and the thrill
intensified. How marvelous to feel his muscles so firm
against her. And more. One hand slid down from his hair
to his arm to his hip. How wanton was that?

But she was a widow, was she not? Was not everyone telling her she had license to do as she pleased? It pleased her to touch him. Although she was not quite brazen enough to touch that hard part of him that thrilled her most of all.

"Lorene," he groaned as his hands pressed against her derriere, intensifying the sensations in all sorts of ways. "We should stop."

She did not want to stop. "Why?" She kissed his neck. "I am a widow. Are not widows permitted?"

"Do not tempt me," he said, though his hands caressed her.

She moved away, just enough that he could see her face. "If you do not want this, then, yes, we should stop, but I do desire it, Dell."

For a long time, she realized. Since she'd first met him. He was the man she had dreamed about in her youth, a good man, kind, honorable, handsome. But something more, something that made her want to bed him.

Make sure to read…
BOUND BY THEIR SECRET PASSION
by Diane Gaston, available April 2017 wherever
Harlequin® Historical books and ebooks are sold.

www.Harlequin.com

THE WORLD IS BETTER WITH

Romance

Harlequin has everything from contemporary, passionate and heartwarming to suspenseful and inspirational stories.

Whatever your mood, we have a romance just for you!

Connect with us to find your next great read, special offers and more.

f /HarlequinBooks

🐦 @HarlequinBooks

www.HarlequinBlog.com

www.Harlequin.com/Newsletters

H HARLEQUIN®

A Romance FOR EVERY MOOD™

www.Harlequin.com

SERIESHALOAD2015

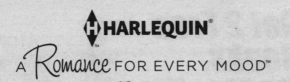

HARLEQUIN®

A *Romance* FOR EVERY MOOD™

JUST CAN'T GET ENOUGH?

Join our social communities
and talk to us online.

You will have access to the latest
news on upcoming titles and special
promotions, but most importantly,
you can talk to other fans about your
favorite Harlequin reads.

Harlequin.com/Community

Facebook.com/HarlequinBooks

Twitter.com/HarlequinBooks

Pinterest.com/HarlequinBooks

Into Historical Romance?
We have the perfect read for you!

Looking for more reads from Harlequin®?
Go back in time with Harlequin®
Historical and Love Inspired® Historical
for stories of life and love set across many
time periods.

✦ HARLEQUIN®

ⓗISTORICAL

Where love is timeless

Love Inspired
HISTORICAL

Historical romance of
adventure and faith

Be sure to check out our
full selection of books within
each series every month!

www.Harlequin.com
#WhateverYoureInto
www.LoveInspired.com

HIBC2016

ℋISTORICAL

A battle of wills!

When Lady Sara Herriard's husband dies in a duel, she turns her back on the vagaries of the *ton*. From now on, she will live as she pleases. She won't change for anyone—certainly not for the infuriating Lucian Avery, Marquess of Cannock!

Lucian must help his sister recover from a disastrous elopement and reluctantly enlists Lady Sara's help. She couldn't be further from the conventional, obedient wife he's expected to marry, but soon all he craves is for her to surrender—and join him in his bed!

"A tale filled with poignancy [and] passion."
—*RT Book Reviews* on
The Unexpected Marriage of Gabriel Stone

$6.50 U.S./$7.25 CAN.

ISBN-13: 978-0-373-29920-1

50650

9 780373 299201

E A N

S

CATEGORY
HISTORICAL

HISTORICAL

harlequin.com